DEMON BORN

THE WITCHES OF CANYON ROAD: BOOK FIVE

CHRISTINE POPE

DEMON BORN

ISBN: 978-1-946435-19-4

Copyright © 2019 by Christine Pope

Published by Dark Valentine Press

Cover design by Lou Harper

Ebook formatting by Indie Author Services

Don't miss out on any of Christine's new releases—sign up for her newsletter today!

1

A GENTLE NIGHT BREEZE STIRRED THE GRAPEVINES, which shimmered under the light of a nearly full moon. Cat Castillo stood in the covered entry of her newly remodeled home, thinking she could almost catch a glimpse of the dark fruit nearly hidden beneath those broad leaves. In that moment, she wondered if she'd made the right decision in selling the grapes, rather than attempt to continue making wine here at what had once been the Rio Luna vineyard. Sure, she didn't know anything about viticulture, but she could have hired someone to help her. She'd been watching these vines since they began to bud in April, had shared every thrill when they reached a new milestone, experienced every pang of fear when the weather forecasts called for a late frost. After investing so much time in them, they almost felt like her children, and surely it was a terrible thing to sell your children on the open market?

After that thought crossed her mind, though, Cat wanted to shake her head at herself. Of course those grapes weren't her children. She might have helped to nurture them, but they were only a crop, an asset she could sell to help earn back some of the truly alarming amounts of money she'd spent getting the house that had come with the vineyard updated and ready to be lived in.

No, although she really didn't want to admit such a thing to herself, she knew the real reason for her current maudlin state was the news that her brother Rafe and his wife Miranda—the Castillo clan's *prima*, or head witch—had just relayed at their father's birthday dinner. Although the ostensible reason for the get-together had been Eduardo's fifty-sixth birthday, Cat had been able to tell from the moment she'd laid eyes on them that Rafe and Miranda were bursting with news they wanted to share.

It had come out soon enough—they were expecting their first child, who was due sometime around the beginning of January. And even though Cat had known this sort of announcement could come along at any time, since Miranda and Rafe had been frank about trying to get pregnant, she still couldn't help experiencing an odd pang of…what? Jealousy? Melancholy? She couldn't even be sure what the emotion really was, because she knew she was also happy for the two of them, had a feeling that she would be closer to this particular niece or nephew than she was to the children of her sisters Louisa and Malena. At the same time, she couldn't quite stop herself from wondering whether she would ever be a mother herself. So far, the answer seemed to be no.

Restless, Cat stepped out from the shelter of the high vaulted roof of the entryway, moving toward the orderly rows of vines that were planted to the south and east of the house and its various outbuildings. The night air was so mild, she didn't need a sweater or shawl, despite the lightweight dress she wore, which she'd put on earlier so she'd have something nice to wear to her father's birthday dinner.

She wanted to be happy for Rafe and Miranda. No, she really was happy, only…

…only she wanted that same kind of happiness for herself. It had been exciting to oversee the renovation of the house, the remodel of the winery's former tasting room into the fiber arts studio of her dreams, but now that Cat had moved in and was here all by herself, she was starting to realize how big the house really was, how her footsteps seemed to echo off the stone floors, despite all the expensive rugs she'd bought to cover them. And night times were the worst, because at least during the day she had Roberto, the vineyard manager, and his son Miguel around the property. It didn't feel empty the way it did now.

The syllables seemed to drift on the air, barely louder than the rustle of the grape leaves in the night wind.

Catalina....

She froze, heart pounding as she scanned the moonlit landscape for signs of an intruder. Everything appeared as it should be, the track that led from the house to the former tasting room empty, the gravel bleached nearly white under the light of the moon.

There was no one here.

Her pulse slowed somewhat, but still she stood where she was, arms wrapped around herself, the night breeze pulling at the loose strands of hair that had freed themselves from the French braid at the back of her head. No one called her Catalina except her parents. Her mother was dead, and that voice hadn't sounded at all like Eduardo's. It was smooth and deep, with the barest trace of an accent she couldn't quite place. The voice felt almost familiar, and yet she couldn't remember where she might have heard it before. It teased at her memory, plucking at threads of recollection that had been buried deeply for months and months.

He stepped out of the vines, the night wind blowing his black shoulder-length hair away from his face. Cat blinked, blood in her veins going to ice, even as she cursed herself for being stupid enough to leave her cell phone sitting on the table just inside the entryway. How the stranger knew her name was secondary to the chilling realization that they were all alone here. The property was large enough that she knew her nearest neighbors wouldn't be able to hear her even if she screamed with all her might.

Then he spoke again. "Catalina. You do not remember me?"

As he asked the question, he moved closer. The moonlight was bright enough that she could see the handsome, sculpted planes of his face, the sensual fullness of his lips, the faintest trace of stubble on his strong chin. He was goddamn gorgeous, that was for sure, but he still had intruded on her property.

She found her voice. "I've never seen you before in my life."

He smiled. "Perhaps not in this guise."

It would have been easy to blame what happened next on too many glasses of wine at dinner, but Cat had drunk only one, knowing that she needed to drive back to her home in Pojoaque after the dinner in the heart of Santa Fe ended. She was, if not dead sober, at least the next thing to it.

The handsome man who stood a few feet away from her shifted, his face and form melting like overheated wax. He grew taller by more than a foot, even as black, leathery wings emerged from his back, spreading out into a span that stretched more than ten feet across. His features grew harsh, monstrous, skin darkening, eyes flaring with red.

And despite all this, Cat experienced only a brief rush of fear, gone as quickly as it had come. Because, incredible as it was to admit such a thing to herself, she knew this being.

The Lord of Chaos, summoned by the dark warlock Simon Escobar to be his slave. That scheme hadn't exactly gone to plan, and the Lord of Chaos had turned out to be an unexpected but very welcome ally in the Castillo clan's fight against Escobar.

His voice echoed in her head. *You know me.*

Yes, she replied. *Why the disguise?*

I fear I am somewhat conspicuous in my natural form, he said. *I thought it better to blend in.*

And just like that, he was once again human in appearance, if one of the best-looking humans she'd ever seen.

Despite herself, Cat grinned. "I hate to tell you this, but you're still pretty conspicuous in this form."

The Lord of Chaos looked down at the human body he now wore. For the first time, Cat realized he was wearing a plain black T-shirt and dark jeans, motorcycle boots covering his feet. "Am I?"

he asked. "I did not have much frame of reference, so I chose something that would be agreeable to most of the people I met."

Oh, it's agreeable, Cat thought. *Maybe a little too agreeable. Because...damn.*

"I can see why you'd think that," she said. "But...why are you here?"

He frowned slightly, and she wished she could take back the question. It had sounded pretty rude, as though she didn't want him here, that she thought he was intruding on her solitude uninvited. And although it might have sounded strange to admit she was happy to have a disguised demon lord suddenly show up on her property, she actually was glad to see him. Even in the brief exchanges they'd shared when they were working to defeat Simon Escobar, she'd felt strangely comfortable with the Lord of Chaos, which she guessed was not the normal reaction to the presence of that sort of being.

"I mean," Cat went on hastily, glad that he hadn't replied right away, "it's been eight months. You said you were going to find someone to help you get back to your own world, and so when none of us heard anything...."

"Yes," he said, sounding more resigned than anything else. "That endeavor did not go precisely as planned. I found no one who could assist me, and so I thought it best if I returned here. At least you and your brother and your *prima* know what I did to aid you in your fight against Simon Escobar, and so I hoped...."

The demon lord stopped there, as though he was vaguely ashamed that he'd been forced to return here once all his options had run out. A stir of pity went through Cat, and she said quickly, "Yes, we do know, and we'll never forget. Why don't you come inside?"

He hesitated, his gaze moving from her to the warm yellow light that spilled out of the living room windows of her house. "Are you sure?"

"Of course I'm sure," she replied immediately. "Are you hungry? I've got some tamales my Aunt Rosa sent home with me. She thinks I'm living on frozen food and yogurt out here." *Which isn't all that far from the truth....*

"I don't know what a tamale is," the Lord of Chaos said, a frown once again pulling at his brows.

"Well, then," Cat responded, "you're definitely coming in."

This was crazy, wasn't it? She sat across from the demon lord, watching as he demolished a plate of pork and beef and sweet corn dessert tamales. Obviously, he wasn't too worried about maintaining the trim, muscular human form he'd assumed. Then again, she supposed if he could make himself look like anyone or anything he wanted, then it didn't really matter how many calories he consumed.

And if he's still himself under there, she thought, reaching for the glass of wine she'd poured for herself, *then he probably needs a lot of food to even begin to maintain his weight.*

He slowed down enough to take a sip from his own glass of Tempranillo. Estate-grown, too, from one of the bottles that had come to her with the sale of the house. "It's all very good," he said. "Thank you."

"It's no problem," she responded, although inwardly she knew she probably wouldn't pass the Lord of Chaos's compliments regarding the tamales on to her Aunt Rosa. The source of the praise would have been way too difficult to explain.

Another flicker of worry passed through her mind, the fear that she might have made herself vulnerable by allowing him into her house, openly inviting him here. No, that was silly; that sort of rule pertained to vampires, not demon lords of unknown origin. Besides, vampires weren't real.

Cat sipped some more wine, then said, "So... what happened? Was Simon Escobar really the only warlock with the power to send you back to your own world?"

The demon paused, fingers tapping against

the stem of the glass he held. "It would appear so. That is, I had to be discreet in my inquiries, because the last thing I wanted was to attract the attention of yet another person who was only interested in exploiting my powers, but I came across no one with that sort of skill. It seems that all you witches and warlocks have been very serious about ignoring any fields of inquiry that have been deemed remotely unsavory, and so there doesn't appear to be anyone who can list demon-summoning on their resumes."

His tone as he said this sounded almost amused, as if he'd already moved far past his disappointment and had done his best to come to terms with his current situation. Cat wondered if she should leave it alone, but she couldn't help asking, "Not even in Central America? That's where Simon's father came from, right?"

Expression unreadable, he answered, "That was the first place I looked."

After delivering that somewhat quelling comment, the Lord of Chaos returned to eating his tamales. Cat noticed that he'd left most of the sweet corn tamale alone as he ate the other two, although once those were gone, he devoured that one with relish as well. Saving it for dessert? Maybe. She supposed she should be glad that his table manners were pretty much impeccable, especially since she'd never thought of demons as the sort of beings who'd be handy with a knife and fork. Knives, maybe, although their talons had certainly seemed sharp enough on their own.

"I'm sorry," she told him after a pause, since she really didn't know what else to say. "But you're welcome to stay here for as long as you need to."

That offer made him look up from his plate, dark eyes intent. Cat had to make herself sit still and return his gaze, which was harder than she'd thought it would be. He really was insanely good-looking.

Not really, she reminded herself. *This is all just window dressing. Underneath....*

Well, underneath he was an eight-foot-tall demon with red eyes, sharp teeth, and bat wings that could probably knock you into the next county if you weren't careful. For some reason, though, that mental image didn't bother her as much as it should have, probably because the last time she'd properly seen him in that guise, he'd been busy helping to save all their asses.

"You mean that?" he asked. He sounded genuinely surprised.

Cat wondered exactly what he'd been through these past eight months, what he'd seen, what seamy undersides of the witching world he'd explored in order to find the one person who could send him back to his natural plane of exis-tence. Even for a being with his powers, it couldn't have been easy, or fun. No wonder he appeared so startled by her offer of hospitality.

"Yes, I do," she said. After all, the house was large, with four bedrooms and three and a half baths. It wasn't as though they'd be tripping over each other if he hung out here for a little while. "If you're done eating, I can show you where you'll be staying—that is, if you want to, of course."

He lifted his wine glass and drained the last of its contents before setting it down once again. "I am ready."

There was enough left in Cat's own glass that she knew she wouldn't be able to finish it off in one swallow. Instead, she took a sip for courage, then got up from her chair. "All the bedrooms are upstairs. This way."

She led him up to the second floor and then down the short hallway to the space she'd designated as a guest room. It wasn't overly large, but it had a balcony that looked to the north and the magnificent cottonwood trees that marked the northern perimeter of the property, and a ceiling fan overhead that helped to move the warm air that had collected here during the daytime.

A few steps across the room, and she'd opened the French doors to let in some of the evening breeze. "Because this side of the house faces north, you shouldn't have to worry too much about the sun waking you."

As soon as she'd spoken, though, Cat

wondered if she'd just made herself sound like an idiot. After all, she had no way of knowing whether demons—or demon lords—even had to sleep. The thought disquieted her. She didn't want to think of the Lord of Chaos awake and roaming the house while she was asleep in her own bedroom down the hall. Her guest might have seemed friendly enough, but, after all, he wasn't human.

He didn't correct her one way or the other, only stood there for a moment in silence as he inspected the room. Did he think it was too plain? She'd been going for a Tuscan farmhouse style in her decorating, and the furnishings in here were simple, just a queen bed with a dark wood frame without any adornment, a writing desk placed up against one wall, and a ficus tree in a basket in one corner. Also, she'd hung a cross of pierced tin above the writing desk. At the time, she hadn't thought much about it; being Catholic was all part of being a Castillo, the same as being a witch or warlock, but maybe a demon had different thoughts about overtly religious symbols.

Not that he was the sort of demon talked about in the Bible, as far as Cat had been able to tell. These demons were simply beings from a different plane of existence, given the name mostly because it served to describe them better than anything else humans had been able to come up with. As for what his world was even like, she really had no idea. It must have its attractions, though, or he wouldn't have been trying so hard to get back there.

Then he spoke. "That sounds very comfortable."

Which didn't tell her a damn thing. She knew she didn't have to worry about him shriveling up in sunlight or anything like that, because it had been broad daylight when he'd appeared at the house in La Cienega and had driven off the lesser demons Simon Escobar had summoned. But the demon lord still hadn't dropped a single clue as to whether he really did need to sleep or not.

And that also meant the next part of her instructions might be pointless as well. However, since she'd already embarked on this endeavor, Cat figured she had better plow ahead.

Taking a breath, she said, "The bathroom's the first door on the right. There are towels and soap and shampoo, and in the top drawer of the vanity, you'll find an unused toothbrush and some tooth-paste. I don't really have any spare clothes, but—"

"Catalina."

His tone was quiet, but it was enough to stop the flow of words. She paused and made herself look at him again. Now he was smiling, and she didn't quite know what to make of that.

"You're being very generous with your hospi-tality," he said. "There is no need for you to worry about clothing, or any other items I might require. I will simply conjure them as the need arises."

"Of course," she replied, feeling her cheeks heat somewhat. Good thing the light built into the ceiling fan wasn't very bright. Or maybe his demon senses were so acute that he would have been able to see her blush even if they'd been standing in pitch darkness. "I suppose I should have thought of that."

"Well, this is probably the first time you've had a demon lord stay overnight," he said, again with that amused note in his voice.

"The first time I've had anyone stay over," she admitted. "Well, my cousin Ignatio passed out on the couch the night of my housewarming party, but since he got up sometime before dawn and drove himself home, I guess that doesn't really count."

As if a demon lord cares about whether your cousin had too many shots of tequila....

But again he smiled at her. "Then I feel honored to be your first guest. Again, thank you for your hospitality."

For all their friendliness, his words had a note of dismissal to them, and Cat decided it was better to take his lead and call it a night. The day was beginning to feel very long to her, and she knew she needed to go to bed.

Whether she'd actually be able to sleep was an entirely different matter.

"Then good night, um—" She stopped there, realizing she had no idea what to call him. "Lord of Chaos" wasn't exactly the easiest phrase to slip into everyday conversation.

"Loc," he said. It rhymed with "woke."

"'Loc'?" Cat repeated, hoping she'd heard him correctly. It was an unusual name, but then she supposed a demon lord probably wouldn't go around calling himself "Tim" or something else equally innocuous.

"For 'Lord of Chaos,'" he supplied. "A small joke, I suppose."

"Oh, right." It did suit him, in an odd way, suited the dark handsomeness of his borrowed features. The nickname also made him sound like a musician or model or something, but Cat supposed that might work to his advantage as well. "Loc it is. If you need anything, I'll be right down the hall."

"I'm sure I will be fine, but thank you," he said, gravely polite.

That seemed to be her cue to leave the room. She managed to send him what she hoped was an encouraging smile, then turned and headed down the hall to the master suite. The door to his room shut quietly behind her, and although she knew she should be glad that he was respecting her privacy—and his—she couldn't help wondering what he might be doing behind that closed door.

Getting ready for bed, just like you should be, Cat

scolded herself as she went into the master bedroom and then made sure her own door was firmly shut. It didn't have a lock—she hadn't thought there would be any reason for one—and right now she found herself wishing for some way to latch the door, even as she realized a lock wouldn't keep out an ordinary witch or warlock, much less a demon lord like Loc.

He's not going to come in here, she told herself. *Just because he looks human doesn't mean he* is *human. He doesn't have human needs or wants.*

That realization reassured her somewhat. It had been an impulsive move to invite him to stay here, and she definitely didn't need to allow that kind of nonsense to take up space in her mind. She'd do what she could to help him, because she and the whole Castillo clan owed him one, but that would be the extent of their connection.

All the same, she couldn't quite keep herself from brooding over what she'd done as she lay down once her usual nightly routines were completed. The house was quiet, with no sound at all coming from the room down the hall.

She shut her eyes and thought, *Rafe is going to kill me when he finds out about all this....*

2

Loc lay on his borrowed bed, eyes open, gaze fixed on the wood-beamed ceiling above his head. Although he himself did not need to sleep, the body he wore required rest, just as it also required food and needed to relieve itself at regular intervals. During the months he'd been trapped on this world, he'd learned to deal with such mortal requirements, and yet tonight he found it difficult to sleep.

Truly, he had not expected Catalina—*Cat*, he reminded himself, knowing that she preferred the whimsical nickname—to offer him a place to stay. He had come here because he knew this was the place where she had settled, and he'd recalled how he had found it so much easier to reach out and touch her mind than it was with other mortals. At the time, he had simply thought that he needed the reassurance of someone familiar, someone to speak to, if only for a few moments. It had never entered his mind that she would offer him a much-needed place of refuge.

This world was a confusing, chaotic place, and to be lying here now, with the whisper of the leaves telling him tales carried on the night wind, seemed so far from what he had experienced during his time on this plane that he was not quite sure what to make of it. Oh, he had never feared for his life; the borrowed body he wore might be weak enough, but the soul it concealed was as fierce as ever, and he knew he could have easily snuffed out anyone who dared to lay a hand upon him. It was more that he'd never before encountered such a cacophony of souls, a place where so many fought for their own agendas, their own petty triumphs. On the plane where he had sprung into existence, he had always been the lord and master, and the lesser beings who dwelt there had known to obey his every command.

Here on this world, he had no such authority, and knew that he must do whatever he could to blend in and pass as one of them, even though there was much about this place he found grating, from the constant traffic in its cities to the way most of the denizens of Earth seemed to spend their days with their faces glued to their phone screens, rather than interacting with one another. More than once he had had to swallow his pride, only because he knew that to annoy one of those whose assistance he sought would surely do him no good.

But none of those witches and warlocks, those hoarders of black texts and brewers of forbidden potions, had possessed the knowledge required to send him back whence he had come. He had kept his true identity secret, of course, and had pretended to be a mere mortal seeking the power to summon demons, and yet it had not been enough. All he had for his efforts was an indecent proposal from a witch in Barcelona, who'd told him that she couldn't summon demons from hell but would like to send him to heaven, if only for one night.

He was not so innocent that he didn't understand what she was asking. However, he had no interest in such things, and his refusal had not been polite. Blazing with wounded pride, she had ordered him from her house. He'd left because it was certainly not worth his time trying to explain to her that he had no interest in participating in such distasteful acts with anyone, and that his rejection had not been personal.

At the same time, he'd wondered whether he should select a human appearance that was less appealing. Doing so might have helped him to avoid such awkward encounters, and yet he was reluctant. Although he was not sure he wished to admit such a thing to himself, somewhere in the back of his mind, he had harbored the notion that he'd chosen this form because he thought Cat Castillo might like it, and if he ever needed to see her again, better to do so wearing a face that would not be cause for fear or alarm.

Not that she'd reacted to him in such a way when she'd first seen him, so many months ago. She had been startled, of course, but he hadn't seen any disgust in her expression, only interest and curiosity. Perhaps it was because she'd already touched minds with him, and therefore knew he was nothing she should fear.

Which could also have been another reason why he'd come here when all his other options had been exhausted. Her spirit had drawn him toward this place like a beacon, and it had felt all too natural to speak to her again, although he had not reached out to her mind until they had physically spoken, since he thought that might have been intruding too much.

She had shown no fear earlier this evening, either, when he'd taken on his true form for a few seconds to prove to her who he was. That same flare of awe, but nothing else.

All this made him wonder why he lay here so wakeful tonight. The bed in this room was much more comfortable than many he had slept on while he performed his search, and the fan overhead kept the air from feeling too warm and stagnant. And since he had begun his day many, many hours earlier, in a slum outside Sao Paulo, he should have been happy to be here in the sanctuary that Cat had provided.

And yet….

She had looked well, in her pale, filmy dress with her arms bare. When he had seen her before, she'd been wearing bulky clothing that might have sufficed to keep her warm but was also very good at hiding much of her form. Now, he had seen far more of her than he had previously, and although there was no good reason for him to do so, he found himself dwelling on that first glimpse of her he'd caught as she'd come down the gravel path from the house, loose strands of hair waving around her face in the breeze, that same breeze blowing the thin silk of her dress against her long legs.

Why was he thinking of such things? Human women held no allure for him, as that witch in Barcelona had found out quickly enough. For some reason, though, Catalina Castillo seemed different, possibly because of the way he could touch her mind. He was unable to do such a thing with anyone else, and that peculiar quality made her stand out that much more from the throngs of humanity.

And perhaps…just perhaps…it was also because he knew that she would never recoil from him, no matter which form he wore.

Do not let your thoughts wander there, he told himself as he turned over onto his side. In a way, it was exciting to have so many different positions available to him in this body, where his wings would never get in the way. True, he hadn't needed to sleep while inhabiting his true form, but still....

She has offered you sanctuary because she knows you have no place else to go. It is pity and nothing else that led her to make the gesture.

Loc did not think he liked the sound of that. He certainly did not wish to be pitied, he who had once commanded legions of demons and called an entire plane of existence his own, who had dwelled in a tower of basalt and whose every need was met instantly. But, thanks to that miserable waste of flesh Simon Escobar, it seemed all that power and majesty had been stolen from him. Whether Loc would ever get it back was certainly debatable at best.

You will, he thought, more because he knew he must believe in eventual success if he was going to continue to exist on this alien world. *In the meantime, though, you have a place of refuge, and must do your best to manage until something changes.*

What that change might be, he had no idea.

Cat woke up earlier than she normally did, probably because she knew there was a disguised demon in the spare bedroom down the hall, and the last thing she wanted was to have him knocking at the door while she was still lying in bed wearing the tank top and panties that were her summertime sleeping attire. Just the mere thought was enough to spur her to climb out of bed and go to the bathroom, then get in the shower and give herself a quick spritz. Luckily, she'd washed her hair the day before in preparation for her father's birthday party, and so she didn't have to bother with it much. The braid she'd worn it in had left fun little ripples all along its length, so she combed it out and left it loose on her shoulders, figuring she could always braid it up again if it got too warm later in the day.

Jeans and a sleeveless embroidered Mexican blouse she'd bought down at the Plaza, and flat sandals and some silver jewelry, and she figured she was fit to be seen. Well, almost—she quickly brushed on some mascara, followed by lip gloss, then slowly opened the door to her bedroom and peeked down the hall.

The door to the guest room was still shut, and she couldn't hear any sound coming from within. Did that mean the demon lord—*Loc,* Cat told herself—actually was still asleep, or had he disappeared sometime during the night, deciding that it wasn't such a good idea after all for him to be staying here?

Such a departure would make her life a lot easier, although she found herself experiencing a pang of disappointment at the thought that he might already be gone.

Crazy, she thought, and headed down the stairs. Still there was no sign of life in the guest room, so her other theory, that he was here but awake and waiting for her to make the first move before he emerged from his bedroom, seemed to be off the mark as well.

Trying not to shrug, she went into the kitchen. After a moment's hesitation, she started a pot of coffee, making enough for two people just in case Loc really was still around. She could save the leftovers for iced coffee later in the afternoon, although generally she tried not to drink too much caffeine late in the day.

Just as she was pouring some into her favorite hand-glazed mug, a deep voice said, "Good morning."

Somehow, she managed to keep herself from splashing the hot liquid on her hand as she started. "Good morning," she said evenly, then turned to see Loc standing at the entrance to the kitchen. Once again, he wore human clothes, faded jeans and those same scuffed motorcycle boots he had on last night, although today he wore an untucked shirt in a deep purple shade with a rough weave of brighter colors worked through it.

Guatemalan, her mind instantly catalogued, recognizing the fabric as the kind produced in home-based textile shops in that Central American country. Well, he had hinted that he'd traveled the world in his search for someone to send him back to his own plane of existence.

"Coffee?" she added, hoping she sounded normal and not at all rattled by the presence of a demon lord in her kitchen at eight o'clock in the morning. "I mean," she added hastily, "if you drink it."

"I've acquired the habit," he replied as he came farther into the room. "That smells good. Sumatran?"

"Yes," she said. "It sounds like you've become something of an expert."

"I've had many varieties in my travels."

Since Cat wasn't sure how she should respond to that comment, she settled for giving him a nod while at the same time fetching another mug from the cupboard. Once it was filled, she handed it to him. "I have cream in the fridge if you want it. And the sugar is in that little blue bowl over there on the other counter."

His gaze traveled to where she'd indicated, but he shook his head. "Black is fine."

Black as his bat wings, which were now hidden...black as the heavy dark hair he'd pushed back from his brow. Seeing him now, in the morning light that poured in through the window over the sink, Cat saw he was really even more spectacular than she'd thought, with those long lashes that partially hid his dark eyes, and the muscles that bulged against the short sleeves of the shirt he wore. And the thing that made him all the more gorgeous was his complete ignorance of his appearance. She got the impression that he'd chosen this form because he thought it would make it easier to work with humans, and cared very little as to whether it was attractive or not. For all she knew, he really had no frame of reference when it came to human beauty.

Which meant that putting on even the minor cosmetics she now wore had probably been a waste of time, but she figured she'd worry about that later. In a way, it was sort of freeing to be around someone who had no concept of appearance and all its myriad ways of affecting behavior.

On the other hand, though, he was just so damn *distracting*.

She cleared her throat. "I don't have a lot of breakfast food on hand. Usually, I just have yogurt or a piece of toast. But I can run down to the market and get something else if you want." That seemed the safest thing to do; she didn't think she was quite up to taking him out to breakfast.

Her offer elicited a small smile—a genuine one, though, with nothing mocking in it. "Catalina, that's not necessary. I told you last night that I can get anything I need...or anything you need. It is only fair, considering you have offered me shelter."

"Then get yourself whatever you usually eat for breakfast," she said briskly, figuring that should be safe enough.

One eyebrow lifted as he considered her suggestion. "I have had many things—scrambled eggs and bacon in Portland, Oregon, a baguette in Paris...some kind of steamed dumplings in Beijing. Most of them have been good in their own way. Human food is actually quite fascinating. So why don't we have something to eat that you would like?"

Cat hesitated. She hadn't been much of a breakfast person for quite some time now, but, on the other hand, she didn't want to offend her house guest. And it had been a very long time since she had eaten one of her childhood favorites.

"Chilaquiles?" she suggested, and he frowned slightly.

"I'm not sure I've ever eaten that."

His response surprised her a bit, since chilaquiles were a popular breakfast dish in Mexico, and it sounded as though he'd hit quite a few places during his trip around the globe. "Get me the ingredients, and I'll make them for you."

Once again, he frowned. "I did not intend to put you to work."

"It's fine," she said quickly. "I actually have

some salsa verde in the fridge, so all I need is fresh eggs and corn tortillas—I ran out the other day."

Almost before she'd finished speaking, the ingredients had appeared on the kitchen island. "Will that do?"

"Perfect," Cat replied, reflecting that it might be kind of handy to have a demon lord around if it meant avoiding trips to the grocery store. It was better to have slightly drier tortillas for the chilaquiles, but she'd make do.

As Loc watched, she tore up the tortillas and fried them in oil, then drained them and added the salsa verde. At the same time, she got a batch of scrambled eggs going in a skillet, then assembled the cheese and cilantro and *crême fraiche* to use as garnish. Luckily, Cat had helped her mother make this meal many times, so the rhythm of the preparation came back to her quickly enough. In about fifteen minutes, she had two heaping plates of chilaquiles put together.

She handed one to her guest and said, "We can take these into the dining room. It's just through that doorway."

Loc took his plate and headed in the direction she'd indicated, while she paused to grab a couple of napkins. All the cutlery was stored in the sideboard in the dining room, so after Cat had set down her plate, she went and fetched them some knives and forks, then sat next to Loc, who'd already claimed the spot at the head of the table.

He'd done so naturally, as though it was only expected that he would take the place of honor. She supposed he might see it that way, since he'd been the master of his particular plane of existence back where he'd come from.

Their coffee mugs magically appeared on the table, and she shot him a quick glance.

"I did not see the need to go back and fetch them," he explained.

"Well, thank you," Cat said. "I hope you like the food."

Loc didn't reply, but instead scooped up a forkful of chilaquiles, took a bite, and then another, this one observably more enthusiastic. After the third or fourth bite, he slowed down enough to say, "These are very good."

His comment sent a shiver of relief through her. It wasn't that she'd feared what he might do if it turned out that he didn't like the dish—after all, he could probably make whatever he wanted appear in front of him—but that she was glad he enjoyed something she also liked. The way he was able to communicate mentally with her seemed to indicate that they had some sort of strange connection, although Cat wasn't sure she wanted to explore the ramifications of their unexpected synergy quite yet.

"Thank you," she said simply, and had a few

bites, followed by a sip of coffee. After that, she set down her mug and added, "We're going to have to come up with some sort of cover story to explain you."

"'Cover story'?" Loc repeated. He still held his fork, but it was idle now as he sent her a quizzical glance.

"To explain who you are and why you're here." She tapped her fingers against the rim of her plate, pondering the conundrum. If she'd only had to worry about Roberto and Miguel, the vineyard overseer and his son, then she could have simply told them that Loc was a Castillo cousin visiting from the southern part of the state. However, while Rafe and Miranda didn't come up to the winery all that often, Cat knew that sooner or later their paths might cross, and so the "Castillo cousin" story wouldn't exactly fly.

"What's wrong with the truth?" Loc's voice sounded mild enough, but his eyes narrowed as he asked the question, so clearly he didn't see any reason for her to lie about who he was.

"Well, my overseer and his son are both civilians, so it's not as though I can just casually tell them that my guest is a disguised demon lord."

A lift of his heavy arched brows. "'Civilians'?"

"Nonmagical people. Not born of witch-kind."

"Ah." Loc was silent for a moment, appearing to consider what she'd just told him. "They come here often?"

"Every day except Sunday," Cat replied. Before this moment, she'd been grateful for Roberto and Miguel's work ethic, knowing that they had everything handled, and that they would take as good care of the precious grapes as if they were their own. "In fact, they're probably here already, since it's after eight."

"You let them come and go as they please?" Now there was a slight note of disapproval in Loc's tone, as if he didn't think much of her handling of the situation.

Well, he could disapprove all he liked. This was her property, and the grapes were her crop, and how she managed things was really none of his business. "Yes," she said, her voice a bit sharper than she'd intended. "Usually, they get here fairly early, and then leave in the mid-afternoon. They don't generally come to the house and interrupt me unless they have a specific question or concern."

"Ah." Loc picked up his mug of coffee and drank from it again; he'd probably consumed enough already to have finished what she'd poured for him originally, although Cat guessed he could give himself a refill whenever he felt like it.

"Anyway," she went on, "it's not Miguel and Roberto who're the real problem. It's Rafe and Miranda."

"Your brother and his *prima* wife."

"Yes. To be fair, I'm pretty sure Miranda won't care if you're here, but Rafe is a different story."

This remark made the demon lord's brows lift again. "Why would he care? You offered assistance to me, nothing more. And he is somewhat indebted to me."

Well, that statement was true enough, but Cat doubted Rafe would enjoy having it pointed out to him. Of course, he'd been just as glad as everyone else that Simon Escobar had been defeated, but she knew it still rankled her brother to admit that he hadn't been as able to participate in that final confrontation as he would have liked. In the end, it had been Miranda who'd taken down the dark warlock, with a very valuable assist from the Lord of Chaos. And it was probably because of his help that Cat hadn't hesitated too much about allowing him to stay here. Witch families made sure to take care of those who had given them aid.

With Loc staring at her, depthless dark eyes fixed on her face, Cat found herself hesitating. The one thing she really didn't want to say out loud was that Rafe would have issues because the demon lord now looked like a very attractive human male, and might present too much of a temptation to his long-single sister.

God knows, she would be the first one to admit that her brother might be right about that. Cat had to keep reminding herself of the true nature of the being who sat next to her at the dining room table, because otherwise she might start to dwell way too much on the romance of the situation, the dark-eyed stranger taking refuge here at her home.

"He does owe you a debt," she said distinctly, reaching for her mug of coffee as a distraction more than anything else. "But...he's my big brother. He tends to be a little over-protective."

This remark only made Loc frown again. "Why? You are a grown adult as your people measure such things, aren't you?"

"Yes," Cat replied. A grown adult with her own home, her own responsibilities, even though she still had days where she felt like an interloper, as if someone was going to burst in and show her for the fraud she was, thanks to those times when she felt as if she was still only twelve years old. "But there's not exactly a cut-off date for when older brothers stop feeling protective."

Loc was silent then, obviously thinking over her words. How much had he known of human society before he was called here? Did he have any frame of reference at all?

Well, if nothing else, the eight months he'd spent stuck here had to have been highly educational.

At last he spoke. "I think I understand what you are trying to tell me. If you prefer that your brother not know who I am, then what is this... cover story...going to be?"

Luckily, she'd already come up with an idea last night as she tossed and turned in bed, but at least it was something that sounded remotely plausible. "You can be a visiting fiber artist I offered to put up at the house. There's a big show in less than a week, one I've been preparing for most of this past spring."

"'Fiber artist'?" Loc repeated, clearly having trouble connecting the two words.

Cat couldn't really blame him for that, since her field was a little obscure to those who expected artists to work with paint and canvas, or bronze and stone. "I can explain it more after breakfast," she said, then added, "Or now, I guess, since it looks like we're both done." She folded her napkin and set it down on the tabletop. "Let me show you my studio."

3

LOC WATCHED WITH INTEREST AS CAT LED HIM OUT of the house and down a stone pathway, one which ended at a long, low building with climbing roses growing on almost all the walls. They bloomed in a riot of different hues—yellow, pink, red, brilliant coral—bright under the sun in its clear blue sky.

The color of the sky was something that still mesmerized him. On his own world, it had always been a dark charcoal shade, one that might roil with clouds but never changed its overall hue. Here, though, the sky could be a brilliant sapphire as it was now, or flushed with rose in the early dawn, or soft gray or midnight blue. Sometimes it was hard to keep himself from simply standing still and looking up, transfixed by the glory of the heavens in this place.

Cat did not appear terribly affected by the

diamond-sharp beauty of the morning, although he did see her pause to admire a particularly lovely rose which drooped just above the doorway to the building that had been her destination. She put her hand on the door handle and turned it. Loc noted how she had no need of a key, but then, that peculiar skill was one all witches and warlocks seemed to share.

Inside, the building appeared to be one large room, with higher ceilings than its low outward profile would suggest. Windows set high up in the south and north walls let in the bright morning light, which illuminated the two looms that took up most of the floor space. Both of the looms had been strung with yarn in deep, subtle hues, and appeared to hold pieces of fabric that were nearly complete.

"You create fabric?" Loc asked. "This is what it means to be a fiber artist?"

Cat nodded, although she said, "It's more than just that. Come over here."

He followed her to an alcove where some of her finished pieces hung. Now he could see what she had meant when she said her art involved much more than weaving. True, the intricate fabrics in the swirling patterns she'd created formed the base, but laid on top of that were more pieces of fabric, embellished with tufts of woolly yarn or bits of metal or even smooth, polished stone beads, all working together to create a landscape that seemed to echo the world outside, from the rich tapestry of the earth to the outlines of tall mountains and dark forests and serene clouds.

Loc could not recall ever seeing anything like it, and he began to reach out to touch the surface of the piece, then stopped. Cat seemed to understand the reason for his hesitation, because she said, "It's all right. It's meant to be tactile."

Thus given permission, he laid his fingertips against one of the tufts of wool, felt it soft against his skin. Next to it was a series of jade beads, and he trailed his fingers across them as well, noting their cool hardness, such a contrast to the woolly yarn. "I see why it is called art. The mixture of shapes and textures is quite pleasing."

Cat smiled, obviously happy to hear such praise. Although she'd been careful to stand several paces away from him, his highly attuned senses felt the way her heartbeat speeded up a little, how a warm flush touched her cheeks. This morning she had dressed simply, in the blue trousers humans called jeans and a top with embroidery that seemed to echo the tapestry in front of them, and yet she still appeared beautiful to him, in a way he couldn't precisely define, except that he enjoyed looking at her.

"Thanks," she said. "I worked a long time on that one, and I'm going to enter it in the juried competition."

"Juried competition?" he asked, thinking that the phrase did not sound particularly inviting.

Another smile as she explained, "It's just a fancy way of saying that it's a panel of judges who inspect and rate the entries in a competition."

Genuinely curious, he said, "What do you get if you win?" Because it seemed to him that Catalina Castillo already had many of the items mortals seemed to value—a large and beautiful home, a piece of land to call her own, the where-withal to indulge in her art without having to worry about earning a livelihood.

Her smile stretched into a grin. "There's a small cash reward, but it's mostly about bragging rights, about being able to put the award on your CV."

"CV?" Every time he thought he'd mastered most of the intricacies of human existence, along came something else to mystify him.

"Curriculum vitae," Cat explained. "It's kind of like a resume, but it's something artists use a lot. Also, the more awards I win, the more the asking price for my work goes up. The gallery owners like that."

"But surely how much you earn is of no real concern, is it?" Loc stared down into her face, watched as her dark eyes wouldn't quite meet his. "That is, I will admit that I am not entirely familiar with the workings of your witch clans, but it seems that most of you have no need to earn any real income."

"You wouldn't say that if you saw how much this house remodel cost," she said, her expression now slightly rueful. At least, that's what he thought it was; he still was not always entirely accurate when it came to reading human reactions.

"My apologies. I thought the Castillo clan was quite a wealthy one."

Now she actually chuckled. "It is. And that means I am, too. I guess it just didn't feel that way as I was signing the checks for all those contractors. Anyway," she went on, clearly ready to move on to a different topic of conversation, "because fiber arts is such a big field, and it can be interpreted in a whole bunch of different ways, it'll be easy enough to pass you off as another artist." A pause as she gazed up at him, and then she nodded. "You look like you could be Spanish. So...you're Loc de la Cruz, a noted fiber artist from Barcelona. You work with...metal threads and stones, making fiber art that's almost like jewelry. Sound good?"

"I suppose so," he replied, amused despite himself by the genuine delight she seemed to take in weaving a tale just as intricate as the piece that hung on the wall before them. "Although, since it seems you do not work with metal threads, I am not sure why this fictional person would be staying with you."

"But I do use a lot of semiprecious stones in my work," she argued. "That should be enough. If Rafe does come by, we'll just explain to him that we met in an online forum and communicated there for a while, and that I offered to put you up when you came here to Santa Fe for the show."

"You seem to have figured out everything," Loc said. Some people might have been dismayed by her apparent talent for prevarication, but he found it more amusing than anything else. Besides, when all these fabrications were being created for his benefit, how could he disapprove?

"Probably not," she said. "Something always seems to slip through the cracks. But at least it's better than telling everyone I have a demon lord sleeping in the guest room, right?"

Loc couldn't really argue with that logic. Since he'd been hiding his identity for many human months now, he knew it was better to remain discreet. "Yes, I suppose you're right."

Someone knocked at the door to the studio, then called out, "Cat, are you in there? I need to ask you something."

For a second, she froze. Then she seemed to relax slightly, and a certain glint entered her dark eyes. "All right, Loc—time to see if our cover story holds water."

She opened the door to the fiber studio, all too aware of how she was holding her breath. Silly, really, since Roberto worked for her. But even though she wouldn't allow herself to look back, she knew that Loc stood only a few paces behind her, would be all too obvious as soon as Roberto had a second to focus on the interior of the building.

"Hi, Roberto," she said breezily, knowing the best thing to do was balls her way through this and hope for the best. "This is Loc de la Cruz, a fiber artist from Spain. He's visiting right now."

Although she'd noticed the way Roberto's eyes had narrowed as soon as he caught sight of Loc, he seemed to relax a bit as he heard her explanation for his presence. "Ah, from Spain?" His gaze moved to the demon lord. "*Buenos días, encantado de conocerlo.*"

Oh, hell. Despite her clan's origins, Cat's Spanish was limited to a few words and phrases, and she had no idea whether Loc had picked up any other languages during the months he'd spent scouring the globe for someone who could assist him.

But then Loc said smoothly, "*Mucho gusto, señor,*" and it was all Cat could do to prevent herself from collapsing in a relieved heap right there on the doorstep. As far as she could tell, his accent sounded perfect, and really, she didn't know whether Roberto would be able to detect anything off about it anyway, since she knew his family had emigrated here from Mexico in the 1960s and so he probably couldn't detect a true Barcelona accent any better than she could.

Then Loc went on, deftly switching back to English, "Yes, Catalina was kind enough to open her house to a fellow artist. Your vines are very beautiful, by the way."

Smooth operator, aren't you? she thought, although she had to be grateful for the way Loc had deflected the conversation away from himself.

Roberto beamed. He was a slender man just a shade under six feet tall, his olive skin deeply tanned from all his work outdoors. "Yes, it was the vines I wanted to talk to you about, Cat."

Although nothing in her vineyard manager's expression or posture showed anything particularly alarming, she couldn't quite prevent the flash of panic that went through her. "Is there something wrong?" she asked. "Did those last two rainstorms get some fungus going on the vines or something?"

At once, he shook his head. "No, nothing like that. It's only that Miguel and I just got done surveying the fields, and it looks as though the harvest is going to be even better than we thought. I wanted to get your permission to hire more help when the time comes."

Again, relief flooded through her. "Oh, sure," she said, airily waving a hand. "However many people you need."

"It shouldn't be too many," he replied. "This is not a large vineyard. But an extra two or three people could make all the difference."

"Then that's fine. Thank you for asking—and thank you for taking such good care of the vines."

"It's a pleasure." Roberto nodded at Loc. "You have come at a beautiful time of year, sir. Enjoy Santa Fe."

Then he was off, heading back to the vines. As Cat watched him go, she saw him meet up with his son Miguel where the path to the house crossed the one to the vineyard. They stood there for a moment, having some kind of discussion, and Roberto pointed briefly toward the fiber studio. Miguel glanced over. Even from this distance, Cat could see the way he scowled.

Loc's deep voice came at her ear. "Who is that?"

"Miguel, Roberto's oldest son," she replied

"He doesn't look very happy."

No, he didn't. And she thought she knew exactly why. However, she figured it was better not to say anything, and instead shut the door.

"What is it?" Loc asked.

She made an off-hand gesture. "Nothing. I

think Miguel has a teeny crush on me. He probably wasn't very happy to hear that you were staying at the house."

Loc's brows pulled together, and he glanced over at the now-closed door. "I don't understand. Why would my presence affect him in any way?"

Now she wished she hadn't said anything at all. Attempting to explain the situation to a being like Loc was going to be awkward at best. Still, since he now watched her with an expectant look on his face, she knew she would have to say something. "Generally, if a man feels attracted to a woman, he also feels threatened if there are other males around who might be rivals. That's all."

The demon lord appeared to process this explanation for a moment, frown deepening. "But I am not a rival. I am not even human."

"Well, you know that, and I know that," Cat said. "But Miguel doesn't know that. He just sees a guy in his twenties." *A gorgeous, exotic stranger from Spain, and an artist to boot. No wonder Miguel looked so pissed off.*

"Ah. Of course." A long pause, and then Loc asked, "Do you have feelings for this Miguel?"

"No, of course not," she replied immediately. "He's a couple of years younger than I am, and besides, we don't have anything in common." *Plus, he's not my type.*

But there was no way she would tell Loc that, because then he might ask what her type was, and the last thing she wanted to reveal was that he happened to be *exactly* her type—handsome, dark, movie-star-perfect.

Otherworldly.

"Anyway," she went on, "it doesn't really matter, because it's not like he's underfoot in the house or anything. He's out in the vineyard with his father all day, so our paths shouldn't cross too much."

"That is something." Loc was silent for a moment, as if still considering everything she had told him. "Where will your paths go, then?"

Good question. A normal day would have included some puttering around the house, and then at least four or five solid hours of work here in the studio. Cat knew she couldn't do much more than that because she started to get brain-fried, or at least cross-eyed from staring down at the threads on her loom or the embroidery yarn of a nearly finished piece. That was fine, though, since she usually knocked off around five-thirty or six, and sat down at her favorite stone table in the garden to have a glass of white wine. This pleasant practice would have to come to an end when the weather started to really cool down, but that day was still a few months off.

Problem was, she knew there wouldn't be any such thing as a "normal day" with Loc staying here. When she'd made that impetuous offer to give him a place to crash for a while, she really hadn't thought too far ahead. Now she had to figure out what on earth they would do to keep themselves occupied.

Possibly sensing her unease, he said, "There is no need to do anything other than what you would normally do. I had no intention of disrupting your life when I came seeking a place of refuge."

Maybe not, but he was disrupting it nonetheless. However, Cat knew she was also on a tight schedule to get her final piece ready for the fiber arts show, which was now in less than a week. Normally, she would have been farther along than this, but even though the house had been mostly done for some time and she'd been living here for more than a month, there had still been innumerable last-minute chores and snags to take up more of her day than she'd planned.

"Well...." she began, then gave a helpless shrug. "I still have a lot of work to do on my final piece for the show, so yes, I am going to have to concentrate on that if I want to meet my deadline. But what will you do?"

Loc glanced away from her, his gaze moving toward the windows set high on the wall, although she wasn't quite sure what he was looking for. "My search is not over. I came here because I needed someplace where I could pause and gather my thoughts, but there are still places I haven't visited. Do you mind if I use your home as a base of sorts? It would make matters less complicated."

Part of her wanted to shake her head at being used as a sort of glorified short-term vacation rental by the demon lord, but Cat understood why he had made the request. He hadn't yet given up hope of returning to his home— although, judging by the few things he'd said about that particular plane of existence, she couldn't quite understand why anyone would want to go back there. Still, it wasn't her place to comment. And really, it would make the situation a lot easier for her if he wasn't around all the time. She might actually be able to focus on her work.

"No, I don't mind," she said, hoping the relief in her voice wasn't too obvious. "Do you know where you're going to go first?"

"Probably New Orleans," he replied. "I had not visited there yet, but I have heard the city has some powerful practitioners of magic."

Cat hoped he would be able to tell the difference between a true witch or warlock and some charlatan hawking fake voodoo dolls in the French Quarter, but she refrained from comment. After all, he was a demon lord, not some wet-behind-the-ears kid who'd just started to grow into his magical powers. Of course Loc would know immediately if someone was trying to sell him a bill of goods.

"That sounds promising," she said carefully. "And I've heard New Orleans is an amazing city."

Without hesitating, he responded, "Would you like to come with me?"

The request surprised her so much that at first she wasn't sure how to reply. Then she shook her head. "No, I can't do that. Like I said, I have a lot of work to do. Also, I'd have to get permission to visit, and the *prima* of the clan there—the Dubois clan, I think—would want to know why I was coming. That might be kind of hard to explain."

"Ah, yes. I had forgotten that you witches and warlocks cannot go freely between yours and other clans' territories."

Was that a hint of condemnation in his voice? Cat couldn't tell for sure, because his expression was neutral enough. Maybe he thought it was silly, the way clans stuck to the lands they'd claimed decades or centuries earlier, but it did help to keep the peace. "It's a courtesy," she said, trying her best to keep her own expression as bland as his. "That's all. Anyway," she went on, thinking it a good idea to change the subject, "where did you learn to speak Spanish so well? On your travels?"

The smile he gave her now was almost indulgent. "If I have heard a few sentences in one of your languages, then I know it. Simple as that."

She blinked. "Simple as that," she repeated, mind reeling. Of course, she knew he possessed powers far beyond those of any witch or warlock, but....

"Yes. It's something that comes naturally to me. The patterns are easy enough to decipher, once I've heard a phrase or two. Luckily, you chose a homeland for me that is a place I've already visited. If I'd had to speak Inuit or Bedouin, I might have had a problem."

Loc wasn't joking. No, he stood a few paces away, looking at her with his mouth slightly pursed, as though doing his best to determine why she should be so surprised.

Cat realized it probably wasn't a good idea to be staring at his mouth. Like the rest of him, it was way too distracting. "Um…okay. Well, that's handy, I suppose. How long do you think you'll be in New Orleans?"

"Oh, just for the day. That should be enough time to either find what I'm looking for, or determine that New Orleans is another dead end, just like all the other places I've explored over these past months."

It would have sounded utterly strange to ask, *Oh, you'll be home for dinner?*, so she didn't. She figured she'd deal with that situation when the time came. Clearly, it wasn't a problem for him to conjure a meal if necessary, so she'd rely on that peculiar gift to take care of dinner, should he come back here in time. If not, she had plenty of frozen stuff on hand.

"All right," she said. "It's probably better if you leave from the house. That way, Roberto and Miguel will see us leaving from the studio and won't wonder why you never came out. You can't really see the garage from the vineyard, so if they say anything later, I'll just tell them that you took your rental car and went into town."

"An elaborate charade," Loc remarked.

"A necessary one," Cat said firmly. "Or would you rather I told them the truth about you?"

Those night-black eyes fastened on hers, and she forced herself to stare back without flinching. It was still so hard to remember that he wasn't human, that the nightmarish shape of his true form still lurked behind the model-handsome features of the man who faced her now.

"No," he said after a long pause. "I suppose that wouldn't do at all."

"Okay, then." She put her hand on the doorknob and turned it, then pushed the door open so they could go outside. Although the studio was stocked with expensive yarn and the even more expensive stones she used in her finished pieces, she didn't bother to lock up. She trusted Miguel and Roberto, and besides, she'd be back here soon enough to get to work once Loc had gone off on his fact-finding trip to New Orleans.

That thought sent a little pang through her. Yes, it would be much easier with him gone and out from underfoot for the day, but....

But nothing, she told herself as they walked up the gravel path that led to the front entry of her house. *Be glad that he has something to do with his time. That way, even if Rafe and Miranda do drop by unexpectedly at some point, there'll be a pretty good chance that he won't even be here. Easier for everyone.*

And if he did find what he was looking for, the one witch or warlock with the power to send him forth from the confines of this plane of existence? Well, then, she'd have to be happy that he was able to go home. This was no place for him, a world where every second of every day, he had to conceal who and what he truly was. What kind of life was that?

"You appear troubled," Loc said as they went inside and she closed the door behind them.

"Oh, I was just thinking," she replied, hoping he would leave it at that.

"Then it seems whatever you were thinking about troubles you."

Cat supposed she could tell him it was none of his business, but that sort of reply sounded awfully rude. Better to dig up a little white lie, something that wouldn't cause him to probe any deeper. Thank God that at least he didn't seem able to tell when someone was lying to him, despite all his powers.

"Oh, I have to make some design decisions before I go forward with my final piece for the art show," she said. "Faceted or smooth garnet beads for one, and I'm still not sure whether I'm going to use onyx or hematite to go along with the garnet. Things like that."

"It seems you're already thinking of your work. Good. Then I will leave you to it."

For just the barest second, it was as though she could see Loc's true self, the great leathery wings, the gleaming black skin, the sharp harshness of his features. Then he was gone, and she stood alone in the foyer, wondering why she could suddenly smell the scent of a bonfire. Had it come from him?

Maybe. Now, though, she was alone, and had work to do.

She hoped to hell she'd be able to concentrate on it.

4

THE AIR TOUCHED HIM FIRST, HEAVY AND HOT AND wet, like a damp blanket someone had folded around his body. If he had been in his true form, Loc probably wouldn't have even noticed the discomfort, but now he found himself wondering how anyone could live in such miserable conditions.

Still, he was here on a mission, and some temporary misery caused by the local climate certainly wasn't enough to keep him from pursuing his goal. Instinct had led him to reappear in an alleyway, a place where he wouldn't be observed by the locals. Now he emerged from the dingy spot and headed out to the sidewalk, where he paused for a moment to get his bearings.

Despite the heat and the humidity, the streets and walks here were crowded with cars and people. The scent of exhaust and frying food and blooming flowers he couldn't name hung on the heavy air, all of it overlaid by a dark, damp smell that probably came from the river, which was only a few blocks away. No one seemed to pay any attention to him, except a gaggle of young women a few years younger than Cat, who stared at him, giggled, and then leaned their heads together as they indulged in a whispered conversation of some sort.

After spending more than eight mortal months in this form, Loc guessed well enough why they were paying attention to him. However, he was not here to attract foolish girls, but to find the person who could free him from the bonds of this world. He walked a few paces and then paused, pretending to be engrossed in the offerings presented in the window of an antique shop, while in reality he was sending his hyper-attuned senses outward, searching for the ripple in the fabric of this place that would tell him he was in the presence of the one he sought.

He'd sensed such a fold in the world when Simon Escobar first brought him to Santa Fe. Miranda Castillo had created yet another, even though Loc had known immediately that she did not possess the necessary skills to send him back. The strongest witches and warlocks always sent out these eddies of power, and yet merely possessing power was not enough. That power had to be married to the knowledge of certain arcane practices and spells, a combination that had proved exceedingly difficult to find.

Still, he had to start someplace.

There was something here...or rather, several somethings. One seemed quite close, probably only a few blocks from where he stood. The other seemed to be farther away, perhaps as much as a mile or more, although that was not so very far in the grand scheme of things.

Well, he would start with the closest one, that strange vibration of power only he could feel. If that venture proved unsuccessful, then he would move on to the next. Loc tried not to think, '*When that venture proved unsuccessful,*' for truly, after so many failures, he had no reason to believe this one would be any different.

His senses led him to a brick building with black shutters, one that appeared to house yet another of the old city's innumerable antique stores, although this one seemed to focus on jewelry and other small accessories rather than furniture and paintings. Well enough. He could pretend to be there searching for a gift for his woman. Not that he had one, of course, but the important thing was the illusion of having a significant other to shop for.

Or you could purchase something for Cat, he thought as he mounted the concrete steps, now worn by the passing of too many feet. *Something to say thank you for allowing you to stay in her home.*

Loc had never before thought of buying a gift for anyone, and the concept was so novel, he had to pause and consider it for a moment. That was what people did, wasn't it? Of course, he'd barely entertained the notion that she would refuse his request, would tell him that he must find some-place else to go, for it seemed only logical that she would do what she could to provide him a refuge. But now it seemed he must acknowledge what she'd done for him, and a gift seemed the best way to do it. Money was not an issue, for he made sure that his wallet always had exactly what he needed at any particular moment.

A necklace, perhaps...one he could drape around her lovely throat. He thought of how soft her skin must be, how exciting it would be to push her wavy dark hair aside so he could fasten the clasp.

His body stirred and he frowned, willing the strange reaction away. By necessity, he'd learned something of what humans did together when procreating or merely indulging in a few moments of pleasure, and yet he'd never found himself interested in any of those pursuits despite the human form he wore while here. This was the first time his assumed body had reacted to any kind of sexual stimuli.

And for that stimuli to be something as innocuous as placing a necklace around a woman's throat....

Loc was not sure what to do about that. He'd allowed himself to admire Cat's beauty, but he'd thought that admiration something in the abstract, certainly nothing he would ever act upon. Now, though, he realized it wasn't just this body that wanted her.

He wanted her.

You can ponder that conundrum later, he told himself as he pushed the door open and entered the antique store. A string of bells dangled from the knob, and they chimed faintly, signaling his arrival.

But if he was successful here, would there even be a later? He would leave this world and everything in it—Catalina Castillo included—far behind. For the first time, such a prospect did not seem particularly appealing.

To Loc's relief, the shop was empty. It would be easier to determine if its proprietor was the one he sought without a crowd of humans muddying the water. Gilt-framed cases hung on the walls, showcasing pieces set with sapphires and emeralds and rubies, pearls and topazes and garnets. A freestanding case stood near the opposite wall, which was covered in rather garish floral paper.

As Loc stared at it, feeling again the pulse of the power that had led him here, a door in that wall opened, and a tall black woman emerged. Her hair had been plaited into a thousand tiny braids ornamented with bands of gold, and they jingled faintly as she moved toward the counter. It was difficult for him to determine her age; he thought she was no longer young, but there was no gray in her black hair, and the warm brown eyes that regarded him coolly had very few lines around them.

"Can I help you?" she asked. Her voice was as rich and dark as her hair, with a certain lilt he recognized from the island nations he'd visited during the course of his quest.

Loc cleared his throat and stepped forward. This was always the most difficult part, for while he could sense the magic in others, they could not do the same with him. He had to find a way to broach the topic without giving too much away.

"It depends," he said. "So far, I haven't been able to find what I'm looking for. But I was hoping your shop might be different…just as you yourself are different."

She understood at once what he was saying, for her eyes with their thick liner narrowed slightly, and she put her hands on her ample hips. No, she was not heavy, but rather curved in the precise way a human female should be, bosom full and waist narrow, the width of her hips echoing the roundness of her bust. "You're sayin' I'm different, then?"

"Yes," Loc replied simply. "And it's because you are different that I thought you might be able to help."

The woman regarded him out of her still-narrowed eyes. "And are you different, too, sir?"

"You can't tell?"

For a long moment, she was silent, appearing to survey him. "I'm not sure," she said, her tone frank. "That is, I can't feel your difference the way I should, and yet...."

"And yet?" Loc prompted.

"And yet you're standin' there with that pretty face of yours, and that body a woman would want to know better, and there's something' about the way you're wearin' it, like it was a suit you aren't sure fits the way it should."

"Very perceptive," he said. "Yes, there is a reason why I can feel your power, but you can't feel mine. I don't think I need to say anything more than that, do I?"

The woman couldn't precisely go pale, but something about her mouth tightened, revealing lines that didn't seem to have been there a moment earlier. "What do you want?" she whispered.

"I want to know who here in New Orleans can reach out to my world," Loc replied. "Can you?"

At once she shook her head, the metal rings in her hair clinking against each other like strange little chimes. "Nossir," she said. "There's a darkness in that magic I know better than to touch. It's the sort of thing that can eat away at a person. But...."

"'But'?" he echoed.

She cast a glance over one shoulder, although it was obvious that she and Loc were the only occupants of the store. "None of 'em like to talk about it," she said, again in that low murmur which was barely above a whisper.

"Them…who?"

"The Dubois witches," the woman replied. "I'm not one of 'em—they took me in when I sought refuge here—but I know what happened."

"What exactly did happen?" Impatience made the question sound harsher than Loc had intended, and the woman went even more tense, knuckles standing out against her dark skin as she clutched the edge of the display case, the only thing separating the two of them.

"*Him*," the woman said. "I'm not going to say his name, because even one of us whispering it is enough to call his attention. Over in the Garden District is where he abides. Darkness hides there. The Dubois witches keep him away from us here in the French Quarter, but they're not strong enough to drive him out of New Orleans altogether."

"This warlock isn't part of the Dubois clan?"

Another fierce shake of her head. "Nossir. I don't know who or what he is. Only that he's there. And if it's those sorts of dark spells you're wanting, then he's the only person who could help. Not that he's in the habit of helping anyone but himself."

The woman's obvious fear might have given some people pause, but Loc knew there was no warlock in this world whose powers were great enough to best his. Yes, Simon Escobar had been able to summon him to this plane, thanks to the one peculiar flaw in a demon's nature that allowed them to be called in such a fashion...but that human warlock hadn't been able to control Loc once he was here. Conversely, another witch or warlock could send him back, but would have no other power over him.

"The Garden District," he said. "Where is that?"

"'Bout a mile from here. A taxi would take you."

"An automated car, you mean?"

For the first time, the shopkeeper witch smiled, as though reassured by this evidence that he didn't seem to know everything. "No. The taxi union lobbied to keep those things out. Only human drivers in the Quarter."

Interesting. Loc knew about the self-driving cars that operated in every city in the world, because of course he'd availed himself of their services during those instances when it made more sense to ride than to magically move from place to place. It seemed that tradition had prevailed over technology here, however.

"A taxi, then." He paused, glancing down for the first time at the display case in front of him. All manner of jewels sparkled there, but his eye was caught by a necklace with a series of heavy, smooth, graduated emerald drops that dangled from a fine collar of diamonds set in black gold. It would look magnificent encircling Cat's slender throat. "And that necklace. The emerald one."

The woman's eyes widened. "I—I can't just give it to you. The owner—"

"I want to buy it, not take it," Loc cut in. He might be a demon, but he wasn't a thief.

"You what?"

"It is for sale, is it not?"

"Yes, but…." For the first time, the strange witch looked more puzzled than frightened. "It's eighty thousand dollars."

"Good thing I carry plenty of cash, then." He produced the wallet from his front pocket, and calmly began pulling out hundred-dollar bills, stacking them on the counter. Since the woman appeared to be frozen in shock, he said, "Perhaps you could take out that necklace and wrap it up for me? This is going to take a while."

A blink, and she said, "Yes, sure."

The case rattled a bit as she opened it. Realizing that having enormous stacks of hundred-dollar bills lying out on top of the glass would be rather conspicuous if anyone else were to come into the shop, Loc instead produced a satchel from the air, then made sure that eight hundred of the hundred-dollar notes were stacked neatly inside. He set it on top of the counter as the woman straightened up, the emerald necklace dangling from her hand.

"I—I'll just get a box for it, sir."

She went into the back room, presumably to search for the aforementioned box. In her haste, she left the jewelry case unlocked, but Loc had no intention of pilfering its contents. If he'd wanted to, he could have taken anything he desired, but he had found the perfect piece for Cat and had no wish to acquire anything else.

The witch returned, a dark green leatherette case clutched in one hand. She opened it to reveal the emerald necklace displayed against a bed of white satin, several discreet pins holding it carefully in place.

"That will do very well," Loc said, allowing himself to admire the piece for a moment before he shut the case and pushed the satchel an inch or two toward the woman. "Your payment."

Her long, clever-looking fingers wrapped around the satchel's handle. She appeared to hesitate, as if wrestling with a question she knew she shouldn't ask, then said quickly, "Who is it for?"

"A friend," he replied. That seemed to be a safe enough answer, especially since he wasn't quite sure he could articulate to himself how he felt about Cat Castillo, let alone explain such a thing to a stranger.

"A very lucky friend, I think." The witch paused again, dark eyes searching his face. "This friend knows who you are?"

"She knows what I am," Loc said smoothly. And that, he thought, was perhaps the most remarkable thing about his current situation. Cat had known from the beginning who he was and where he came from, and she still had offered him a place to stay. How many other human women—even witches—would have done the same thing?

The woman standing behind the display case appeared to absorb his reply, then said, "Then go to her, and take her the necklace. Don't go to see *him*. You'll regret it."

"Are you a seer?" That seemed the most rational explanation for her urgency. Perhaps she had seen something….

But the strange witch shook her head. "Nah, not me. Estelle Dubois, *prima* of the clan here—she's a seer. That's partly why she's been able to keep *him* at bay—she can see him comin', so to speak. She can't see everything, though, and that's why—" She stopped abruptly there, as if she had just realized she was about to reveal secrets that were not hers to tell.

"Why what?"

"Nothin'. Or at least, no concern of yours. Better to go back where you came from, take that necklace with you. I figure you must be trapped here, or someone like you wouldn't be seekin' help. But sometimes it's better to leave such things alone. Exile isn't the worst thing that can happen to a person."

Although Loc wanted to know more—a certain sorrow in her big dark eyes seemed to indicate that she understood the pain of exile all too well—he guessed she would not reveal more unless compelled to do so, and he had no wish to inflict pain upon her. She had clearly already suffered her own share, and besides, such behavior would not reflect well on the Castillos if the Dubois witches ever figured out where he had come from.

Perhaps her words were wise ones. However, Loc had set himself on this quest, and he would not shy away now. He had already crossed paths with some workers of very dark magic and had never suffered any ill effects for it. They, like he himself, knew that he could not be bested.

"Thank you for your help," he said politely, and took the jewelry case and left her. From the sorrow in her face, she appeared to realize he planned to ignore her advice, but she made no move to stop him, or protest further.

Wise woman.

As she'd informed him, taxis painted a variety of bright hues constantly trolled the streets of the French Quarter, looking for fares. Loc supposed they must occasionally leave this district, or at least he hoped they did. Otherwise, he would be forced to go the rest of the way to his destination on foot.

He flagged down a taxi painted a shocking orange, then climbed in the back and told the driver, "The Garden District."

The man, whose looks were as classically patrician as the Castillo witches Loc had met in Santa Fe and whose accent proclaimed him to be from somewhere far north of Louisiana, said, "Want to narrow it down? There's a lot of places you could go—zoos, parks, museums, Lafayette Cemetery—"

"The cemetery," Loc said immediately. He wasn't quite sure why, but for some reason he'd experienced a strange prickling along the back of his neck as soon as the driver uttered the words, "Lafayette Cemetery," as though the power within him had recognized the destination as significant, even if he had no real way of explaining why.

"Gotcha," the driver said, and began inching along through the heavy traffic.

At this rate, it might have been faster if he had walked, although Loc didn't know whether even the young and healthy body he wore would have been up to the task of slogging more than a mile in this heat and humidity. At least this time in the back seat of the taxi gave him some time to mentally prepare to face the nameless warlock who resided in the Garden District. In general, witches did not frighten easily, and so the very real fear the witch in the jewelry shop had shown must be based in some sort of harsh reality.

Even so, Loc knew he had no reason to be afraid. In fact, fear was not an emotion he understood very well, since he had yet to truly experience it for himself. Yes, he was not precisely happy at the thought of having to remain here in this world for all eternity, but even with all that, he couldn't exactly call the emotion he felt at the thought of such a prospect *fear*. Trepidation, perhaps, but that was about as far as he was willing to go.

At last they were out of the French Quarter and its crowds of milling tourists, but their progress still wasn't what anyone could call swift. Eventually, though, the driver stopped the taxi under a large oak tree whose roots had all but destroyed the sidewalk around it. On the other side of that ruined sidewalk was a brick wall, its whitewashed surface faded and patched.

"Lafayette Cemetery," the driver said. "The entrance is around the block, but there's generally no place to stop there."

"Not a problem," Loc replied. He produced a hundred-dollar bill from his continuously resupplied wallet and handed it to the man, whose expression shifted from guarded boredom to outright surprise.

"I'm not sure if I have change for that—"

"Keep it."

Loc opened the door and got out. The driver, apparently not wishing to stay around to see if his fare changed his mind about the size of the tip he'd just given, pulled away from the curb in some haste, narrowly missing the front bumper of a truck that had just turned the corner.

Perhaps the citizens of the French Quarter should rethink the carte blanche they've given the taxis, Loc thought with some amusement.

That amusement faded abruptly, however, as he felt it drifting toward him, like a foul odor being carried on the wind.

Evil.

Some might argue that by his very being, Loc himself was evil, but he knew that was not precisely true. Demons could only act according to the natures with which they'd been born. There was nothing evil about such behavior, even if those acts might occasionally impinge on human health and happiness. Although he, as a demon lord, was not as controlled by his nature as his vassals, he still existed outside the moral code that bound most mortals.

However, humans could not claim that same privilege. They knew the difference between right and wrong, had the free will that allowed them to make decisions based on such knowledge. If a human turned away from the right-hand path, explored areas of learning that should have been shunned...well, then one could only call them evil.

And that was what he sensed now. A darkness that lived here amongst these gracious old houses and narrow streets, that hid its nature from those around it. But it could not hide from Loc, because his inner senses were far more attuned to such things.

He turned away from the faded, whitewashed wall that bounded the cemetery, and regarded the house directly opposite where he stood. It was barely visible from the street, thanks to the high brick wall that enclosed the property and the old, old trees which crowded the grounds. He was able to make out a tall house, also made of brick, with several chimneys and dark green shutters, but he could not see much more detail than that.

From this vantage point, he could not detect anything like a gate in that high wall. Perhaps it was located on the side that bordered the driveway, which was long and empty. Not that it mattered; even a wall as high and forbidding as the one he faced now was not enough to keep him out.

In an eye blink, he was inside. The sense of evil was even stronger here, like having to walk through the miasma of a skunk spray, although the front garden itself seemed ordinary enough, the tall trees shading a lawn of lush green, white camellias gleaming like familiar spirits along the edge of the front porch. Jaw clenched, he stowed the jewelry case he carried in the back pocket of his jeans, although it should not have been able to fit in such a confined space. However, the laws of physics did not constrain him the way they did ordinary mortals, and so the case with its precious cargo fit in his pocket well enough.

That task done, Loc made himself approach the porch, even though he was beginning to wonder if this had been such a good idea after all. Never in all his travels had he encountered anything like the cloud of darkness that seemed to envelop the house in front of him. Then again, he already knew that the magic required to send him home was not anything a light-worker would touch. If the sense of evil was so terribly strong here, that must mean the warlock who was its source must be equally strong.

Up the front steps, five in number, and then Loc paused at the door. It was ordinary enough in appearance, painted dark green to match the shutters on the windows to either side, with a fanlight above it and a plain brass knocker.

As he stared at that door, willing himself to reach up and knock, it slowly swung open. The man who stood there did not appear either young or old, but someplace timelessly in between. His skin was far lighter than that of the witch in the jewelry store, but still dark enough to show he was probably of mixed blood. Features regular, but neither handsome nor ugly. The one striking element of his appearance were his eyes, a pale, icy shade somewhere between blue and gray.

Those eyes fastened on Loc, and the man smiled slightly, showing very white teeth. "Hello," he said. "I've been expecting you."

5

CAT TRAILED HER FINGERS THROUGH THE BOWL OF stone beads that sat near her elbow. This was a normal practice for her, since she liked to feel their shapes beneath her fingertips, get a sense of their weight, before she began selecting the ones she intended to use in a particular piece. Now, though, she had the feeling she was doing this more to kill time than because she was getting any closer to enlightenment when it came to her current work-in-progress.

Although at the time she'd thought it a good idea for Loc to get out and continue his search for someone with the power to send him home, now she was reevaluating that particular plan. She had all this work to do, and yet all she seemed capable of was sitting here and thinking about what he might be doing at this moment.

Which, she realized, was stupid, because of course he'd tell her about it when he got back.

If he got back. If he was lucky enough to find someone who could help him, he might just leave then and there, and not bother to come back here to say goodbye.

Cat realized she was expecting a lot from a person that she'd probably exchanged a few hundred words with at best, and yet...she didn't want to think of him disappearing and not giving her a proper chance to offer him at least a "fare thee well."

He's a demon lord, she told herself. *He's going to do what he's going to do. And you'd better get your ass moving on this piece, or it's never going to be ready in time.*

Suddenly purposeful, she tipped a quantity of garnet beads into the wide, shallow bowl she used to make it easier to thread them onto wire. They glinted in the light coming down through the high windows of her studio, a light that had shifted a good bit since the time Loc had disappeared out of her living room.

She didn't keep a clock in the studio, because she didn't want her work dictated by the hour. Now, though, she let out a frustrated huff of breath and reached for her phone so she could check the time.

One-thirty. That meant he'd been gone for almost three hours.

So? she thought. *New Orleans is a big place.*

Or at least she thought it was. She'd never been there, of course. Just another on a long, long list of places she'd never been. It wasn't the first time she'd chafed at how circumscribed her life was, but now it felt even worse, possibly because she couldn't help thinking of all the places Loc must have visited on his quest, cities and countries that were just a dot on a map to her but must be exotically alive in person. Paris and Milan and Berlin…Kyoto and Casablanca and Singapore. Of course, she had no way of knowing that Loc had actually been to all those places, but….

She allowed herself another sigh but also went to work, needle flashing as she stitched the garnet beads on top of the fluffy yarn that rested atop the hand-woven linen base. The colors did go beautifully together, and she found herself relaxing as she worked, occupied—for the moment, at least—by the intricacy of the details, the need to keep every stitch as neat and precise as possible.

Thus occupied, she was able to push Loc out of her thoughts.

Almost.

"Come inside," the man—the warlock—said. "It's insufferably hot out there."

Loc couldn't argue with that description. It

was brutally hot and humid. And, although he could still feel the evil that seemed to flood every corner of the house, he was unable to detect any spells directed at him, whether to trap him here, or possibly attempt to tap into his own enormous powers.

"Thank you," he said politely, and stepped into the foyer.

At once the man closed the door, although again, the movement didn't seem particularly sinister, but rather an attempt to keep any more of the precious air conditioning from seeping outside. The foyer was small, furnished in the sparsely elegant style of the Biedermeier period. A landscape of a rolling green countryside hung above a small table.

"This way," the man said, and Loc followed him down the hallway into another room, a salon of some sort, with a pair of couches upholstered in dark green velvet, and striped wallpaper upon the walls. A fire burned in the hearth, but it was not a natural fire, for no logs rested on the grate, and the flames flickered in shades of acid green and cobalt blue. The warlock must have noticed the way his gaze moved to it, because he said, "I suppose you think it an affectation."

"The colors are quite bright," Loc replied, his tone neutral.

"I find them soothing." The warlock went to a

side table, where a crystal decanter and several matching tumblers awaited. "Bourbon?"

"None for me."

"It is safe, you know."

It wouldn't have affected him even if it weren't, but Loc saw no reason to explain such a thing to the warlock. "I am more of a cognac man."

The man smiled, once again showing off his white teeth. "A refined demon. How…unusual."

"You know what I am."

"Of course. If you throw a stone into the center of a still pond, the ripples always spread out, don't they?" He busied himself with pouring several fingers of bourbon into a tumbler, then paused with it lifted halfway to his mouth. "I am Nicholas Toulouse. What should I call you?"

Loc knew it was safe enough to give the name he had been using, since it was not his true name and therefore had no real power. "Loc is good enough for now."

The warlock nodded and took a sip of his bourbon, and said, "Loc, then. What brings you to our fair city?"

"You don't know?"

Nicholas Toulouse paused for a moment, seeming to consider the question. "I can guess. But I don't know for sure."

"What is your guess?"

The warlock set his tumbler of bourbon back

down on the table next to its mate. "Well, since I know that you possess powers equal to or greater than my own, I believe there is only one thing you could need from me, the one thing you can't do for yourself. And that is to be sent home."

Even though he had been halfway expecting such a response, Loc couldn't quite prevent a small chill from moving down his spine. It was never easy to have another guess one's weaknesses quite so accurately.

Instead of directly admitting to such a failing, Loc asked, "Can you do it?"

"Yes."

He had not been expecting such a direct answer. Perhaps noting Loc's surprise, Toulouse went on, "Oh, there will be a cost. Such things always have a cost."

Loc narrowed his eyes at the warlock's presumption. "I do not barter."

That declaration earned him a thin smile. "Possibly you don't, but I do. I have the power, but I do not yet have the means. You will get me what I need for the incantation, and then I will cast the spell to send you home."

"And what is it you need?"

"A certain grimoire, a book of spells that contains the exact incantation, the precise sigils, that are required to direct all my power into sending you back to your plane." The warlock's pale eyes lit with something that could only be called mischief. "That grimoire is now in the keeping of the Castillo witch clan."

There were times Loc very much regretted the human body he was forced to wear, for it tended to react in ways that his own demon form never would. As soon as he heard Nicholas Toulouse's requirements, a cold finger of dread trailed its way down his spine. At least, he assumed that's what the unpleasant sensation was. Perhaps he should have realized that the Castillo witches would have all of Simon Escobar's belongings in their possession, including any spell books he had left behind, but Loc had departed immediately on his quest to find a magic-worker capable of such powerful incantations, and therefore hadn't been around for the aftermath of Escobar's defeat.

"You want me to steal it from them?" Loc asked, his voice steady.

"'Steal' is such an ugly word. And really, the book isn't even theirs. Its rightful owners are the de la Paz clan in Arizona, although, since they've been so careless with their belongings, it only makes sense to have the grimoire come to someone like myself, someone who will treat it with the respect it deserves."

Cat's face flashed into Loc's mind then, the earnest expression on her lovely features as she'd offered her house to him. Surely he couldn't betray her—betray all of the Castillos—by taking such a thing from them.

And yet...this was not his world. What did it really matter, so long as he was able to go back where he belonged?

"I have not sensed the presence of any such grimoire," he said slowly, which was only the truth. By the time he'd returned to Castillo lands, it must have been long since hidden away somewhere.

"That does not surprise me. The Castillo *prima* is young, but she is powerful, and intelligent enough to recognize what has fallen into her hands. She would have done her best to secret it someplace within Castillo territory. You, Loc, must track it down and take it."

"The Castillos control all of New Mexico," he pointed out. "That is a great deal of territory to cover."

Toulouse shrugged. He was wearing a plain black dress shirt and dress slacks, but the dark power swirled around him so strongly, he might as well have been wearing sorcerer's robes. "I doubt they would have hidden it very far from where their *prima* lives," he replied, apparently not at all perturbed by Loc's objection. "You must go and ingratiate yourself to them—it shouldn't be too hard, considering the face and body you have chosen to wear. Surely there is someone in the Castillo clan who would be susceptible to your charms—if memory serves, the former *prima*'s youngest daughter, Catalina, is still unattached. She should be your target."

Those words made another finger of cold trace its way down Loc's back. How could this warlock know what had transpired between him and Cat? But no, Toulouse had given no indication that he realized the two of them even knew one another. He had made a lucky guess, no more.

Still….

"I will see what I can do," Loc replied, which he hoped was a noncommittal enough response. He knew better than to promise this warlock anything. Words could be binding, even for a being such as he. Otherwise, Simon Escobar would not have been able to summon him here.

A thin smile. "I'm sure you will be able to do quite a lot."

"Nicky?"

Both men turned toward the doorway, where a pretty young woman in her early twenties stood. She had honey-blonde hair that fell in ripples down her back, and she wore a flowered sundress that was demure in style and yet still managed to show off the curves of her slender body. Her feet were bare.

"Ah, Celeste," said Nicholas Toulouse. "I'm almost done here."

She nodded, but her gaze moved toward Loc, questioning.

Wearing an indulgent smile, Toulouse said,

"Celeste, this is my new friend Loc. Loc, this is Celeste Dubois, my...very special friend."

Dubois? Loc felt his brows pulling together in a frown, even as he did his best to smooth out his expression. Surely this girl couldn't be....

"Yes," the dark warlock said, apparently divining his thoughts. "She is one of that clan. The *prima*'s youngest daughter, actually."

Noting more clearly the almost blank look on the girl's face, Loc realized she must be under the control of some sort of spell. And he very much doubted that the Dubois clan had given her up willingly, unless her presence here was some sort of guarantee to prevent any kind of action against her family.

He forced himself to say, "It's very nice to meet you, Celeste."

She smiled, but he noticed the way her eyes went immediately to Toulouse and did not linger on him. Because Loc had spent the greater part of eight months wearing this face and body, he knew this was not the sort of reaction he typically elicited from a young woman. Yes, her keeper had definitely placed some sort of dark spell on her...which meant he might attempt the same thing with Loc. Already he knew this warlock was not to be trusted, although he tried to reassure himself with the thought that, while this body was human, the soul it encased was not...and therefore not susceptible to Nicholas Toulouse's dark magic.

"Nicky," the girl said. "You told me you were going to take me shopping, and it's almost two. How much longer are you going to be?"

"Just a few minutes, my pet," he replied, still wearing that indulgent smile. "Besides, you need to put on some shoes before you go."

She looked down at her feet and giggled. "Oh, I suppose I do. Thank you for the reminder—you always take such good care of me."

A flash of a dazzling smile, and she was gone, leaving the two men alone in the room.

Watching Loc closely, Toulouse said, "Is this going to be a problem, demon?"

"No," Loc said at once. "The affairs of mortals mean nothing to me."

"Good. Then you know what we both have to do."

"Yes." He would say no more than that. The most important thing was to get away from here, away from the dark warlock's stare. He might be mortal, but clearly he was a very dangerous man, someone even Loc might not wish to trifle with.

"I'm glad we understand one another." Toulouse paused for a moment, then said, his tone careless, "You shouldn't worry about Celeste. She is quite happy, you know. I believe the same sort of spell would be quite effective in helping you gain the confidence of the Castillo witch."

Loc allowed himself a shrug. "I will take that under advisement."

The faintest hint of a frown passed over the dark warlock's features. "Do as you like, but if you are really so eager to return to your own kingdom, then I would think you would use whatever means necessary to accomplish your goal."

"Perhaps," Loc allowed. "So far, I have not needed to resort to such measures."

That comment only made Toulouse's expression darken further. Clearly, he understood the subtle insult implied by Loc's words, that someone as attractive as he was had no need to use magic to seduce a woman. Bravado, of course, because in all his time here, he'd never been tempted by a human woman, had never had any desire to be intimate with one of them.

Until now....

He thrust that thought away and said, "I will return as soon as I have the book."

"Excellent." The warlock's expression was neutral once again, showing no hint of his previous irritation. "I hope it will not take too long."

"Does the offer have an expiration date?"

"No," Toulouse replied at once. A glint came and went in his pale eyes, a flicker of greed that Loc immediately recognized. It was clear that the dark warlock wanted that grimoire, wanted it badly. Of course, he was doing his best to conceal his need, because that would weaken his bargaining position, but he'd betrayed himself there. He would wait as long as necessary in order to add such a prized specimen to his collection. "Only that the longer you take, the greater the chance that the de la Paz clan will send someone to collect their property. If they take it back to Arizona, the grimoire will be that much more difficult to obtain, because of course they will doubly guard something that has been stolen from them before."

"I don't see such a thing happening," Loc said calmly. "Considering that the Castillos have now had the book in their possession for more than eight months. But I will keep your warning in mind."

"Good."

That seemed to be the end of that. "I'll return when I have the grimoire," he repeated, then took himself away. It was rather amusing to see the shocked expression on Toulouse's face as Loc disappeared before his eyes. Apparently, for all his magical abilities and powers, that was the first time he'd ever witnessed another living being winking out of existence in the blink of an eye.

Loc did not go directly to Cat's house in Pojoaque, however. Although he was fairly certain that the warlock had no way of tracking him, he thought it safer to detour to Santa Fe itself. Besides, he wanted to walk the streets there, send his senses out in all directions to see if he could possibly detect where the grimoire had been hidden. This was a long shot, because he guessed that Miranda, the *prima*, had made sure it was buttressed behind as many protection spells as she could conjure, but he figured he might as well try.

That would be the simplest thing, really—to find the book on his own, without having to use Cat as the means of locating it. For some reason, he didn't like that idea much at all. He didn't want to abuse and betray her trust. Perhaps he would still be doing so by taking the grimoire in the first place, but that was walking a very fine line. Nicholas Toulouse had only been pointing out the truth when he said the Castillos had no real right to the tome, either.

Conundrum settled for now, Loc trod the crowded streets around Santa Fe's famed Plaza, glad that, while it was still warm here, he no longer had to suffer the sticky, heavy heat of New Orleans. As he walked, he sent his senses ranging forth, looking for anything that felt like a sink of dark magic, but he could detect nothing. Oh, he knew who in the crowd were witches and warlocks, felt the presence of other Castillos as far out as a quarter-mile from where he stood, but their vibrations ranged from neutral to warm and inviting. A particularly bright flare to the east told him that was the *prima*'s house, a large, ancient building that seemed as if it held its own secrets.

But no grimoire, nor any other object of magical significance. A shop a bit farther down the street had a cursed bracelet among its used jewelry for sale, and on the other side of downtown was an antique bedstead that was still haunted by the woman who had died in it. Those two were the only remotely magical items he was able to sense, and neither of them had anything to do with his quest for the grimoire. As he'd thought, Miranda Castillo had done her best to secret the book away.

Well, he had halfway expected as much. Now he would have to set his sights on Cat, and hope that she was privy to the information he sought.

If not...well, he would just have to find a way to have her get it for him.

6

A WARM BREEZE DANCED ACROSS THE GARDEN, setting the leaves of the aspen trees surrounding the patio into a rustling shimmer that reflected the late afternoon sunlight. Cat sat at the little bistro set she'd placed off in the secluded corner, sipping from a glass of sauvignon blanc and trying to tell herself that it was just fine for Loc to be gone this long.

Almost as if she'd summoned him herself, he was suddenly there, letting himself in through the little gate that separated this section of the patio from the rest of its concrete expanse. That same wind blew in his loose, shoulder-length hair, sending raven-hued strands fluttering around his face. They weren't enough to conceal his dejected expression, however.

"No luck?" she asked, hoping she sounded appropriately sympathetic despite the small stab of relief that went through her. If he was here, then he must not have been able to find the magic-worker he sought.

"None at all," he replied. His gaze moved from her to the bottle of sauv blanc in its metal cooling sleeve, the extra glass she'd set out in the vain hope that he might be back in time to have a drink on the patio with her.

"You look like you could use a glass of wine," Cat said. "Come and sit down."

"A drink might be helpful." He came over and pulled out the other chair, then sat in it somewhat heavily.

Without speaking, Cat poured a generous amount of white wine into the other glass and handed it to him. He took it from her and allowed himself a large swallow.

"That is better. Thank you."

"No problem." She sat up a little straighter and sipped at her own wine. "Do you want to talk about it?"

"What is there to talk about?" His shoulders lifted. "I am able to sense workers of magic when they are anywhere near me, sense if theirs is the kind of magic that would be useful to me. I found no one like that in New Orleans. Oh, there are witches there, but only the ordinary kind."

"'Ordinary kind'?" Cat echoed, lifting an eyebrow. "Should I be offended?"

He sent her a weary smile, one that still

managed to make her knees feel somehow weak, even though she was sitting down. "I meant no offense, Catalina. Only that it is a dark magic which will send me back to my world, and the Dubois witches and warlocks are much like the Castillos and all others of witch-kind that I've encountered so far. They have no wish to take the left-hand path, and while that is admirable, it does not help me at all."

"I didn't realize it was dark magic," Cat said, feeling a bit chastened. She supposed if she'd thought about it, such a spell would have to be, since demon summoning was some of the blackest magic of all, and a spell to send a demon back to his own world would have to tap into some of the same energies.

"Not as dark as what brought me here, since at least in this case, it would be a spell cast to return to the natural order of things. Still…." Loc didn't exactly sigh, but he did let out a breath before he retrieved his glass of wine and sipped from it. "Since today's witches and warlocks tend to avoid any magic that has any hint of the forbidden to it, there is no one who can do what I need, it seems."

"No one in New Orleans," she said gently. As happy as she was to have him back here, and not disappeared off to his own plane of existence, she didn't want him to think that he'd already exhausted all his resources. "Maybe the person you need is in a small town somewhere. Maybe they're in…Poughkeepsie or something."

His lips lifted slightly at her whimsical comment. "Possibly. But it would take a lifetime to visit all of America's small towns, let alone all the towns and villages of similar size across the globe. I've traveled to many, many cities, thinking that a practitioner of such magic would more easily hide him- or herself in a place with a large population. Perhaps I was going at this from the wrong angle, however."

It did make more sense for a dark warlock to conceal himself someplace where there were a lot of people around. After all, Simon Escobar had managed to hide his true nature for years, first in Southern California, and then in the greater Phoenix area. No one seemed to have had any idea that he was there, or what he was up to.

But just because that kind of strategy had worked for Simon, it didn't necessarily mean that every witch or warlock who was messing with the wrong kind of magic had decided to do the same thing. Cat could see all sorts of reasons why a smaller town—or not even a town at all, but an isolated house in the middle of nowhere—might be a far better choice. It was hard for people to figure out what you were up to when there was no one else around to see what you were doing.

Cat wasn't sure whether she should say any of this to Loc, however. He was intelligent, and had certainly been around far, far longer than she had. No doubt he'd done the mental math, too.

"It sounds as though you've been pretty methodical about it," she said.

"Possibly too methodical. For someone others have called 'the Lord of Chaos,' I am not being terribly chaotic."

Both his voice and his expression were rueful as he delivered that statement, and he leaned back in his chair and drank some more wine once he was done speaking. Cat pursed her lips, considering his words. What he'd said seemed true enough—she hadn't seen much evidence of chaos in his behavior, although she supposed Simon Escobar might have something different to say on the topic, if he were around to say anything at all. The demon lord had definitely thrown a giant monkey wrench into Simon's plans, that was for sure.

"Why do they call you that?" she asked frankly.

To her relief, Loc didn't appear offended by the question. He reached for the bottle of wine where it rested in its silvery cooler, poured a bit more for both of them, and then replaced it. Glass in one hand, he regarded her for a moment before saying, "It was a name given to me long ago by someone who had summoned me to do his bidding. Because he was sloppy, his magic had called me here, but it could not compel me to do what he asked. He ended up sending me back, calling me the Lord of Chaos and cursing my name. Word got out, I suppose, because that is what I have been called ever since."

"Do you get summoned a lot?"

"Not after that," he said, a glint in his dark eyes.

Clearly, he didn't have too much of a problem with the moniker that had been attached to him for God only knows how many centuries. "So what's your real name?"

The amused expression left his face. "You couldn't pronounce it."

"Really?" Cat had the feeling that wasn't the whole reason why he didn't want to give it to her. Maybe if she knew his real name, she'd be able to control him, just like that long-ago warlock had attempted to do…the same thing Simon had tried and failed at so miserably, thanks to Miranda.

Not that Cat wanted to do such a thing. She wasn't really sure exactly what she wanted, only that she liked sitting here with him, talking and drinking wine, and letting the warm, grass-scented breeze blow over them.

"Loc is good enough," he said, in a tone that didn't seem to allow for more discussion on the topic. But then his expression suddenly brightened, and he reached into a pocket and pulled out a green velvet jewelry case that looked far too large to have been hidden in his jeans. "I got this for you, though."

"For me?" Cat asked, staring down at the case. It was the sort of thing that usually hid a very expensive piece of jewelry. "Why would you get something for me?"

"Because I thought you would like it," Loc replied, sounding careless...a bit too careless. "And to say thank you for your hospitality."

She would have to open it. Part of her really didn't want to, because she was worried that maybe he'd stolen it, seen it in a shop window in New Orleans and decided to bring it back to Santa Fe with him. After all, he was a demon. Did he even have much concept of right and wrong?

Holding her breath, Cat slowly opened the case. A gasp escaped her lips as the air she'd been holding in abruptly escaped. That was...a necklace for a queen. Or maybe a movie star on the red carpet at the Academy Awards or something, but not for Cat Castillo, who lived in jeans about ninety-five percent of the time and had to be forced into a dress.

Those huge teardrops of green stone had to be emeralds, and the necklace of black rhodium was studded with diamonds as well, smaller ones in the links that formed the necklace itself, larger ones of at least a half-carat apiece sitting on top of the joins between the links. It was fabulous, mesmerizing…and she absolutely could not accept it.

"I can't," she said, while Loc stared at her, his expression puzzled.

"You can't what?"

"I can't—I can't take this from you. It must be worth—"

"Eighty thousand dollars," he said calmly.

"How do you know that?"

"Because that is what the Dubois witch who sold it to me said it was worth."

"She—she *sold* it to you?"

"Of course. You did not think I stole it, did you?"

Warmth crept into her cheeks, because of course that was exactly what Cat had been thinking. She swallowed. "How in the world did you have that kind of money?"

Now Loc smiled, as if he'd determined why she had been so worried about the necklace's origins. "Catalina, I can have all the money I need. You see?" He pulled his wallet—a battered brown leather thing, the same kind she'd seen her brother Rafe carry—out of his jeans and began pulling hundred-dollar bills out of it and setting them on the table. The breeze threatened to begin blowing them away, and she quickly grabbed the half-empty wine bottle and set it on top of the stack of bills before they could escape.

"Okay, I get it," she said, knowing she

sounded more than a bit shaken. "That's—I guess I should have realized you'd have a way to pay for things as you were traveling."

"This was the simplest thing I could think of," he admitted. "The currency changed, of course, depending on where I was, but I found very few places that wouldn't take cash."

Probably not. The world seemed to run on plastic these days, but that was mostly for convenience. Cat had no doubt that Loc had been able to convince waiters and shopkeepers and hotel clerks to take cash. And if he didn't have to worry about exchanging currency as he went from place to place, all the better.

"But…." she began and trailed off, not sure what she wanted to say.

"But what?"

"I'm not sure that giving you crash space is enough to merit a piece of jewelry that's worth so much."

"I think it is. Shouldn't that be enough?"

Flummoxed, Cat stared down at the necklace. The slanting afternoon sunlight warmed the heavy teardrop cabochons of the emeralds, making them almost look as though they were glowing from within. "I don't even know where I would wear it."

"To this art competition you spoke of?"

He actually had a point there. On the opening night of the exhibition, there was a fancy reception held at the gallery that was hosting the event. The dress code was "dressy cocktail," which could be interpreted as almost anything...except blue jeans. She still hadn't picked out a dress because she'd been waffling on whether she even wanted to go or not.

"Maybe," she allowed. A thought struck her, and she asked, "Would you go with me? They have cocktails and hors d'oeuvres. If you're still here, of course."

Loc looked genuinely surprised by the request. "You wish me to take you to this party?"

"Well, technically, I'd be taking you, but yes. It's a week from now, and I know you're still looking for someone to send you home, but—"

"I have been here eight months, Cat," he said, cutting her off. "I believe I can manage an extra week."

Well, that seemed to settle things. She wasn't sure where she'd found the brass *cojones* to ask a demon lord out on a date, but....

"I think I would like to see you wear it before then, however," he said, and got up from where he sat so he could come over to her. Before she was able to utter a protest, he'd lifted the necklace from where it rested in the box and draped it around her neck, fingers brushing against her skin for the barest of seconds before he locked the clasp in place.

Her heart was racing, but Cat didn't know

whether that was from the weight of the expensive jewels encircling her throat, or from that featherlight touch of his fingertips. He'd been very close, too, body scant inches away from hers before he took a step backward and went around the bistro table so he could resume his seat.

"It looks very well on you," he said.

She reached up to touch one of the emerald drops. It felt slightly warm against her skin, probably because it had been lying in the sunlight for a few minutes. "I don't know what to say."

"Thank you, perhaps?"

Of course. She managed to smile at him and then said, "Thank you, Loc. It's beautiful. It's an antique, isn't it?"

"Yes, I think so. I suppose I should have asked something of its provenance. I was occupied with other matters at the time."

Like trying to find out if there was anyone in New Orleans who could help him. Cat had the feeling he was leaving out something of the story, but she supposed it really wasn't any of her business.

"The party and the hors d'oeuvres you spoke of are still in the future," he went on. "What about dinner tonight?"

"We can have something here, I suppose. Obviously, you can get me whatever I need to make something." That sounded safest. She'd rather not have to cook for him every night—

although she did make a mean pan of chicken enchiladas—but staying in seemed far, far safer than venturing out to dinner someplace where they'd have to be seen together in public.

Obviously, Loc didn't share her thoughts on the subject. "Wouldn't you rather go to dinner somewhere? You have already made breakfast for me—I can't expect you to be my cook the entire time I'm here."

Since she'd been thinking basically the same thing, Cat didn't have a retort ready. About the only protest she could offer was, "There aren't a lot of places to eat around here, unless you go down to Santa Fe. Or there are a couple of restaurants at the Buffalo Thunder Casino."

"Is it close by?"

In for a penny…. "Yes. It's just about five minutes away."

"Is their food good?"

"Quite good, yes." And expensive, at least in the casino's top-shelf establishment, but with the way Loc could peel hundred-dollar bills out of his wallet without blinking an eye, the cost of the meal really wouldn't be a problem.

"Then we will go there." He glanced down at his faded jeans and dark T-shirt. "I assume I will need to change."

"We both will," Cat said. Her attire was just as casual as his, and wouldn't really be appropriate for the casino's fanciest restaurant, especially on a

Friday night. "Assuming we can get reservations, that is. They're usually pretty busy on weekends, especially during the summer."

"That will not be an issue."

"You can fix reservations?"

"Of course."

Of course. She supposed she should have thought of that. It seemed that Loc could handle pretty much everything that came his way... except for finding someone to cast the spell he needed to go home.

"It's almost six now. Why don't you get a reservation for seven-thirty? That'll give us enough time to get cleaned up."

The smile he sent her was almost indulgent. "Oh, it doesn't quite work like that. It's more that when we arrive, a table will be ready for us."

Did she want to ask how he made that happen? Probably not.

"Okay," she said. After lifting the bottle off the stack of hundred-dollar bills he'd produced, she handed them back to him. "I'll cork this up and put it in the refrigerator, and I guess you can save those for paying for dinner tonight."

"I'm looking forward to it."

Was she? Maybe, a little bit, but that didn't keep her nerves from knotting up her shoulders. "I'll meet you down in the entry at seven-fifteen."

He nodded, and she made her escape, box that had held the incredible necklace clutched in one hand, the half-empty bottle of sauvignon blanc in the other. At least she knew what she planned to wear—she had a dead-simple draped silk tank in a shade of green that would go perfectly with the emeralds. A skirt would be too much, but with the only pair of dressy jeans she owned and some high-heeled sandals, she might be able to pull it off...maybe.

Look on the bright side, she told herself as she got out of her faded jeans with the frayed hems and into a nice new dark pair. *It's not as if anyone is going to believe this necklace is real.*

Her fingers went up and touched one of the emeralds. The necklace was like something you'd see in a museum, or maybe a catalogue for a high-end auction house such as Sotheby's. For all their money, Cat knew no one in her family owned anything quite so impressive. The Castillos were not about flash, because it attracted attention. And no witch clan wanted to draw any more attention to itself than its members absolutely had to.

Well, this necklace was probably going to attract a lot of notice. Even if it were actually fake, it was still big and...flashy wasn't exactly the right word, because the cabochon drops gave it a certain earthy gravitas, but it was definitely impressive.

As she'd thought, her silk top went perfectly with the jewels. She didn't have enough time to wash her face and start from scratch, but she put on a little more makeup than she normally wore, darkening her lids with some shadow, using a sheer lipstick in a dark wine color rather than her usual nude gloss. A few minutes with a big-barrel curling iron to give some body to her hair, and she figured she was done.

Mostly.

When her grandmother Isabel had died, she'd left careful instructions to have her jewelry divided equally amongst her grandchildren. Cat had inherited a pair of delicate diamond drops in white gold, as well as a diamond eternity band and matching bracelet. These items hardly ever saw the light of day—she realized the last time she'd worn the earrings had been for Rafe and Miranda's cathedral wedding—but they would work well with the necklace, coordinating with it rather than fighting it the way other emerald pieces might have.

After putting on the diamond earrings, Cat paused and surveyed herself in the mirror. Her reflection looked impossibly glam compared to the way she presented herself most days, and she wondered if she'd gone too far. The last thing she wanted was for Loc to think she'd done all this to impress him…even if, deep down, she sort of hoped she would.

A glance at the clock on her nightstand told her it was now about ten minutes after seven. She supposed her demon visitor could have magically transported the two of them to the Buffalo Thunder resort, but she thought it was safer to drive, or at least more reassuring.

Her regular purse—an embroidered backpack she'd bought in one of the import stores in Santa Fe—really didn't work with the outfit, so she hurriedly stuffed her wallet, phone, and car key fob into a small black bag that was her default for whenever she needed to look ladylike, then went downstairs. Loc was already waiting in the entry, his casual outfit from earlier in the day traded for a pair of black dress pants and a dark gray shirt.

Looking at him, Cat wondered how he knew exactly what he should wear for this sort of occasion. Then again, he'd spent months and months exiled here on Earth, so he had to have picked up some of the finer details about existing in modern society. She knew it was safer to ponder these sorts of questions rather than pay too much attention to how drop-dead gorgeous he looked.

It's all a façade, she reminded herself. *He doesn't really look like that.*

But then he smiled up at her as she descended the stairs, and she felt a stab of guilt for dwelling on the ugliness of his true form. That smile had been a genuine one, no matter what the face doing it looked like underneath.

"Are you ready?" he asked. There had been the slightest hesitation before he asked the question, as though he'd wanted to comment on her appearance but then had decided against it.

"Yes," she replied. "I'll drive—we have to go out through the kitchen to get to the garage."

For a second, he appeared puzzled. Had he thought he was going to whisk the two of them away to the restaurant?

If he had, he didn't seem too put off by the change in plans. A nod, and he said, "Lead the way."

She managed to smile, then headed toward the kitchen. Alarms were already starting to go off in her head, but she knew she couldn't really back out now. No, all she could do was hope they would have a quiet dinner, and that she wouldn't bump into anyone she knew. At the moment, the last thing she felt like doing was explaining Loc to a fellow Castillo.

As they went into the garage and he climbed into the passenger seat of her Mercedes SUV, she sent a silent prayer to the universe.

Dear God, let me survive this dinner....

7

Loc knew Cat was tense, although he couldn't determine the exact reason for her obvious nervousness. Was she afraid he might embarrass her in some way? He wished he could reassure her on that front; by now, he'd spent enough time in human company that he knew how to comport himself well enough. Perhaps he wasn't aware of the etiquette involved in a state dinner, for example, but for a meal in a regular restaurant, he thought he should do just fine.

Or perhaps she feared they might encounter someone she knew, and she would have to explain his presence to them. Again, such a meeting didn't necessarily have to be problematic, for she'd already concocted a false identity for him, along with a reason for being here in New Mexico at this time. Even if their paths crossed with someone from her clan, no witch or warlock would be able to detect anything out of the ordinary about him unless he wanted them to, and of course he knew he needed to be discreet. No, she had nothing to worry about on that front.

The third possibility was one he was not sure he wanted to acknowledge. Was Cat on edge because she was battling some sort of attraction to him? He thought he'd sensed something earlier, but subtle nuances of human behavior sometimes eluded him, especially in an area as unknown as human sexuality. There had been a certain light in her dark eyes as she caught sight of him standing there in the foyer. He thought he might have recognized that spark simply because he'd experienced much the same thing as he looked up at her as she descended the stairs. The emeralds had gleamed at her throat, and the clothing she wore did far more to show off the slender curves of her body than most of the garments he'd seen her wearing so far. And the shape of her mouth under the gloss of its dark lipstick…he'd had to force himself not to stare, because he wasn't sure he had ever seen anything so beautiful.

He was not supposed to find her beautiful. She was only a human being, after all, albeit one who possessed certain supernatural powers. Still, he knew he should not be dwelling on her outward appearance. That was no way for a demon lord, a master of his own plane, to behave.

But she smelled good, too….

He forced himself to look out of the window and not at her as Cat backed the SUV out of the garage, then engaged the self-driving mechanism, sending them down the narrow lane that led to the main road. Apparently, that road led away from here and up through the mountains, and would eventually bring you to Taos and its environs, but Loc had never been that way.

At least at this time of year, everything around them was lush and green, thanks to the monsoon rains this part of the world tended to get every summer. Loc watched the tall cottonwoods and low-spreading poppies go past outside the window, until Cat took them down a side road that brought them in around the rear of the casino complex.

To tell the truth, he had not expected it to be quite so large. Cat had referred to a casino, and he had seen several of those during his travels. This was more than merely a casino, but also a large hotel and convention complex, and apparently a golf course as well, since he could see the well-tended lawns off to his left as she brought them through the casino's parking lot and up toward the main entrance.

Someone was backing out of one of the closest spaces just as they approached, and Cat pulled into the open spot, a small smile playing around her mouth. Once she'd turned off the engine, she glanced over at Loc. "Your doing?"

"As I said, I can often...smooth the way, so to speak."

Her smile didn't fade. "That's useful."

"It can be." He didn't say anything more than that, and so she gave a small shake of her head, then picked up her purse from where it had been resting in the footwell and climbed out of the vehicle.

Loc followed her across the small expanse of asphalt that stretched between the parking spaces and the sidewalk that fronted the casino. People were coming and going, some of them as well-dressed as he and Cat, others so casual, he wondered if they had bothered to look in a mirror before leaving the house.

Well, perhaps they had come here only to gamble, and so what they were wearing didn't matter so much. It appeared that the casino itself was on the lower level; Cat ignored the escalators and led him to a restaurant off to one side of the large hallway that seemed to split this floor of the building in two. The entrance did not front on the corridor, but was built into one side of their desti-nation, making for a more private, intimate feeling.

A young man who appeared to be Native American was watching over the host station. "Do you have a reservation?" he inquired as Loc and Cat approached. She looked dubious, but Loc knew they had nothing to worry about.

"I was hoping you might have an open table," he said.

The man seemed to frown for a second, but then he smiled and said, "Actually, we do have one available. Right this way." He gathered up two menus in leatherette covers and took them through the open space in the center of the restaurant and over to a secluded table off to one side.

As they followed, Cat shot a sideways glance at Loc, and he couldn't help grinning back at her. Why had she doubted him? He could always makes things go his way…all save one, of course.

After they were seated, she remarked, "I think I'll want you around the next time I try to go to dinner at Sazon."

Loc had never heard of the place, but he assumed it must be a popular restaurant in Santa Fe. "Of course, I am happy to go to dinner with you anytime you like."

She appeared somewhat taken aback, as though she'd just realized that she'd tacitly agreed to another dinner date with him. But then she lifted her shoulders and said, "Sure. Although I think tomorrow we should stay in. Going out to dinner can get old after a while."

"If you say so." He was perfectly content to stay at her home with her; that would be quite cozy as well.

After that exchange, they were silent for a few moments as they studied the menus. A waiter came by to take their drink orders, and Cat requested a single glass of wine. That surprised Loc somewhat, since he'd thought it was customary to order a bottle to go with dinner. Once the waiter had left, though, she said, "I had a glass and a half of white wine at home, and we have to drive back. I know the self-driving function handles most of it, but I still need to be in control."

"Of course," Loc said. He did not entirely understand her caution, but he knew arguing with her was not a good way to start off their evening.

"Does it affect you at all?" she asked. "Alcohol, I mean."

He shook his head. "Not in the way it does you. That is, I can feel something from it—just a bit of elevation—but I could drink ten bottles of wine in a row and not get drunk."

"Good to know," she replied, then made a rather ostentatious show of drinking some of her water, as if she wasn't quite sure what else to do.

Sitting across the table from her like this was somewhat awkward. He'd felt much more comfortable when it was just the two of them together at her home, rather than out in public like this. Well, it was too late to change his mind now. This had been his idea, and so he needed to see it through.

Besides, Loc thought he might as well try to

get whatever information about the grimoires out of her that he could. He waited until the waiter had returned with their glasses of wine and had taken their orders, knowing that they should be undisturbed for some time now.

"I was thinking of something after this last trip also proved fruitless," he remarked, fingers playing with the stem of his wine glass.

"Of what?" She'd taken a small sip of her pinot noir, but clearly, she intended to nurse this one glass through their entire meal.

"I thought of how Simon Escobar brought me here. But I know he did not do it entirely on his own—in addition to drawing on your sister-in-law's power, he also used certain books of magic. I was wondering...do you know what happened to those books?"

At once, she shook her head. "No. I mean, things were kind of crazy afterward, what with getting Miranda settled as *prima*, and then her and Rafe's wedding." Cat paused there, dark eyes intent on his face. "Are you thinking that maybe you could use the books yourself to get back?"

The idea hadn't even crossed his mind, mostly because he knew it was an impossibility. These were not the sort of spells one could cast on oneself. However, Cat didn't know that, and she'd now unwittingly given him the perfect excuse to probe deeper. "I was considering it. I thought that perhaps I didn't need to find a magic-worker to perform the spell, that if I had access to those books, then I could try to send myself home."

"I could ask Miranda," she offered.

No, that wouldn't do at all. Because if Cat started making those sorts of inquiries, then the *prima* would want to know why she was asking now, after so many months had passed. While Cat might not understand all the ramifications of the spells contained in those books, Loc had an idea that Miranda just might. And if she didn't, she'd reach out for help, for someone to clarify the matter, and would learn that there was no way any of those spells could be worked in such a manner.

"No, don't do that," he said quickly, and one of Cat's eyebrows shot up. Doing his best to recover from such obvious backtracking, Loc went on, "That is, she must be very busy. This is only a theory of mine. I was merely wondering whether your clan still had Simon Escobar's spell books."

Cat still looked puzzled, but she seemed to give an inward shrug as she reached for her glass of wine. "Well, Miranda does have a lot on her plate, especially now."

"Now?"

"She just told the family that she's expecting. I think the baby will be born around the first of the year."

Perfect. Although Loc had never paid much attention to the gestational habits of human beings, the Castillo *prima* being pregnant gave him the perfect excuse to make sure she stayed out of all of this. "Congratulations to her," he said. "But it's very important that she not go near those books, because the dark magic contained in them could affect her child."

Cat's dark eyes widened, and she abruptly set down her wine glass. "Then I have to say something to her—"

"Yes, go ahead and warn her. Only it is probably better that she not know where the warning came from."

This request didn't seem to trouble Cat, as Loc already guessed that she had expended considerable mental energies on ensuring that the rest of her family knew as little as possible about her improbable house guest. She gave him an abstracted nod, then said, "Do you mind if I send Rafe a quick text? Not that I think they're keeping the books in the house or anything, but...."

"No, it's fine," Loc replied. He also doubted that the *prima* had the books on her property, but it was possible that she checked on them regularly to make sure they were still safe. Now she would do whatever she could to stay far away from them...which could only work to his benefit.

Cat's fingers flew across the screen. When she was done, she set the phone on the tabletop rather than putting it back in her purse, as if she knew that her brother would reply sooner rather than later.

Which of course he did. Once again, Cat typed out a hasty message. When she was done, she sent him an apologetic smile. "Sorry, but he sort of freaked out."

"Has she had any contact with the books since she became pregnant?"

Cat sent another message, then held the phone as she waited for a reply. It came soon enough, and she sent him a relieved smile. "No. Rafe says she hid the books and protected them with a bunch of wards months and months ago, and she hasn't seen them since. They're safe at the house of one of my cousins here in Santa Fe, and she checks regularly to make sure they're still there, but Miranda hasn't gone near them."

No wonder Loc had been unable to catch even the faintest whiff of the books. Any wards Miranda Castillo set would be very, very strong. He wished he could ask the name of the cousin who was guarding the grimoires, but he feared such a question would be too obvious. At least he now knew for certain that the books were in Santa Fe, which would narrow down his search considerably.

"Then that is good news," he said. "And good news that the books are safe. I will try to do more research as to whether I can even use them, but in the meantime, I will also keep up with my search."

Cat smiled a little uncertainly at those words, probably because she herself was ambivalent about the prospect of him leaving this plane forever. No, she would never come right out and say it, but he could tell that she did not look forward to that day with any real joy.

To tell the truth, now he was not sure whether he did, either.

Cat watched Loc place a couple of hundred-dollar bills in the little case that held their check and let out a mental sigh of relief. Except for that scare about the grimoires—which turned out to be nothing, after all—the meal had gone smoothly enough. No one had bothered them, tucked away at their secluded table, and Loc had asked her more questions about fiber arts in general, and her own work in particular. She figured that was because he wanted to make sure he could lie plausibly on the subject if asked, and maybe also because he could tell that talking about the grimoires or his search for someone who could send him home upset her on some level, in a small, secret place in her soul that she really didn't want to acknowledge.

Now all they had to do was walk back to the

car, get in, and go home. Easy peasy. Soon the night would be over.

Except….

As they exited the restaurant, Loc paused and looked across the wide hallway to a neon sign that spelled out the word "Echoes" in a vaguely Art Deco font. A thumping beat was coming out of the doorway just beneath it. "What is that?" he asked.

Cat stifled an inner groan. They had been so close…. "Echoes? It's a nightclub."

"People dance there?"

"Um…yes."

"I want to see it."

"Loc, I really don't think that's a good idea—"

But it was too late. He was already walking over to the nightclub entrance, and Cat couldn't really do anything except trail helplessly after him. The burly man guarding the door told Loc there was a twenty-dollar cover charge, and Loc handed over a hundred-dollar bill without batting an eye, telling the man to keep the change.

"I've always wanted to go in one of these places," he told Cat as she came up to him.

"They're nothing special," she said. "Bunch of people getting drunk and dancing badly."

The scene that met her eyes didn't give the lie to that statement. It was early in the evening, and so the club's attendees hadn't had a chance to get truly wasted yet, but Cat had no doubt they would, given enough time. The dance floor was fairly crowded, everyone bumping and grinding against each other. She hoped Loc didn't expect her to dance, although the thought of moving with him like that was enough to send a little shiver down her spine.

"I see an open table," he said after scanning the inside of the club for a few seconds.

Of course he did. For Loc, there would always be empty tables at clubs and restaurants.

He led her over to the table in question and she sat down, figuring she was a little less conspicuous that way. Sure, it was dark in here, and she hadn't seen anyone she recognized, but better to play it safe.

"I'll go get us some drinks," Loc said. "What would you like?"

"A white wine spritzer," she replied. Yes, she was drinking like an old lady, but she'd already had enough wine tonight. A spritzer was the most innocuous thing she could think of that still had a bit of alcohol in it.

Loc didn't seem put off by her request, but only nodded and headed over to the bar. Cat remained where she was, pretending to study the little card in its plastic stand on one side of the table, a card that listed all the happy hour specials and proclaimed that Tuesday was ladies' night.

"Cat Castillo?"

She looked up and tried not to groan. Standing

next to the table was Ashley Meadows, someone who'd attended Cat's high school. They hadn't been exactly friends, because Genoveva Castillo had frowned on her children getting too close with civilians, but Ashley was one of those people who just *had* to make you her best friend—for the few minutes she was talking to you before she got distracted by something or someone else.

"Oh, hi, Ashley," she said lamely.

Her former acquaintance seemed mesmerized by the necklace Cat was wearing, but she gathered herself enough to exclaim in her usual gushing tones, "Oh, my God, Cat, I haven't seen you in for*ever!* I didn't know you came to Echoes!"

Good thing the music was so loud, or Ashley's piercing voice could have been heard to the back wall of the nightclub. "Well, I don't, really. I'm just here with a friend because he wanted to check it out."

Ashley's big blue eyes widened. Because of the false eyelashes she wore, they made her look a little like a startled kitten. "He? I didn't know you were seeing anyone. Everyone says you've been living practically like a *nun.*"

Cat didn't bother to ask who "everyone" was, mostly because she knew that there was a small, dedicated group of gossips who seemed to make it their duty to keep up with everyone in their high school class who was still living in Santa

Fe…never mind that they'd all graduated seven years earlier and should have been getting on with their lives. As for the comment about living like a nun, well, she couldn't do much to argue with that particular statement, since it was pretty much the sad truth.

Calmly, she replied, "I'm not 'seeing' him. He's a fellow artist, and he's visiting here for a while so he can find out more about the fiber arts scene in Santa Fe."

"Oh, right," Ashley said, wrinkling her nose a bit. "You've been doing that whole weaving thing or whatever it is."

"Weaving is part of it, yes." Cat figured there wasn't much point in going into any detail about what her work actually involved, since Ashley would probably zone out halfway through the explanation anyway. To tell the truth, she had no idea what Ashley was up to these days, either. She'd gone to the state university in Las Cruces but had promptly returned to Santa Fe when she graduated. The last thing Cat had heard, she was working in a law office—maybe because she hoped to snag a lawyer husband and then not have to work ever again. Ashley had never been very twenty-first-century when it came to her attitudes about women's empowerment.

But then her eyes widened, and Cat shifted slightly in her seat so she could see what her friend was looking at. Sure enough, there came

Loc, white wine spritzer in one hand and something tall and filled with ice in the other. Long Island iced tea? She had a feeling he'd order a drink like that, just to see whether it would have any effect on him at all.

"Oh, my God," Ashley said, her tone almost reverent. "*That's* your friend?"

"Um…yes," Cat responded. She knew there wasn't any way to hide her connection to Loc, so it seemed safest to just come right out with it.

"He's…he's…." Words had clearly failed Ashley, so she just stood next to Cat's table, making no attempt to hide her obvious stare.

"Hello," Loc said, smiling at Ashley as he handed Cat her spritzer.

"Loc, this is Ashley Meadows. We went to high school together. Ashley, this is Loc de la Cruz. He's visiting from Spain for a few days." It seemed safe enough to put a bit of a time limit on Loc's presence here in Santa Fe. If it ended up that he stayed longer, she'd figure out a way to explain the reason for his extended vacation.

"'Spain'?" Ashley echoed. "Wow. I've never been any farther than California."

"Oh, yes," he said. "Travel can be a wonderful thing, although I do find it somewhat amusing to see all the Spanish names here in your desert Southwest. It feels almost as if I never left Barcelona."

"I guess I never thought about it," she said

with a giggle. Then she turned an almost accusing stare on Cat. "And I'll bet this is the first time you've even gotten out and about. Cat was never much of a partier."

That was only the truth, mostly because the dubious fun of partying had to be weighed against the fallout should Genoveva have ever found out what her youngest daughter was up to. Voice a bit strangled, she said, "Loc's been out and around. It's not like I'm keeping him prisoner at my house or something."

"Oh, right—I heard you bought the old Rio Luna winery and fixed it up." A sudden grin touched Ashley's pink-glossed lips, and Cat braced herself, knowing that the other woman had something up her sleeve, something she probably wouldn't like very much. "I know!" Ashley exclaimed next. "You should have a party! That way, everyone can see your new house, and you can introduce Loc to everybody."

"I don't—" Cat began, but she didn't get any further than that, since Loc cut in.

"I think a party sounds like a wonderful idea," he said. "I would like to meet more of your friends."

She wished she could stare daggers at him, but with Ashley standing there and staring down at her expectantly, Cat knew this was not the time to get into an argument. Willing herself to stay calm, she said, "I have a lot to do to get ready for the show next week."

"It's no problem," Ashley said. "I can take care of the guest list. You just need to give me your address so I know where to tell everyone to go."

Cat could think of where she wanted to tell Ashley—and Loc—to go, but that wasn't really an option. Before she could respond, Loc chimed in.

"And I can manage the food and the drinks," he said. "Let us do it Spanish style, with tapas and sangria."

"You're going to make tapas for fifty people?" Cat asked, not bothering to hide the skepticism in her tone.

"Of course," he replied. His dark eyes were dancing, and she realized then that producing tapas for fifty people—or a hundred, or two hundred and fifty—wouldn't be any problem for him at all.

"Oh, that sounds awesome!" Ashley said, her voice almost squeaking with excitement. "Tomorrow night?"

"Sure," Cat said wearily. Might as well get it over with.

"Perfect timing, too, because Channing Ellis is in town—his sister Emma just had her first baby, and he's here for the christening." Now the excited glitter in Ashley's big blue eyes almost seemed more like a scheming gleam, although Cat knew that was probably only her imagination at work. "I know he'd *love* to see you."

"Um, sure," Cat returned. Channing Ellis was probably the last person on earth she wanted to come visit her, but there was no way she would ever tell Ashley that. "Sounds great."

"Okay, what time?"

"Um…seven-thirty?"

"Great. Oh, and your address?"

"Forty-two North Shining Sun," Cat told her, doing her best to ignore the sensation of being caught on the back of a runaway horse. "It's right off the 503."

"Got it," Ashley chirped. "See you tomorrow night. This is going to be so much fun!"

She bounced away then, pausing only a few yards away to talk to a couple around her age. The woman looked familiar, and Cat thought she might be another former schoolmate. It was dark enough that even that small distance made it difficult to pick out many details of someone's facial features.

Loc spoke then. "You don't seem particularly pleased."

"Oh, no, I love the idea of my house getting invaded by a hundred strangers," she shot back, and took a large swallow of her white wine spritzer. Damn it, she should have asked him for something stronger.

"'Strangers'?" Loc echoed. "How can they be strangers if you went to school with them?"

"We all graduated seven years ago," she told him. "And I haven't done much to stay in touch, because my late mother wasn't real keen on having her kids hanging out with civilians. But no worries."

She sipped at her spritzer again, while Loc swallowed some of his Long Island iced tea and appeared to pause for a few seconds, as though evaluating its effects. Then he said, "Who is Channing Ellis?"

"A guy I went to school with. I guess I had kind of a crush on him."

Was that a frown creasing Loc's brow? "He was your boyfriend?"

"No," she said shortly. "My mother would never let me date a civilian."

"Ah." He was quiet again. "Then why would Ashley be so eager to have him come to your party?"

"Because she knows I liked him, and she probably thinks it'll be funny to see how we react to each other after all this time."

Luckily, Loc seemed to accept that explanation, lapsing into silence as he watched the dancers gyrate under the strobing lights set into the ceiling above the dance floor. Thank God for that, because Cat was in no mood to tell him the truth about her and Channing Ellis. No, nothing had happened between them in high school, but when he'd come home from college a year after they graduated, she and Channing had had a brief fling. It was her single greatest act of rebellion against her mother, losing her virginity to a civilian she had no intention of marrying. Channing hadn't seemed to expect anything out of the relationship either, except to scratch his itch, since he'd broken up with his girlfriend a few months before he hooked up with Cat.

She hadn't liked sneaking around, though, and after spending a few days in his company, she'd realized she really didn't like Channing all that much, either. Yes, he was gorgeous, but even an unpracticed virgin like she had been could tell he wasn't all that great in the sack, and it seemed the only things he'd wanted to talk about were football and school. He was pre-law, following in his father's footsteps. It had paid off, because the last she'd heard, he was working for some high-powered law firm in Houston, but Cat had no reason to think Channing Ellis would be any more interesting now than he'd been six years ago. Maybe now he'd talk about his law firm or his stock portfolio rather than his classes, but she had a feeling football would still figure far too prominently in any of his conversations.

Well, he probably wouldn't even come to the party. She doubted he had any more desire to see her than she did to see him. He'd probably get

Ashley's invitation and smile and shake his head, then not bother to show up. That would be the easiest resolution to the situation.

Unfortunately, Cat knew all too well that things were rarely so simple.

8

HE'D THOUGHT HE WOULD ASK CAT TO DANCE— after watching the people on the dance floor for a good fifteen minutes or so, Loc knew he could manage to imitate their moves well enough—but she seemed troubled after Ashley had left, and he had a feeling that any such requests would be summarily shot down. Was Cat troubled at the idea of seeing someone she'd once cared for, or was she merely annoyed that he and Ashley had plotted this party without really asking for her approval?

Probably a combination of both, and so he judged it best to sit with her and finish their drinks, then suggest quietly, "Time to go home?"

"I thought it was time to go home a half hour ago," she replied, her tone tart. "But yes, I'm ready."

She got up from her chair and retrieved the

little black clutch purse she'd brought with her. Loc rose as well, knowing that she was angry and not exactly sure how he should try to soothe her troubled spirit. The problem was, he didn't know why she would be upset about the party, since Ashley had promised to manage the invitations, and he himself would be handling all the food and drink. The house and its grounds seemed very neat and clean to him, so he didn't think there should be much work involved in making sure the place was ready to receive guests.

After they'd left the club, walked across the parking lot, and climbed in to her SUV, Loc said, "I will do everything I can to make sure this party won't require you to put forth any effort. All you'll have to do is attend and have a good time."

Cat had already set the vehicle in self-driving mode, and so it was not unsafe for her to turn her head and send him an unreadable look. "It's not about the work, Loc."

"Then what is it? If it troubles you that Ashley is inviting this Channing Ellis, then message her and tell her to take him off the guest list."

That offer only made Cat let out a huff of an exasperated breath. "Doing that would only make things worse."

Sometimes, human motivations could be very difficult to understand. Here he had given Cat a way to get out of an awkward situation, and she'd refused. Could it be that, deep down, she really wanted to see this Channing person?

Loc couldn't know for sure. What he did know was that it probably would not be wise to push the issue. Cat already seemed upset, and he did not wish to anger her further. He went quiet, watching as the headlights flickered against the massive trunks of the cottonwoods that lined the road leading back to her property. It was very dark out here, for there were no streetlights such as those that lined the roads in more populated areas.

Just as she was turning onto the little private lane that would bring them to the house, she spoke. "It's all right, Loc. I have been living like kind of a hermit out here. I did have that small housewarming party, but it was just for family, only about twenty people. Since it's summer, we'll do everything in the patio area off the old wine tasting room. I haven't really done anything to it except make sure the gardeners keep it all looking nice, so it's still set up for large groups of people. It'll be fine."

"That sounds like a good plan," he said, relieved that she seemed to have come around to the idea of having a party. Truly, he was curious to see how she acted around her peers, because before this he'd only seen her interacting with family members, and that had been during a difficult, highly charged time. "It will reduce the risk to your house, at least."

She sent him a tight little smile, then turned off the SUV's self-driving function so she could guide the vehicle into the garage. "Oh, people will still come into the house, if for no other reason than to use the bathroom. There's one in my studio—the old tasting room—but the last thing I need is someone getting drunk and making a mess while I'm in the middle of working on projects there. It's better for them to go to the house. At least there if someone trashes something, it can be more easily replaced."

Did she really think that her former classmates would be quite so destructive? He couldn't know for sure, because he might have traveled around the world, but he'd always kept to himself for the most part. This would be the first time he'd ever attended a real party. At any rate, if anything got broken, he would help to repair or replace it. However, he realized that even his great magical gifts might not be enough to help Cat if someone damaged some of her art. Better to keep everyone out of her studio and avoid any risk of such unpleasantness.

"I'm sure they will be respectful of your property," he said.

Another of those thin-lipped smiles that ruined the beautiful fullness of her mouth. "For a demon, you sure have a high opinion of humanity."

She pushed the button to turn off the engine, then took her purse and got out of the vehicle. Loc climbed out as well, still searching for a suitable reply to her last comment. If anyone had asked, he would have said that his opinion of humanity was entirely neutral, since there were both very fine and truly horrible examples of the species. For some reason, though, he did not particularly like Cat referring to him as a demon. Yes, he was one—a demon lord, at any rate—but when she spoke of him in such a way, it seemed as though she was doing what she could to create more distance between them.

Not that he hadn't done a very good job of doing such a thing by going along with her friend Ashley's idea of a party. Wouldn't it have been better to have a quiet evening alone with Cat, rather than inviting a horde of humans to invade the quiet sanctuary she'd created here?

In some ways, though, that scenario was even more fraught.

He followed her into the house, where she paused so she could take off the high-heeled sandals she wore. "It's been a long day," she said. "And it sounds like tomorrow is going to be even longer, so I'm going to bed." A pause, and then she added, "Thank you for dinner."

"You're welcome," he murmured, but she was

already gone, sandals hanging by their strap in one hand, her useless little purse tucked under her arm. It was clear enough that she didn't want to spend any more time around him this evening.

Well, all he could do now was hope she would be in a better mood the following day.

Cat was still cranky when she woke up, although she told herself that done was done, and she might as well make the best of the situation. When she went down to have her morning coffee, Loc was already there. He set a mug in front of her and said, "You really don't have to worry about anything. I will make sure the house is ready for the party."

Was a demon lord really capable of managing all the thousand and one details that needed to be taken care of when planning a big get-together? She didn't know, but she figured she'd find out. As she'd showered, she'd told herself that she wouldn't get involved, would stay out of things.

And if the whole damn affair turned out to be an unmitigated disaster, well, at least she could use that as ammunition to make sure no one ever came to one of her parties again.

"Sounds good," she said, and left it at that.

They had a quiet breakfast, and then Cat disappeared into her studio to get as much work done as possible before the hordes descended. She figured she'd have to stop working around six-thirty to give herself enough time to get ready, but even so, she had a whole day ahead of her. Better to make the most of it, because she had no idea how out of it she would be the morning after the party.

Time flew. She'd brought a container of yogurt and some bottled iced tea with her, and so she hadn't had to leave the studio to get any lunch. Part of her worried about what Loc might be up to, but she'd told him he was on his own when it came to the preparations, and she knew she had better stick to her word.

Six-thirty rolled around, and she set the heavy, bead-studded tapestry aside and got up, stretched, and let herself out. Since she left through the door that faced the house, she couldn't really see what Loc had done with the patio, and that was fine. At this point, she'd rather be confronted with something she knew she couldn't change, rather than sneak a peek now and worry about whether she'd have time to get things fixed up before any of her guests started to arrive.

Loc was nowhere to be seen. Cat went into her bedroom and closed the door, then wearily stripped off her T-shirt and jeans. Her back was aching a bit from spending so much time hunched over her worktable, but she figured a glass of sangria might help with that.

No high heels, though. Loc had said the party's theme would be Spanish, and so she got out a skirt she'd bought in a boutique in Santa Fe, black and ankle-length, with an embroidered, fringed overlay reminiscent of a Spanish shawl. The evening promised to be warm—the A/C unit in her studio had been working overtime all day —and so she put on a black tank top and flat black sandals, then pulled her hair back into a loose braid. Some red lipstick to go with the embroidery on the skirt, big silver hoop earrings studded with garnets, and she figured she was good to go.

Loc was just coming down the hallway from his own room as she stepped out from the master suite and closed the door behind her. The briefest widening of his eyes told her he'd registered her dolled-up appearance, and she experienced a flicker of satisfaction. It wasn't that she'd put on this outfit on purpose to entice him or anything, but she did like knowing that she'd gotten a reaction from her demon lord guest.

"I think everything is ready," he said. "Shall we go out to the garden and take a look?"

"Love to."

He smiled, then headed for the staircase. Cat followed, telling herself it was silly to have expected him to take her arm. He might have picked up a good deal about human behavior during his time here, but it wasn't as if he had everything down pat yet.

And even if he did, it's not like he had *to take your arm. He's not your date, after all.*

Although she had a feeling plenty of the people attending the party would think that about the two of them, no matter what she said.

Oh, well.

When she stepped outside, Cat couldn't quite keep herself from letting out an admiring gasp. It wasn't yet sundown, and so the true beauty of what Loc had done wouldn't be obvious for another hour or so, but still, she had to admire the luminarias that outlined the pathway leading from the front door to the patio area, and the white fairy lights that had been twined in the trees.

"It's beautiful," she said.

Loc glanced up at the trees. "You like it?"

"Oh, yes."

"Good. Because there's more."

He set off down the path, walking at a brisk pace. Cat was glad that she'd opted for flat sandals, since the flagstones that made up the pathway weren't completely even. Hopefully, there wouldn't be too many party-goers who chose to wear three-inch heels, because that might be a problem after they'd had a couple of glasses of sangria.

The vines that arched over the path right before it opened onto the patio also had strings of white lights entwined with them, and the patio itself was lit up by criss-crossing strands of the large, clear bulbs that always made her think of Italian restaurants. Candles in little mercury glass votive holders offered their own illumination, making the spot look even more enchanted.

"I can't believe you did all this just today," she said.

Now Loc smiled, a sort of velvety smile that made her knees feel a little weak. However, he didn't seem to notice the effect he had on her, because he replied sensibly, "You forget that I have a few more resources than most people."

Well, that was true. Still, it was one thing to have the power to make a scene like this possible, and quite another to have the sort of vision and artistic flair to pull it off successfully. Had he seen something like this in real life, or possibly on a television show, and merely replicated what another designer had done?

In the long run, it probably didn't matter. What mattered was that the patio looked exquisite. When Ashley saw this, her head was probably going to explode from trying to figure out how they'd managed to do all this in the space of a day.

"And over here," Loc said, "is the food."

Again, Cat couldn't quite keep herself from

gasping. Off to one side of the patio, a long table had been set up, one that was now covered with basically every tapas dish she'd sampled in local Santa Fe restaurants, and a bunch more that Loc must have dug up from a Spanish cookbook. Or maybe he'd eaten food like this in Spain and had re-created everything from his memories. Next to the tapas table was a smaller one that held two large glass beverage dispensers. One contained white sangria, the other red.

Despite the warmth of the evening air and the fact that flies always descended like the plagues of Egypt during monsoon season, the patio was noticeably free of bugs. More of Loc's unique powers at work, she supposed. He could make a killing marketing that particular talent to any of Santa Fe's restaurants that offered patio dining.

"It looks like you've thought of everything," she said.

"I hope so," he replied, and went to fetch a couple of pressed-glass cups for the two of them. "White, or red?"

"Red, please," she said, watching as he filled both of the cups with red sangria. He came to her and offered her one, and she took it from him and drank. The sangria was the perfect blend of sweet and tangy, lively with the flavors of the lemon, lime, and orange slices that had been soaking in it all day.

"Is it all right?" Loc asked, watching her some-what anxiously.

"It's perfect." How he'd managed to achieve the perfect sangria in just one afternoon, she wasn't sure. Concocting sangria and arguing over the relative merits of one version versus another was a long-running summertime activity in the Castillo clan.

"Good." He looked away from her then, head tilted slightly, as if listening to a sound only he could hear.

In the next moment, Cat was able to hear it as well—the crunch of tires on gravel. "Sounds like our first guest is here."

"Probably Ashley," Loc observed. "I got the impression that she would want to arrive ahead of the others, just to make sure everything was all right."

Yes, that did seem like something Ashley would do. Well, since even the most exacting party planner really couldn't find fault with how Loc had set things up, Cat was sure her friend would approve of everything as well.

Which turned out to be the case, because just a few minutes later, Cat heard Ashley's trademark "oh, my *God!*" just as she came down the path into the patio area. She paused for a moment, as if to take in everything, then came over to where Loc and Cat stood.

"How did you two manage to do all this in

one day?"

"Loc works very fast," Cat said.

Ashley's head tilted to one side at that comment, as if trying to decide whether there had been an underlying meaning to Cat's remark. Then she shrugged, apparently dismissing the statement so she could attend to more important things. "Well, it all looks fabulous! Which is perfect, because as of six o'clock today, I had 136 people say they were coming tonight. There will probably be a few more—you know there are always the ones who're too lazy to even click a button to let you know they're going to attend."

One hundred and thirty-six people. Cat could feel her stomach tighten and gulped down some of the sangria she held. No, it wasn't as though she had to worry about running out of food or drinks—she was sure Loc would quietly ensure that wasn't a problem—but still, that was a lot of people to cram into this patio space. She thought they would *probably* fit, but....

"That sounds like a very good turnout," Loc said. "While we're waiting for them to arrive, can I get you a glass of sangria?"

"Oh, that would be great. White, please." Ashley watched him go over to the beverage dispenser and get a cup for her, an expression of something close to envy on her features. Leaning close to Cat, she whispered, "You are so lucky. I don't think there's a single guy here in Santa Fe who even comes close to him."

"I'm not lucky," Cat replied at once. "I mean, I guess I am in a lot of ways, but I'm not with Loc. He's just a friend."

"Well, *you* may think that, but I'm not sure *he* does. I could see the way he was looking at you."

Despite herself, Cat felt a little shiver of pleasure go over her. She tried to tell herself that she didn't want Loc looking at her in any kind of way, except as a friend, but those inner protests fell pretty flat. Even as angry as she'd been with him the night before, she'd found it impossible to ignore the way her heart seemed to beat a little faster whenever his gaze met hers. Maybe her mind knew that acknowledging such an attraction was dangerous and possibly downright crazy, but her body didn't seem to have gotten the memo.

"That's just how he is," she made herself say calmly. "He's kind of a flirt. Spanish, you know."

"Uh-huh. I sure didn't see him looking at *me* like that."

Then they had to fall silent, because Loc was approaching with Ashley's cup of sangria, which he handed to her with a smile, saying he hoped she would like it.

"It's awesome," she said after taking a sip. "The food looks amazing. And how were you able to keep all the flies and mosquitoes away?"

"An old family trick," Loc replied.

Ashley drank some more sangria. "Then whatever it is, you need to bottle it, because you'd make millions."

Unfortunately, Loc's magical nature wasn't something you could exactly bottle. He settled for giving a noncommittal shrug and then said, "I hear some cars coming. It sounds as though our guests are starting to arrive. Good thing there's plenty of parking."

Cat wasn't sure "plenty" was the word to use when you were expecting more than a hundred guests. Back when the winery was operating, it could handle about fifty cars if you got creative, and she hadn't done much to change the gravel area that used to function as a parking lot. Eventually, she thought she'd plow it under and maybe have some drought-tolerant grass put in.

Ashley must have seen the worry on Cat's face, because she quickly added, "I told people they needed to carpool if possible, so it should be all right."

If not, they'd probably end up spilling out onto the highway itself. At least here she didn't have to worry about impinging on her neighbors, since the property was so big that it had a large stretch of roadside right in front of the vineyard.

Cat nodded, and after that, she didn't have time to worry about the parking situation, since people kept arriving and greeting her before heading straight for the food and the drinks. Had she really been friends with this many people in high school? She honestly didn't think so, but she guessed most of these people had come to the party out of simple curiosity or a chance to get a free dinner and some booze. Not that it really mattered, since she just smiled and said hi to everyone as they came by, and hoped she might get a chance at some point to snag some of those tasty tapas for herself.

Her cousin Tony was among the party-goers. Cat supposed she would have been surprised by this, since he had been a year ahead of her in school and therefore probably not on Ashley's guest list...except that Tony could sniff out a good party the way a shark smelled blood in the water. She gave him a resigned wave as he appeared—solo, of course, since she knew he wasn't dating anyone—and approached her. Luckily, Loc was off somewhere else, so at least she didn't have to explain him right off the bat.

"Finally decided to throw a party, huh?" Tony said. Somehow he'd managed to go by the drinks table and get a sangria for himself before he came up to talk to her, but again, that was Tony for you. "I have to say, I'm kind of surprised you did something for the high school gang and not us Castillos."

"It was Ashley's idea," Cat said darkly.

He grinned. "Got it. Next to me, she's probably the best person in the world to make a party happen out of nowhere."

"I'm surprised you never dated, considering you're so alike."

That remark earned Cat a shudder. "No, thanks," Tony said emphatically. "The last thing I want is to marry someone *too* like me. Besides, my mother would have freaked out if I'd tried dating a civilian. She's almost as bad as Genoveva was about that sort of thing."

As soon as the words left his lips, he looked immediately contrite, though, as if he'd realized that making such a remark about Cat's mother when she hadn't been dead for even a year wasn't in the best of taste. However, Cat had reached the point where she could hear references to her mother without either getting angry at the way she'd died, or guilty for maybe not being everything Genoveva had expected from her daughter.

Most of the time, anyway.

She gave a lift of her shoulders, then said, "It's all right, Tony. Because she was completely rigid on that subject—you know, it might be all right for some of the more distant cousins, but never in the world would she let her own children hook up with civilians."

Which was exactly why Cat had done precisely that very thing. When she'd come home after her losing her virginity to Channing Ellis, she'd been terrified, sure that her mother would be able to detect at once what she'd done. But apparently Genoveva's *prima* powers hadn't extended that far, and Cat had never been found out.

Tony nodded and swallowed some sangria. He didn't get a chance to respond, however, because Loc approached them, a smile on his lips but a question in his eyes—and, although Cat wanted to tell herself she was imagining things, just possibly a hint of jealousy in his expression.

"Loc," she said hastily, "this is my cousin Tony. Tony, this is Loc de la Cruz. He's a fiber artist visiting from Spain. He's staying through the show next Friday."

"Nice to meet you," Tony said, transferring his sangria to his left hand so he could reach out with his right.

It seemed Loc was familiar enough with that human convention, because he shook Tony's hand and said, "It's nice to meet someone from Cat's family."

"What, she hasn't taken you to meet Rafe and Miranda and the rest of the gang?" The question was a simple one, but Cat could tell from the way Tony's eyes were dancing that he enjoyed putting her on the spot...and possibly had a few choice questions he wanted to ask her once she was alone again.

"We've been busy," Cat said in quelling tones. "But yeah, I'm sure we'll try to do something next week…as long as Ashley doesn't throw any more impromptu parties for me."

"I assume she wouldn't do that, since it would be when people had to work," Loc pointed out in his precise way, and Tony grinned.

"Exactly. Well, I think I'm going to mingle now. Nice to meet you, Loc." Tony's gaze slid toward Cat, and the smile he gave her came dangerously close to being an outright smirk. "Talk to you later, Cat."

"Okay," she said, not sure she trusted herself to respond with anything more than that. It wasn't that she expected Tony to go to Rafe and blab about Loc to him—for a party animal, Tony could be remarkably circumspect—but more that she had a feeling he had already made all sorts of assumptions about her and Loc, none of which could be remotely true.

Yet.

Loc stood next to her, watching as Tony paused to chat up a group of women in skimpy sundresses. "Your cousin seems to get along with everyone."

"Tony? Oh, yeah, he's always the life of the party."

Her remark earned her an inquisitive glance. "You don't care for that quality in him?"

"No, it's not that. It's just…he makes every-thing look so easy."

"And it isn't?"

She lifted an eyebrow at the demon lord. "What do you think, Loc?"

He drank from his cup of sangria, then said, "Well, in contrast to many others I've observed during the course of my travels, the Castillos appear to lead fairly comfortable lives."

How was she supposed to respond to that comment? On the surface, what he'd said was true enough. It wasn't as though anyone in her clan suffered for want of material comforts. However, spending a good chunk of your life pretending you were something you were not tended to get a little draining after a while. And Loc should know that better than anyone else.

His voice sounded in her mind. *I did not mean to upset you.*

It was the first time he'd reached out in such a way since they'd met in the vineyard the day before last, and Cat startled, even though she realized communicating like this was a lot safer in a big group if the discussion veered into topics you'd rather not have overheard. *I'm not upset. It's just that you of all people should know a little bit about having to hide your true identity. Doesn't it get exhausting?*

Exhausting? A pause, as if he was considering her question carefully. *I hadn't thought of it that way, but I can see your point. I suppose that is why I like spending time with you...you already know what I am.*

Cat almost replied that he had a funny way of showing it, since he'd pushed her to go out to dinner the night before, and then conspired with Ashley to throw this damn party. Although at least the party seemed as if it was chugging along just fine without her.

I'm glad you feel that way, she told him, and then paused, dismay coursing through her.

What is it?

She really hadn't thought he would come. In her mind, she'd visualized him getting Ashley's text invite, then shaking his head and promptly deleting it. Clearly, though, that wasn't what had happened at all, because there he was, looking a bit too dressed up in a black polo shirt and khakis, pausing here and there to stop and say hello to people he knew, but always moving inexorably toward her.

Channing Ellis.

9

CAT'S POSTURE SUBTLY CHANGED—HER CHIN WENT up and her shoulders squared, and she made a too-casual flip of her braid over one shoulder. Loc followed her gaze and saw a tall, handsome man walking through the crowd, clearly intent on coming up to talk to her. The stranger's gaze slid toward Loc and paused there for a second or two, taking his measure, and then he stopped a few feet away from where the two of them stood.

"Hi, Cat," the man said.

"Hi, Channing," she replied coolly. "I'm glad you could make it."

Obviously, this was Channing Ellis, the man Cat had had a relationship with a year after they'd graduated from high school. Loc did his best not to dislike the stranger on sight, mostly because he realized it was foolish to show antipathy toward a person who'd been out of

Cat's life for years, but he didn't know how successful he was. Besides, Loc knew he had no claim on Cat, none at all...and yet he still wanted to shift into his true winged form, take hold of this smiling man in his ridiculous polo shirt with the little horseman embroidered on the left breast, and drop him somewhere from a very large height.

"Oh, I couldn't miss it," Channing said. Unlike many of the party-goers, who appeared to be of either Hispanic or Pueblo extraction, or possibly a combination of the two, he was quite fair, with sandy blond hair, blue eyes, and a lightly tanned complexion. "I'm just glad I happened to be in town at the right time."

"Yes, I suppose it was serendipity," Cat said. Although the words were polite, there was an edge to them that Loc couldn't miss. However, it seemed Channing Ellis wasn't quite that perceptive.

"Exactly." He chuckled, then shifted so he faced Loc and stuck out his hand. "I'm Channing Ellis."

"Loc de la Cruz," Loc replied.

"Right. Ashley said you were an artist or something?"

The way Channing asked the question was deliberately off-hand, as if he didn't think much of being an artist. Since Loc had assumed that identity as an easy way to explain his presence here, he wasn't offended on his own behalf. However, he found himself bristling for Cat's sake. She cared very much about her work, and this insignificant human was belittling the profession simply because it wasn't the same as putting on a suit and accumulating as many billable hours as possible.

However, since Cat had just sent him a sideways, pleading glance, Loc knew he needed to remain civil. She had already said that she no longer had feelings for this person, and so there was no point in causing a scene...even if the desire to drop him off the highest spire of Loretto Chapel had only increased exponentially.

"Yes, I am an artist who specializes in fiber work, like Catalina here. She was good enough to invite me to Santa Fe to attend an international show and competition this coming week."

That was definitely a disdainful curl to Channing Ellis's sculpted upper lip. Artist was bad enough, but for a grown man to be playing with fabrics and yarn? Loc could only imagine the mocking thoughts going through the other man's head.

"Yes, Loc is really talented, and busy, too," Cat put in, obviously conscious of the tension between the two men. "I'm just lucky he was able to carve out a little time in his schedule to come for a visit. We've been corresponding for a while, but we just didn't know until fairly recently whether he was going to make it this year."

"That's great," Channing said, his tone dismissive. "Hey, Loc, you mind if I borrow Cat for a bit? I'd love to get a tour of the property."

She didn't look too thrilled at this presumption, but it also seemed that she wanted to keep everything as friendly as possible, since she said, "Oh, sure, let me show you the rest of the grounds. You don't mind, Loc, do you?"

Of course, he minded a good deal. He did not want Cat going off with this person, but protesting probably wouldn't go over very well with either of them, for different reasons. Besides, when this party ended, Channing Ellis would be sent off with the rest of the party-goers, but Loc would be able to remain here with her.

"No, I don't mind at all," he replied. "I think I'll go get some food."

"Great idea," Channing said. "Better to get yourself something before it gets too picked over."

There was no danger of such a thing happening, because Loc had been monitoring the refreshments to make sure that all the food and drinks remained well-stocked. He couldn't very well point this out to Channing Ellis, and so he nodded and replied, "The tapas have been very popular."

With that, he walked off toward the food table, forcing himself not to look over one shoulder to see where Cat and Ellis might be headed. She'd made it sound as if she only planned to show him the rest of the patio and probably something of the vineyard, but Loc doubted whether her erstwhile boyfriend would be content to have the tour end there. No, he would want to see the house as well. With any luck, he would be content with seeing the ground floor, but what if he pressed her to go upstairs, to look at the bedrooms?

Such jealousy and foolish conjecture were not at all like him. Loc shook his head at himself and went over to refill his glass of sangria. For some reason, he did not have much of an appetite, although he had made it a point to choose food that he'd sampled when he traveled through Spain, all dishes that he'd enjoyed very much and wanted to have again. Food was just one of this world's many wonders; his demon body hadn't required it the way this form did, but he was glad to have to eat and sample the apparently endless variety Earth had to offer.

As he stepped off to one side to allow more people near the drink dispensers, Cat's cousin Tony got up from a nearby table and approached him, expression a little too knowing.

"Looks like Channing Ellis swooped in again to do his quarterback thing."

"His what?" Loc inquired. The phrase sounded vaguely familiar, but he couldn't quite place it at the moment.

"Well, Mr. Ellis was the quarterback of the high school's football team the year Cat graduated. He always was pretty good at interceptions."

Loc could only stare at Tony blankly, not sure what he was talking about.

The Castillo warlock chuckled, then said, "Oh, right. You're from Spain. You probably don't know too much about American football."

"No, I don't," Loc replied, glad that he could use his assumed nationality as a way to explain his ignorance of something that appeared to be an important part of life in this section of the world. Although he'd traveled just as extensively in the United States as he had in Europe and Asia, he hadn't wasted much energy on sports, mostly because they had very little to do with his quest, and the people he was seeking wouldn't have been involved in that sort of thing. "But I assume if he was the quarterback, it was a position of some importance?"

"You could say that." Tony paused to swallow some of his sangria. "I don't think Cat ever cared about it one way or another, like some girls do. But I know she hung out with him the summer after she graduated, because I spotted them together a few times down around the Plaza."

"I know about that," Loc said. He wanted to make sure Tony understood that none of this was really a surprise. "Cat told me."

"Oh, she did? Well, then." He drank more sangria, gazing out over the crowd with a contemplative expression on his face. "You two must be serious if she's discussing her old boyfriends with you."

"No, not at all." Had he sounded a bit too vehement? Loc hoped not, but he also wanted to disabuse Tony of the notion that anything was going on between his cousin and himself. "It's only that Ashley mentioned his name, and I could see that Cat wasn't very happy about his being invited to the party. She explained why she was not too eager to have him come back into her life."

"And yet she's off giving him a tour of the place."

"Because he asked. It's not as though she offered to do such a thing."

Tony was quiet for a moment. He swirled the contents of his cup of sangria, now down to only a few more mouthfuls. "Well, I suppose it's none of my business anyway."

"You're family. It's right for you to be concerned. But really, I am only here as Cat's friend, nothing more. However, just because I am returning home soon doesn't mean that I want her to fall back into the orbit of someone who doesn't deserve her."

That remark earned Loc an approving clap on the shoulder, probably a little rougher than Tony had intended. Loc wondered how many glasses of sangria he'd downed already. It was stronger than it looked. "Well, she's lucky to have a friend like you. You keep an eye on her."

"Oh, I will."

"And over here is where we have the Tempranillo planted, three hundred vines in all. If I demolish the parking lot, I may end up planting more there."

"Cat."

She glanced away from the vines, now muted and golden in the last light of sunset. Channing was standing a few feet away from her, arms crossed, an amused smile on his lips. "What?"

"I don't really need the rundown on every vine you're growing on the property. It's cute that you have a hobby and all—well, besides the fiber stuff you do—but I'd really love to see the house."

The word "hobby" made her bristle...almost as much as his off-hand remark about "fiber stuff"...but she did her best to sound calm as she responded, "It's not just a hobby. These grapes will bring in a lot of cash."

"Great, but I know you did a lot of renovating, and I'd like to see it, maybe get some ideas for my own place."

She raised an eyebrow. "What, you bought a defunct winery and are renovating it, too?"

"No, but I'm looking to dump my condo in the next year and buy a real house, and it always helps to see what other people are doing with their properties."

He spoke so casually of acquiring property, like it was something all twenty-six-year-olds could do. Cat had been in a unique position because of her family's background, but she knew that most of the people eating and drinking on her patio were renting apartments, or maybe scraping together enough to get a lease on a house if they'd been lucky enough to land a decent job.

But Channing Ellis was a different story. His father was a hotshot attorney down in Albuquerque, and Cat had no doubt that he'd pulled whatever strings were necessary to get Channing into law school and then fast-tracked into a good position with a large firm in Houston. He'd probably started earning in the mid-six figures right out of school and never looked back.

"Okay, okay," she said, knowing that continuing to protest was worse than just letting him see the damn house and getting it over with. "But it's not like it's Buckingham Palace or anything."

"Good," Channing said. "Because I hate gold leaf."

Despite herself, Cat couldn't help chuckling a little at his remark. She led him away from the vineyard area, through the now-packed parking lot, and along the path that wound its way to the front entrance of the house. Even though most of the party's action was taking place on the patio, she'd left the house lit up so people could safely find their way to one of the two bathrooms on the ground floor.

No one seemed to be inside at the moment, though. She and Channing went through the entryway with its high, beamed ceilings and antique lantern light fixture, and on into the living room, where the large multi-candle chandelier overhead sent a soft light throughout the space.

"This is pretty amazing," Channing said, looking around. "You did all this yourself?"

"Well, I hired contractors for the remodel, and I had a designer come in and help me smooth out some of the rough spots," Cat replied.

"But still." He rubbed his chin, looking at the large plaster fireplace with its aged oak mantel, the stone tile on the floor. "I guess you inherited a chunk when your mother passed away, right?"

The question sent a flash of anger through her. She didn't know which was more offensive—the off-hand way in which he mentioned Genoveva's death, or the assumption that she couldn't have possibly afforded any of this with her own money. All right, she could see why some people would have a hard time understanding how a fiber artist could earn any real money, but since one of her pieces had recently sold in a gallery for more than ten grand, it wasn't so strange to think that she could have financed the purchase of the house and its remodel with her own funds.

Voice icy, she said, "I don't really see how that's any of your business."

Immediately, Channing raised his hands and said, "Sorry, sorry. It's just—this is a hell of a house." His tone softened further, and he took a step toward her. "You know, I never was happy about the way things ended between us."

"I wasn't aware there was a 'way,'" she responded coolly. "We had some fun, but it's not like we were boyfriend and girlfriend or anything. We just…got together for a while. I always knew you had to go back to school after you were done visiting for the summer."

"And now I'm in practice, and you own a vineyard. Crazy, huh?"

Cat shrugged. True, a year ago, she couldn't have imagined she would end up where she was now, but Channing being a hotshot in a law firm had pretty much been a given. "How about I show you the dining room and the kitchen?"

Channing took another step toward her. "How about we pretend those six years never happened?"

His hands closed on hers, and he pulled her toward him, leaned down so he could press his lips against hers.

The first thought that went through Cat's mind was, *Well, at least his technique has improved a little.* But then it clicked that he was kissing her, even though she was pretty sure she'd given him no indication that she'd be at all receptive to such a move.

She snatched her hands away from his and took a step backward so she'd be safely out of arm's reach. "What the hell was that about?"

"What do you think?" he replied, completely unruffled. "Like I said, how about we pretend those six years never passed? You could show me your bedroom...."

The words trailed off there as Cat stared at him, not sure she could believe he was saying these things to her. She hadn't given him any encouragement, hadn't said or done anything that should have made him think she was eager to rekindle their romance...if you could even call it that. A few lunch dates and stolen tumbles in hotel room beds wasn't exactly enough to make what they'd had a romance, or even a relationship.

"I think I've shown you enough," she snapped. "And really, I think it's better if you just leave now."

"'Leave'?" he repeated, as if he wasn't sure he'd heard her correctly. He moved closer again, and she took another step back—although not quickly enough, because his hand closed on her wrist and prevented her from moving out of his reach. "Seriously, Cat—are you really trying to play coy now, when you were so quick to give it up back in the day?"

Cat's first instinct was to reach up and slap him across the face for the insult. However, she wasn't fast enough, because suddenly Loc was there, fists clenched at his sides and his face dark with fury. She had no idea where he'd come from, but she was overwhelmingly relieved to see him.

"I think Catalina has made it very clear that she wishes to have nothing to do with you," he said, interposing himself between the two of them. He was an inch or two taller than Channing, and broader through the shoulders, and made an effective barrier. "I think you had better leave."

Channing's eyes narrowed, emphasizing how they really were a bit too close set. "Yeah?"

"Yes," Loc replied. His voice was calm enough, but Cat could hear the silky threat lying at the bottom of it and wondered if Channing had any idea how much trouble he was in. "What kind of pitiable creature feels he must take such things from a woman, rather than have them freely given?"

"Pit—" Lips pulling up in a snarl, Channing said, "Cat, I think you'd better tell your little artist friend here to back off. I don't think he knows who he's dealing—"

He didn't get any farther than that, because Loc's fist came up, connecting with Channing's jaw in a perfect roundhouse punch. His eyes went wide, and then he toppled over, rather like a tree giving way under the last blow from a woods-man's axe.

Luckily, a Persian rug was there to break his fall. Even so, Cat could hear the grunt of pain he gave as he hit the floor. He shook his head as if to clear it, then managed to push himself back up to his feet. Blue eyes blazing, he said, "I should call the cops on you for that, you Spanish piece of shit. Assault and battery—"

"And I'll tell them he was defending me from *your* assault," Cat replied coldly, thinking it was far past time to put an end to all this. "I know you think your dad is a big shot, Channing, but believe me—the Santa Fe P.D. and the sheriff's department will take my word over yours every time."

A scowl creased his face. "You sure about that? My father knows people at the State Department. They'll make sure your Spanish friend is deported so fast, his head will spin."

"Say another word, and your life is forfeit," Loc snarled, and before Cat could do anything to stop him—or even see exactly how he'd managed it—he had his hand on Channing's throat and had him pressed up against the nearest wall so his feet dangled helplessly below him. "Understand, vermin?"

"I—I understand," Channing gasped, face going red.

"And you'll leave here, and never come back?"

"Ye-es."

Loc let go of his throat so abruptly that Channing fell to the floor, his legs buckling beneath him. Somehow, he managed to push himself up to a standing position, although Cat saw how he kept one hand pressed flat against the wall to give himself some leverage...and probably to keep himself from falling down again.

"Get out," Loc said.

Was that a flash of red she spied in his dark eyes? Cat couldn't tell for sure; it could have just been a trick of the lighting from the candles that flickered in the chandelier above him. Maybe Channing saw it, or maybe not. Either way, he sent her a baleful, sideways glare before he hurried from the room, fists clenched in impotent rage.

As soon as Channing had left the living room and slammed the front door behind him, Loc came over to her, his expression now only one of concern, all of the venomous rage he'd shown her attacker gone as if it had never been. "Are you all right, Cat?"

Her hands were shaking a little, and she clenched them into fists to make them stop. "I'm fine," she said, although she didn't know for sure whether that was really the truth or not. Channing's assault on her had been completely unexpected. All right—maybe not as unexpected as she'd wanted it to be. She knew she hadn't felt entirely comfortable bringing him inside the house, but still, she really hadn't thought he'd be so brazen, would at least try a little sweet talk before he swooped in for the kill. "Thank you, Loc."

"It's nothing," he said. He hesitated for a moment, then added, "I don't want you to think that I was spying on you. It's just...something your cousin said made me think it might be a good idea to come in here and make sure everything was all right."

Well, thank God for Tony. He often came off as someone who really wasn't paying that much attention to the world around him, but Cat knew better. His devil-may-care attitude tended to mask a man who was actually a keen observer of other people, even if he didn't often step in and try to interfere.

"Even if you were spying on me, I'm glad," Cat said frankly. "And honestly, I never thought Channing would pull something like that. Back...before...he hadn't really seemed any more interested in continuing the relationship than I was. I figured he'd come here more to satisfy his curiosity about how I was doing than anything else."

Loc's dark gaze was focused on the front door, even though Channing was now long gone. "Perhaps. Unfortunately, men who have early success in life tend to think they have a right to anyone and anything that crosses their path."

That sounded plausible enough. Even though Cat had lived in this world far longer than Loc had, she realized that in some ways she was a lot more sheltered than he. At least he'd gone out and traveled, had seen other cultures and probably met all kinds of people. She found it entirely plausible that, in some ways, he was a far better judge of human nature than she could hope to be.

"I should never have invited him into the house," she said, arms wrapped around herself. Even though the night was warm, she felt cold, and she wondered what would have happened if Loc hadn't intervened. If she'd been lucky, maybe someone would have come inside in search of the bathrooms, but….

"Don't do that," Loc replied. "Don't try to make this your fault. You were only trying to be friendly."

"I suppose so," she said, but deep down, she wasn't sure whether or not she entirely believed him. The warning signs had been there, and she'd chosen to ignore them.

He began to reach out a hand, as if to lay it on her arm to reassure her, but right then the front door opened, and a laughing, obviously tipsy couple entered. "Bathroom?" the girl asked. She was clearly younger than her companion, whom Cat thought she recognized from the world history class she'd taken in eleventh grade. Well, hopefully the girl was at least old enough to drink.

"Down the hall," Cat said, pointing, and they stumbled off in that general direction.

The mood lost, Loc turned toward the door. "I should check on the refreshments."

"Thank you."

He lifted his shoulders. "I told you that I would manage the food and drinks."

"That's not what I meant."

For a moment, he was quite still, and only stood there and gazed across the living room at her. Although it was a fairly cozy, intimate space, right then he felt as though he was roughly a thousand miles away. At last he said, "It's fine," and let himself out.

Not sure what she should do, Cat remained where she was, leaning against the couch. Then she realized that she still had roughly a hundred people partying a few dozen yards away, and that she'd better put in some face time with them if she didn't want to be branded as more eccentric than most of her former classmates already thought she was.

Luckily, it didn't seem as if anyone had missed her. Although Loc hadn't really mentioned that he was going to provide any entertainment, now there was a local band set up to one side of the patio, playing Spanish-language songs. Some of the tables and chairs had been pushed out of the way to create an impromptu dance floor, and four or five couples were swaying to the music's beat.

Cat realized her hands were shaking. She had no idea what had happened to the cup she'd been drinking from previously, so she fetched herself a new one and poured some sangria. Several people waved at her and called out, "Great party!", and she made herself raise a hand and wave back. Somehow, she even managed to smile, even though what she really wanted to do was disappear into her room and not come out for roughly a hundred years.

On the other side of the patio, Loc stood talking to Ashley. Was he reporting how badly her invitation to Channing Ellis had backfired? No, it looked like they were both smiling, so they were probably congratulating each other on a well-executed event.

"You all right?"

Cat turned to face her cousin Tony. For someone attending a blow-out party, he seemed pretty serious, his gaze intent, as if he was looking for any sign that she might have run into trouble.

"Is it that obvious?"

He shrugged. His hands were empty, which meant he must be taking a break from drinking for a while. She'd noticed a while back that he tended to carefully space out his alcohol consumption so he could last all night at a party without getting completely plowed. "I saw you walking around with Channing Ellis earlier, and he's conspicuously absent now. It doesn't take a rocket scientist to figure out that something must have gone wrong."

The last thing she wanted to do was tell her cousin about what had just happened. Besides, Loc had made sure to send Channing packing, so there really wasn't anything left to talk about, was there?

She answered with a lift of her shoulders. "It doesn't matter. He's an asshole."

"I'm glad you finally figured that out."

What was that supposed to mean? She'd been very careful to keep her dealings with Channing a secret from her family, so why was Tony talking about her relationship with the guy when no one was supposed to know there had even been a relationship at all?

As she stared at him in consternation, Tony said, "I knew about it, Cat. You thought you were being discreet, but I saw the two of you together a couple of times. Like I said, this sort of thing isn't exactly rocket science."

"Did—?" She broke off, then swallowed. "Did anyone else know?"

"If they did, it wasn't because I told them. I

knew your mother would have raised hell about the whole thing. And then that jackass went back to college and didn't seem inclined to come back to Santa Fe any time soon, so I figured that was the end of it."

"Well...thanks." Suddenly, she felt very tired. If there had been a convenient way to get all of these party guests off her property and back to their respective homes, she would have done it that very second. Actually, since Tony's talent was controlling the wind, Cat supposed she could have asked him to summon a convenient gale to chase everyone away, but that seemed like the coward's way out.

"It's nothing." He paused for a moment, studying her face. "You need me to help you get rid of these people? I can start spreading a rumor about an awesome after-party happening back down in Santa Fe. That should clear out the place pretty fast, especially since I heard a couple of guys complaining about there not being any tequila."

"Would you?" Cat asked, and hated how tremulous her voice sounded. She wasn't going to break down in tears on the spot, was she?

"Consider it done. Cousins have to look out for each other."

Tony gave her a reassuring pat on the shoulder, then went back to mingle with her guests. Sure enough, within a few minutes, people started coming up to her and saying what a great party it had been, but that they needed to get going. Faster than she would have thought, the patio had emptied out, with even Ashley stopping to breathlessly say that it was great and she was really glad to have helped plan the party, but now she had someplace she needed to be. Then she was gone, too, wobbling a little on her platform sandals as she headed back to her car.

The musicians seemed to have disappeared, too. Cat honestly didn't know whether they'd even been real, or some kind of illusion Loc had conjured once he realized the party needed entertainment. It was very hard to understand the scope of his powers, whether they had any real limits. The thought troubled her, but she pushed it aside for later. She had enough to worry about right now.

He approached her as she stood there in the center of the patio, party lights crisscrossing overhead. They revealed all the empty cups and plates left behind, the uneaten tapas and undrunk sangria still sitting on the refreshment table.

A wave of his hand, though, and all that was gone, except a fresh pair of glasses filled with sangria on the table closest to where she stood. Loc picked them up and handed one to Cat.

"Your friends seem rather fickle."

She couldn't help smiling. "Actually, that was

my idea. Tony only implemented it. I just couldn't take any more partying."

"I suppose I can't blame you for that." He raised his glass, and she lifted hers as well so they could clink their glasses together. "Here's to peace and quiet."

Amen. "To peace and quiet," she echoed.

They both took a few sips. While it felt good to have everyone gone, Cat couldn't help realizing that she and Loc were now alone together. True, they'd been alone here before, but this felt different, standing on the patio while the warm wind of a summer night touched their hair and the soft glow of the party lights illuminated just enough of the space to make it seem exotic, enticing.

Or maybe it was just Loc who was exotic and enticing. He looked so handsome standing there in his dark shirt and his jeans, the breeze ruffling his black hair. For the hundredth time, Cat reminded herself that the face he showed the world was only an illusion, that beneath it was something far, far different, and yet…

…and yet, she wasn't sure whether she cared. He'd come to her rescue tonight, had shown that he was perfectly fine with putting Channing Ellis through a wall if that was what it took to get rid of him. No, she'd never thought of herself as the sort of person who needed a man to protect her, knew she could take care of herself, but still, it was kind of nice to know he would be there for her anyway.

Very gently, he plucked the glass she held from her fingers and put it down on the table next to them, then set his down as well. He watched her carefully for a second or two, as if trying to see something in her expression that would tell him to stop.

Cat knew it wasn't there, though.

His hands touched her face, fingertips moving over her skin, slowly, as though he wanted to familiarize himself with the sensation. Heat surged in her veins, even though he'd barely made contact with her. Still, that was enough. Probably more than enough.

There must have been a moment where she could have stopped him, could have said they shouldn't do this. However, that moment passed, and she remained silent, heart pounding in her chest, hoping...

...hoping that he would bend down and press his lips against hers. Once again, his touch was tentative, although Cat honestly didn't know whether that was because he kept expecting her to stop him, or because he'd never done this before and didn't know whether he was kissing her correctly.

Oh, yes, that certainly felt right. Now her entire body was on fire, aching with need, even though the kiss he'd given her was just as chaste as the very first kiss she'd ever experienced, back in seventh grade when Gregory Luna had stolen a kiss from her during a slow dance at the school's Halloween party.

She let her lips part slightly, and she reached out with her tongue—gently, but enough for Loc to know this was how things should progress. He startled slightly, but then his mouth opened as well, and she could taste the sharp sweetness of sangria on his tongue, could feel the way his arms tightened on her, holding her tightly against him, the heavy muscles of his chest pushing against her breasts.

And the whole time that rich, sweet warmth was swirling around her. Cat pressed herself against him, wanted to feel as much of his body as possible, even as she knew this was crazy, that the last thing she should be doing was kissing him. The problem was, she wanted to do a lot more than kiss him, and that was the craziest thing of all.

Then, very gently, he pulled away, although his hands slid down to hold her gently by the arms. If she had wanted to, she knew she could have stepped back and he would have let her go. It was more that he held her in such a way so she would know he hadn't wanted to break the contact, but thought perhaps he should give her enough space if she needed it.

When he spoke, his tone was wondering. "Now I see."

He didn't say anything more than that, but Cat thought she understood. Probably before this moment, he had wondered why humans put such an emphasis on sex and love and desire. When he'd ruled as the Lord of Chaos, it most likely hadn't made any sense to him. Now that he inhabited a human body, on the other hand....

She let out a shaky little laugh. "And I kept telling myself I wasn't going to do this, but here we are."

One hand let go of her arm so he could reach up to lightly trace the curve of her cheek. "You did?" he asked, sounding surprised. "I thought perhaps there might be some kind of attraction, but I didn't want to flatter myself."

"'Some kind of attraction'?" she repeated, and chuckled again. "Something like that. Only...." Her thoughts roiled, and she wasn't sure whether she should say anything at all. The moment had been so perfect, she really didn't want to spoil it. But sooner or later they would have to hash this out.

He was studying her in that way he had, his dark gaze speculative. "Only what?"

"Only...what's the point, Loc? You want to go back to your own world, and I can't stop you." Channing Ellis's sneering face rose in her mind, and she resolutely pushed it back. He hadn't been her only fling, although she had been "living like a nun" lately, to use Ashley's careless phrase. But even when she was having those brief affairs, Cat had known she wanted something else, something more, even if the perfect warlock hadn't yet crossed her path.

Now she had the perfect man, except he wasn't really a man at all. Even ignoring that fact, if they went further with this, became truly intimate, what then? Loc would still be gone as soon as he found the right person to cast the right spell that would send him back to where he'd come from.

Cat was pretty sure her heart couldn't take that.

Loc's brows drew together, his expression darkening. "True. This is not my world."

"Well, there you have it." She pulled in a breath and hoped it wouldn't choke her, since she could already feel her throat tightening. "I—I like you a lot, Loc. But I think we need to leave this here, because it's not going to work. It just isn't."

He didn't move, but his dark eyes met hers, imploring. "Can't we enjoy the time together that we have?"

"We will," she said firmly. "I'll take you to museums and my favorite restaurants and whatever stupid action movie is out right now. We'll have a good time. But we won't—we won't—" She faltered there, and he gave a grim nod.

"But we won't have that sort of connection," he said. "I understand." For a second he was quiet, surveying the patio. The only signs that a party had been held there not even a half hour earlier were the lights twined in the trees and swagged across the open area between the grapevine trellises. However, he added, "I'll finish cleaning up here. You go on to bed."

"Loc, I—" Cat began, although she wasn't even sure what she'd intended to say.

His tone was inflexible. "Good night, Catalina."

Any further protests would have sounded ridiculous. She swallowed, hard, and turned away from him to head up the path that led to the house.

She made it halfway there before the tears came.

10

Loc sat on the roof of Cat's house, watching as the great filmy expanse of the Milky Way moved in the dark heavens above him. He knew she was asleep because he had made a heavy veil of weariness drape itself over the house, forcing her into slumber. Otherwise, he feared she would have wept far too long, and he could not have that.

With everyone gone, and another subtle form of magic making sure that no one would come here before the next morning, he had allowed himself to take on his natural form. It had felt good to stretch his wings and fly up here where he could have a commanding view of the dark landscape around him. Now, though, as he looked down at the black-scaled skin of his hands where they rested on his knees, he couldn't prevent himself from frowning.

If Cat looked at him now, would she recoil, realizing that these were the hands which had held her, that it was this inhuman body she'd pressed herself against?

He didn't want to believe that, because in the past she had seemed remarkably unconcerned by his hideous—to humans, at any rate—appearance. But Loc wasn't sure she would be quite so calm about it now that she'd allowed herself to share such intimacies with him.

One hand went up to touch his mouth, claws tracing the outline of his upper lip. Hard to believe that she had kissed this, had opened her mouth to his so they could taste one another.

And she had been delectable.

He was not even sure why he had done it, except she had looked so sad and tired, and yet so exquisitely lovely, that it had seemed the most natural thing in the world to bend down and touch his lips to hers. Perhaps the human body he had been wearing had also contributed to the act, its own hormones driving him to do something he would not otherwise consider.

Well, that was a pretty fiction, anyway. If he were going to be completely honest with himself, though, he would recall how he had thought of Catalina Castillo as he made his lonely way through this world, how visions of her beautiful face and the kindness in her dark eyes had visited him even during the times when he had taken back his natural form to give himself some respite. He might not have wanted to acknowledge it, but even his demon body had experienced desire for her, his soul aching for hers in a need he knew he could never explain.

Had such a thing ever happened before? Loc could not say for certain; his existence had spanned century upon century, and he had met beings and entities from a variety of worlds, and yet until he had met Cat, he had never thought of his life as a lonely one, had never looked on a human as anything except a form of life far below his. Was he not the Lord of Chaos? Did he not command legions of lesser demons? Had he not visited world after world and known they must answer to his command? A single human being could never compare to that kind of power.

And yet, strangely, Cat Castillo did.

The night air flowed over his wings, enticing, but he knew better than to take to the skies, even in as sparsely populated an area as this. It was one thing to fly from the balcony outside his window up to the roof directly above, and quite another to go drifting over the houses and ranches and the slow-moving river he could smell not quite a mile away. In this world, people had drones and surveillance systems and all manner of technology that might lock on to his presence. He could keep people away from Cat's property so they might have some privacy, but he could not keep the entire world at bay once he left this haven.

Well, he would just have to resume his search with a vengeance the next day. Where that search would take him, he wasn't sure, since he had already exhausted most of the likely prospects. Clearly, Cat wasn't willing to let their relationship advance any further, not when she knew it had no chance of lasting, and so there was very little else he could do.

Because of course he could not allow himself to consider the possibility of staying here with her....

Her mouth tasted gummy, and there was a crick in her neck, as if she'd spent far too much of the night before sleeping in the wrong position. Actually, she couldn't remember very much of what she'd done after she'd gotten to her room and shut the door. Her clothes and shoes had been dropped carelessly to the floor instead of being put in the hamper or returned to the closet, and that wasn't like her. Neither was sleeping in just her panties, but that was all she had on when she woke up.

For all she knew, she hadn't even brushed her teeth before she collapsed into bed. That would account for the gumminess in her mouth and the overwhelming feeling of ick that seemed to surround her as she pushed herself up from the bed.

Or maybe that was because she'd let a demon kiss her the night before...and that she'd kissed him back.

Demon lord, she reminded herself, going into the bathroom so she could start the water running for her shower. Even with all the new plumbing she'd put in, it still took a minute or two to get comfortable. *Wouldn't want anyone to think you were slumming with a regular old garden-variety demon.*

Somehow, that thought didn't cheer her up very much at all.

And now what? Loc had said he was going to resume his search, so if she was lucky, he wouldn't be around much, but even so, things were probably going to be a teensy bit awkward until that time when he actually found someone to help him.

What if he doesn't? Cat asked herself, kneading shampoo into her scalp with a bit too much vigor. *Are you going to let him crash here indefinitely?*

She wasn't sure how to answer that, although some traitorous part of her mind muttered that if he never located a way to get home, then that would solve their current situation pretty neatly, since her biggest issue had been that she didn't want to get involved with someone she knew was going to disappear in the near future.

Then she wanted to laugh at herself. Yes, the biggest problem was Loc not sticking around, and not the fact that he just happened to be a *demon lord*.

Even though Cat knew it was probably smarter to keep quiet and hope that her demonic house guest would leave sooner rather than later, she found herself wishing she could talk to Miranda about all this. Funny how she immediately thought of her sister-in-law as a possible confidant, rather than her own flesh-and-blood sisters, but neither Louisa nor Malena had ever been much of a comfort. They were enough older that they tended to view her problems as inconsequential, or at least something that experience would have told her would blow over soon enough.

I can just imagine the lecture I'd get from Louisa, Cat thought as she rinsed the last of the conditioner out of her hair. *Letting myself fall for a demon lord? I'd never hear the end of it.*

Whereas Miranda seemed a lot more likely to be sympathetic. After all, her relationship with Rafe hadn't run all that smoothly in the beginning either, although at least Rafe was a normal human warlock and not a demonic being from another dimension.

Sigh.

Cat decided to forego the blow dryer and the curling iron, and instead worked some serum through her hair in the hope that it would dry into passable waves on its own. The weather had been humid enough lately that she didn't hold out any great hope, but she was so on edge this morning that the thought of spending another half hour on her hair was intolerable.

Of course, being so quick to get ready also meant that she'd have to face Loc that much sooner. If he hadn't already disappeared for the day. He could have already headed off to Oslo or Vancouver or Timbuktu.

Or Poughkeepsie.

Her lips twitched a little, even though she was in no mood to be amused. Right then, she was still angry with Loc for kissing her…and angry at herself for responding rather than shutting him down the second he tried to make a move.

She looked in the mirror and scowled at her reflection. Those were definitely some dark circles under her eyes, but she wasn't going to bother with any concealer. She likewise scorned the mascara and lip gloss. Might as well go down-stairs looking like complete and utter crap. With any luck, she would scare Loc off so completely that he wouldn't spare another glance on her.

When she went down to the kitchen, though, it was deserted, with no sign that Loc had been here at all this morning. True, with the way he could snap his fingers or twitch his nose or whatever else it was he did, he could have made himself a whole pancake breakfast and she would have been none the wiser. The door to his room had stood open, the bed completely unrumpled, so she knew he wasn't up there, either.

Then she caught sight of a small piece of white paper sitting on the island in the kitchen. She went over to it, saw the delicate scroll pattern at the corners of the paper, and realized it was one of the little notepapers she kept in their own matching box. That box usually was hidden away in one of the drawers of the sideboard in the dining room, but clearly Loc hadn't had any trouble finding it.

The piece of paper contained one word, written in careful block letters.

Searching.

To anyone else, that single word would have seemed completely cryptic, but Cat thought she knew what it meant. Just as he'd said he would, Loc had gone off somewhere to continue his quest for the one person who could send him home.

As she stared down at the paper, a burst of anger went through her, and she crumpled the little note in her hand. Why she was so upset, she really didn't know, because this was what she'd wanted him to do, after all.

Wasn't it?

Since Cat really didn't want to answer that

question, she threw the wadded-up piece of paper into the trash and headed over to the coffeemaker. Once it was going and the rich scent of brewing coffee began to fill the kitchen, she'd calmed down a little. She knew she needed to get into a better head space, or she'd never be able to focus on her work today. Now she only had four days to finish up the two pieces she was entering in the competition, since everything had to be submitted by five o'clock on the Thursday before the show started.

A few sips of coffee did help to improve her mood somewhat. She went to the kitchen window and looked out just in time to see Roberto and Miguel pull up in their big white pickup truck. Well, at least all the mess from the night before had been cleared away, so she wouldn't have to explain why the patio still looked like a bomb hit it.

Right then, she felt more tired than anything, despite the coffee. She didn't want to have to go out and say hello to her vineyard manager and his son, and she really didn't want to go out to her studio and get any work done. What she really felt like doing was to get her emergency carton of Moose Tracks ice cream out of the freezer, then sit in the TV room and slowly consume the carton's contents while she watched every stupid rom-com she could find on her various on-demand channels. If nothing else, it might make her feel better to know that all those fictional heroines found their happily-ever-afters, even if they'd started out in even direr straits than Cat was now in.

Of course, none of those rom-com heroines had lip-locked with a demon lord, either.

Mouth tight, she forced herself to go over to the fridge and get out a carton of yogurt. Even though it was her favorite organic brand with blackberry fruit on the bottom, she couldn't muster any particular enthusiasm about eating it.

Despite herself, she couldn't help wondering what Loc was up to.

He sat at an outside table at the Café du Monde, eating a beignet and sipping a cup of chicory coffee as he watched the world go by. If asked, Loc wasn't precisely sure he could say what he was doing there. Something had drawn him back to New Orleans, even though he knew he had nothing substantive to offer Nicholas Toulouse yet. Yes, now he knew that the books were being kept somewhere in Santa Fe, but that piece of information was far too flimsy to offer to the warlock currently holed up a few miles away in the Garden District.

But at least Loc had put some distance between himself and Cat, and that could only be a good thing. Perhaps it had been cowardly to flee so early this morning, but he hadn't wished to confront her before he had a chance to think about what he truly wanted. A night of restless sleep hadn't provided any answers, and so it seemed best to get away for a while.

He thought of the warlock who desired Simon Escobar's books—well, to be fair, the books Escobar had stolen from the de la Paz clan. And then he couldn't help thinking about the young woman he'd clearly enslaved, the youngest daughter of the Dubois clan's *prima*.

Surely she should be rescued and taken back to her family, but Loc knew that if he undertook such a venture, he would incur Nicholas Toulouse's wrath, and that could only mean the end of any partnership between the two of them.

Would that be such a bad thing? he wondered. *After all, the only thing you have from him are promises. There is a very great chance that he will have you bring the books—once you've located them—and then offer nothing in return.*

Doing such a thing would be very dangerous, for even though Loc wore a human body, he still retained all his powers. He could blast Toulouse into the next plane of existence if he so desired. Of course, if he did something like that, then he would have to begin his search all over again. The dark warlock was the only one Loc had encountered so far who claimed to have the power and skill necessary to cast such a spell, and although Loc commanded many powers of his own, he could only affect the dark warlock physically, couldn't force him to cast his spell. No, as unpleasant as the prospect was, he would have to be bribed with the grimoire.

Which was why Loc had to tread carefully. If Toulouse were gone....

You might be exiled here forever, Loc thought.

Exiled in a place where he would be trapped in this human form. There were no kingdoms here for him to command, no legions of willing demons to build him temples and fortresses and palaces. He would be ordinary, nothing.

And that was why he knew he must go back, even though his own world had no such beauties as this one, no blue skies, no bright sparkling streams or golden-hued autumn trees or snow-capped mountains.

And no Cat.

He scowled and drank some more coffee, then took another bite from his beignet. To tell the truth, he thought it far too sweet and could not see why humans made such a fuss about the place, although he did have to admit that the view here was spectacular. And as varied and inter-esting as Santa Fe might be, it still could not come close to the parade that passed by on the side-walks of Decatur Street, tourists and musicians and street performers and artists milling about

Jackson Square or heading down the various side streets to have their own adventures.

A young woman strolled by hand in hand with her companion, a handsome black man in a loose white shirt and khaki trousers. The woman —girl, really, probably no more than twenty—had long blonde hair almost the same honey color as Celeste Dubois, and Loc found himself frowning.

If nothing else, he needed to know more about how the *prima*'s daughter had ended up in the hands of such a monster. More than once during his travels, he'd seen young women forced into terrible circumstances and had stopped himself from intervening, knowing that he was not a crusader, but for a witch to be trapped in such a situation troubled him more than he wanted to admit.

He wore no watch and didn't own a phone, but Loc knew it was now almost ten o'clock in the morning. By the time he'd walked the few blocks to the jewelry store where he'd purchased the emerald necklace for Cat, the shop should have opened. He had to hope that the same witch would be working there today, because he thought he might be able to get some answers from her. If this was not her day to work, he would have to start all over again with someone new.

Plan fixed in his mind, he put a ten-dollar bill down on the tabletop and set his plate partly on top of it so the wind wouldn't blow it away. Then he got up from his chair and began heading north on St. Ann Street, going deeper into the heart of the Quarter.

The crowds grew even thicker as he approached Bourbon Street, but soon enough he was on the other side and had turned down onto Dauphine, where things appeared to be a little quieter. Soon enough, Loc spied the brick building with black shutters that housed the jewelry store he sought.

And there on the front stoop was the witch he had met before, the gold rings in her braided black hair glimmering in the morning sunlight. She had just finished watering the geraniums in the window boxes, apparently, for she had a tin watering can in one hand.

Her eyes met his. Loc could see the way she startled, but she held her ground, remained standing there as he approached. Tone wry, she said, "Why did I have a feelin' I hadn't seen the last of you?"

"I have a question," he said, and she raised the hand that wasn't holding the watering can.

"Not here," she warned him. "Come inside."

He didn't waste time with protests, but followed her into the shop. All seemed to be very much the same here, although he noted that the spot the emerald necklace had occupied was now filled by a heavy gold and turquoise and enamel collar in the Egyptian Revival style.

"Your friend didn't like the necklace?" the witch asked.

Loc thought of the way the necklace had draped around the smooth, lightly tanned skin of Cat's throat…how soft that skin had been when he touched it as he fastened the jewels at the back of her neck. Forcing that image—and the arousal that threatened to stir in him—aside, he said, "No, she liked it very much. I've come here about something else."

The woman's full lips thinned. "You saw *him*, didn't you?"

"Yes, I did," Loc replied smoothly. "How could I not, after you were so kind to give me directions?"

"Well, it seems you lived to tell the tale, so I don't know what else you need from me."

Despite the briskness of her words, he could tell she was troubled; her eyes wouldn't precisely meet his, and she seemed preoccupied with wiping down the surface of the display case, even though it looked immaculate to him. "I want you to tell me about her."

"Her who?" But still the witch was looking down at the glass of the case, preoccupied with a smudge that didn't exist.

"Celeste Dubois. The *prima*'s daughter."

The rag came to a halt on the top of the case,

pressed flat by a hand whose knuckles showed pale against the witch's dark skin. "Don't be sayin' her name," she said. "Probably better if you don't even think it."

"Why not?" Loc pressed. "Surely the *prima* must want her daughter back."

"No, sir," the woman replied. "That girl is dead to her."

"'Dead'?" Loc repeated. "Why? I could tell that she was in Nic—"

"Don't say it. Don't even think his name."

Loc wanted to shake his head at the admonition, because he knew that even if Nicholas Toulouse were suddenly to appear in this shop, summoned by his name as the witch seemed to think, then Loc could drive him off easily enough. However, as he didn't want to waste his time on arguments, he lifted his shoulders and said, "Very well. At any rate, it seemed obvious enough to me that she was under some sort of spell, that she certainly wasn't there of her own volition. Surely your *prima* would understand that, and not blame her daughter for her actions?"

"You're the one who doesn't understand," the woman replied. "Celeste should have been able to withstand him. The problem was, she didn't want to."

Loc frowned at her words, not sure what she meant.

"It's not a pretty story," the witch said.

"Celeste was always headstrong, always wanted more, even though she was the *prima*'s daughter and could have had pretty much anything she wanted. Problem was, what she wanted was more power, or at least the opportunity to use her own powers more. She didn't like bein' told to hide her abilities, even though every witch and warlock alive knows that's the only reason our clans have been able to survive down through the centuries. Well, Celeste found out about *him,* and was intrigued. Didn't matter that he was old enough to be her father, and dabbled in magic that had turned his soul black. So she went to him, and let him make her his own."

None of this made very much sense. Oh, he supposed he could see how a child of a witch family might want to rebel, as they did have a peculiar set of restraints they must all live under, but it sounded as if Celeste Dubois was Nicholas Toulouse's willing partner, rather than the bewitched sex slave Loc had thought she was.

"But why does it seem as if she's under a spell if she went to *him* under her own volition?"

The witch laughed, but there was no humor in the sound. "I told you his soul was black as night. She's under a spell because it amuses him, and because he knows it will upset Estelle Dubois even more than knowin' that her daughter went willingly to such a dark warlock. That's how it's been for the past year, and I don't see it changin', least not until he tires of her and throws her back to her family. And of course they'll have to take her in, because witch families always look after their own."

"I see." Actually, Loc wasn't sure he did, not completely, but understanding human motivations was still difficult for him.

Another chuckle, although this one seemed almost genuine. "Don't tell me you came chargin' back here thinkin' you were going to rescue the girl, were you? Because you can put that notion right out of your mind. Even if you managed to do it somehow—and maybe you could, seein' what you are—that girl would just go crawlin' right back to him. No point in wastin' your energy."

Apparently not. Had Nicholas Toulouse sensed his presence here in New Orleans, and was even now attempting to determine what had brought his demon lord friend back to the city so soon after his last visit? Perhaps. Loc's powers should not have been detected in such a way, but he still didn't have a very clear grasp of what Toulouse was capable of.

"He asked me to get something for him," he said, surprised that he'd allowed himself to be so frank with this witch whose name he still didn't know.

"Whatever it was, you won't be doin' yourself or anyone else a favor if you give *him* what he wants," she said darkly. "I don't care what he promised you in return, although I can guess. Somewhere else on this earth is someone who can help you, someone who won't cheat you."

"But what if there isn't?"

Her big dark eyes, a warm chocolate brown, fixed on him. "Like I told you before, there are worse things than exile. Best you get your priorities straight."

Loc wanted to laugh at her, laugh at the presumption that had led her to think she could lecture him, when he'd once been master of an entire plane of existence. However, she was regarding him calmly, brown eyes shrewd, and he had the sudden thought that perhaps laughing at her wasn't the best idea. "My priorities are in order, I assure you."

"Hmm." She crossed her arms, and the gold bangle bracelets she wore clinked faintly. For the first time, Loc wondered at the lack of activity in this shop, how no one else ever seemed to come in here. But then, perhaps this witch's talent was keeping away those she didn't want straying into her orbit. He supposed he could have asked, although it was generally considered rude to ask a witch or warlock what their particular gift might be. Arms still folded under her ample bosom, she said, "I'm goin' to give you some advice."

He lifted an eyebrow at her. "I'm not sure what good the advice of a human will do me."

This time, she actually threw back her head and laughed, a deep, throaty laugh that seemed to echo through her entire body. "Well, that's for you to decide, but I'm goin' to give it anyway. You were in here lookin' for somethin' for yourself, but you left with somethin' for someone else. Maybe it was no big deal to you, seein' as you can make hundred-dollar bills appear out of nowhere, but even though it wasn't hurtin' your wallet, you still had to be thinkin' of that other person, thinkin' of something they might like. And that means you've made a connection here, whether you like it or not. The more you make those sorts of connections, the harder it'll be for you to leave. So consider well whether it's worth all this effort, if the answer has been in your own heart all along."

For a moment, Loc was silent. He thought of how Cat had looked as she stood under the patio lights the night before, her dark eyes alive with desire, even if she hadn't been aware of her need. He remembered how sweet she had tasted, how warm her skin had been...how his body had responded as she pressed herself up against him. And then how she had rebuffed him, because she hadn't wanted to be hurt, hadn't wanted to open up her heart to someone whose only goal was to leave her.

"Ah," he said at last.

It seemed that was enough, because the witch

said, "Exactly. 'For what shall it profit a man, if he shall gain the whole world, and lose his own soul?'"

Those words sounded familiar, although Loc couldn't recall where he'd heard them before. "Some might argue that I do not have a soul."

She smiled. "Oh, you do. Otherwise, you wouldn't have come back here, askin' worried questions about Celeste Dubois…and you wouldn't have bought that necklace for your friend. What you need to do is look into that soul and listen to what it tells you."

Would he be able to hear such a voice? He supposed there was only one way to find out.

"Thank you," he told the witch, and she shrugged.

"Don't thank me yet."

"Why not?"

"Because I don't think that dark warlock in the Garden District is goin' to be too happy when he finds out you don't want his 'help' any longer."

11

THE SUNLIGHT FLASHED OFF THE BROAD GRAPE leaves, barely reaching the clusters of fruit that hung underneath. Weeks remained before those grapes would be ready to be picked, but they were still beautiful, tantalizing. Roberto had given Cat his usual Monday report, letting her know what he thought the yield for each of the varieties would be, but he and Miguel had left about a half hour before. Now she walked amongst the vines, letting the warmth of the sun do its best to work out some of the kinks in her neck. She'd put in a good six hours' worth of work on her tapestry today, but she'd been glad of the interruption Roberto had provided. It was time to set aside her needles and scissors and go outside, try to clear her head a bit.

Loc had been absent all day, and now that it was nearly five, she wondered if he was going to return at all. Once again, she tried to tell herself it was probably better that way, although she really didn't believe those inner admonitions. Even if —*when*—he ended up leaving, she had to think it would be better if she had a chance to say goodbye.

Eventually, she left the vineyard and made her way up to the house. To her surprise, she saw Loc standing in the shelter of the covered entry, clearly waiting for her.

His expression was very solemn, and a sudden, sick feeling seized her stomach. Maybe he had found someone to help him, and he'd only come back here to let her know he was leaving. Suddenly, the opportunity to share a formal farewell didn't sound nearly as appealing as it had just a few minutes earlier.

When she approached him, though, he said probably the last thing she'd been expecting.

"I'm sorry."

Cat blinked at him. "Sorry for what?"

"For last night. For not understanding that such an advance wouldn't be acceptable to you."

Oh, boy. Did she really want to do this right now? Whatever Loc had been up to today, it seemed that he'd spent some of his time engaged in a bit of soul searching. "It's—it's all right," she said. Was it? But he looked worried, as if he feared she wouldn't forgive him for that one transgression. "You just caught me off guard."

He nodded, but his expression remained troubled. "There is more to it than that."

"There is?"

"I think we should talk inside, or at least on your patio—the one in back of your house," he added. "Not the one where we held the party."

"Um...sure." More than ever, she was convinced that he planned to tell her he'd found someone to send him home, and he was only here now, making apologies, because he wanted to clean up whatever messes he'd made in this world before he returned to his own. "Is this the sort of thing that could use some wine?"

For the first time, he smiled, the somberness lifting from his expression. "That might be a good idea."

Still puzzled, Cat led him inside the house, making a detour into the kitchen so they could collect a pair of stemless wine glasses and a bottle of Chenin blanc from the fridge. Thus armed, they went out to the patio, where the sun was filtered through the vines that climbed on the pergola overhead but still offered plenty of warmth.

After she'd uncorked the bottle and poured some wine for both of them, she asked, "What's this about, Loc? Are you leaving?" Because she figured it was better to get it out in the open rather than keep dancing around the topic.

"Leaving? No. At least," he continued, as her heart began to beat a little faster, "not immediately. But there are things I need to tell you. I want you to know the truth, even if it makes you angry with me."

Cat didn't like the sound of that very much, but she told herself she needed to wait and hear what he had to say. Then again, someone who had once earned the epithet "the Lord of Chaos" could have been up to all kinds of mischief. "All right, Loc," she said, after sipping at her Chenin blanc. "What is 'the truth'?"

"You know I've been searching for someone to send me back to my home."

As truths went, that one wasn't exactly earth-shattering. "Yes."

"I found someone in New Orleans who said he could help me."

The wine she'd just swallowed seemed to be stuck somewhere near her esophagus, but Cat managed to say, "Oh, really? Well, that's good news, isn't it?"

"Not necessarily." Loc leaned forward, strong sun-browned fingers wrapped around his wine glass. "You see, this warlock said he had the strength to work such a complex enchantment, but the only way he could so was by utilizing the spell books Simon Escobar had left behind—the same spell books that were used to bring me here in the first place."

For a second, all Cat could do was stare at him. Now that strange conversation they'd had about the grimoires made sense—Loc had been trying to find out if she knew anything about them, especially their current location. And of course he had to shut that line of inquiry down as soon as she offered to ask Miranda about the books. The last thing he would have wanted was for the clan's *prima* to know he was here and looking for such powerful magical artifacts.

Anger surged through her. "So what was the necklace about? Trying to butter me up so I would tell you whatever you needed?"

"No," he replied at once. He actually looked offended, which was sort of rich, considering what he'd just told her. "I saw the necklace in a shop in New Orleans and thought you would like it. There was no plan to 'butter you up.'" To her surprise, he reached across the table and laid his hand lightly on top of hers. She could feel a faint coolness to his skin, probably from holding his wine glass, but for some reason, she didn't want to pull away. "And today I realized that what I was doing was wrong. I should have told you the truth about those books, and about Nicholas Toulouse."

"He's the warlock in New Orleans?"

"Yes…and a very evil man."

The comment surprised Cat, because she wasn't quite sure if Loc even thought in terms of such absolutes as good and evil. He had done things which seemed altruistic, and then gone on to act in ways that appeared utterly selfish. Maybe that sort of behavior wasn't entirely surprising in a being whose frame of reference was completely different from that of an ordinary human, but still, she'd had a hard time trying to figure him out. However, if a demon lord from a different dimension considered someone evil, then she supposed they must be.

"But you still would have gotten the books for him."

Loc released her hand, dark eyes full of remorse. "Yes, I fear I would have...until today."

She pushed herself against the back of her chair, putting some extra distance between the two of them. "What made you change your mind?"

"Some advice from a very wise woman. I realized that I could not give Nicholas Toulouse those books because he would never use them wisely, but would utilize them in the pursuit of power, of influence."

Cat was silent for a moment, thinking of Simon Escobar and how close he had come to taking control of her clan. The last thing she wanted was for the people she cared about—or anyone else, really—to have to face someone just as dangerous as Escobar. "How powerful is this Toulouse character?"

"I don't know for sure. I was able to sense

something of his power, but I got the sense that far more was hidden than was revealed."

"Worse than Simon Escobar?"

"In terms of native ability, probably not. But Toulouse is much older, has had more time to hone his talents."

Well, that sounded just great. Cat ran a hand through her hair, feeling the sun-warmed strands slip over her fingers. Normally, such a sensation would have reassured her, but she was finding little reassuring about the world just now. "Is he part of the clan in New Orleans?"

"No. He is somehow apart from them, but I have no idea where he came from, or which clan he was originally born to. He has a house in the Garden District and is barred from entering the French Quarter where the Dubois witches live. That is their only real power over him, though."

All of this was sounding uncomfortably like what had happened to the Santiagos, the witch clan in California that had been taken over by Simon's father, Joaquin Escobar. However, it seemed as though at least the Dubois witches and warlocks were hip to this Nicholas Toulouse's game, even if they weren't strong enough to get rid of him altogether.

"What are you going to do now?" Cat asked. "I mean, this dark warlock was your only real lead, wasn't he?"

"Yes," Loc replied. However, he didn't look nearly as dejected as someone who'd just suffered such a setback should. Actually, he appeared almost relaxed, as if it had taken a huge weight off his shoulders to have told her what he'd been planning.

And strangely, even though she'd experienced a burst of anger earlier when he first confessed what he was up to, that anger had gone as quickly as it had appeared. Maybe it was mostly relief that it didn't seem as though Loc would be going anywhere anytime soon.

"But," he went on, "if Nicholas has such powers, then someone else in this world must possess them as well. I don't want to believe that the only person with such skills must be irredeemably evil."

"If he even was capable of sending you back where you came from," Cat remarked. "He could have been lying to you to get you to bring him those books." A thought occurred to her, and she asked, "Unless you can always tell when someone is lying to you?"

"Unfortunately, no," he replied. "Sometimes I can pick up on small signs and nuances, since I have been studying human behavior closely in order to imitate it as best I can, but that only goes so far. My own powers don't extend to such an ability, so I fear that it is entirely possible Toulouse could have played on my desire to return to my world in order to trick me into getting the books for him."

This response wasn't entirely reassuring, but she was glad to know that Loc wasn't all-seeing and all-powerful. Not that she intended to lie to him anytime soon, of course, and yet it was a bit of a relief to know that he couldn't instantly pick out the subtext of anything she said, just because his power as a demon lord allowed him to look into her mind and soul.

Then again, he'd done a pretty good job of it the night before. Even though she'd resisted those sensations as best she could, it was hard not to recall the touch of his mouth on hers, the way the hard muscles of his chest had felt as he held her close.

And now it seemed as if he was going to be sticking around, at least for a little while longer, and Cat really didn't know how she was supposed to deal with that.

"We'll need to tell Miranda," she said, and Loc's black-lashed eyes immediately flared with alarm.

"Why?" he asked. "I just told you that I have no plans to cooperate with Nicholas Toulouse."

"I know," she said, trying to keep her tone gentle. "But still, now there's a dark warlock in New Orleans who knows the Castillo clan is sitting on some very valuable and dangerous books. I don't know how much of a threat he is, whether he'd attempt to get them on his own now that he won't have you to do his dirty business for him, but the *prima* of this clan needs to know that a threat is out there." Cat stopped then, another suspicion entering her mind. "Are those books really dangerous to her unborn child, or did you just say that so she'd stay far away from them?"

Loc sighed, one finger tracing its way through the condensation on the surface of his wine glass. "I fear I made that up. At the time, I was only thinking of what I needed to do to make sure she wouldn't go near them before I had a chance to steal them for Nicholas Toulouse."

Should she chastise him for lying to her? But no, he'd already apologized, and clearly he was ready to tell her the truth now, no matter how bad it made him look. Cat wasn't sure how many human men would do the same thing.

"Well, Miranda and Rafe will be relieved to hear that," she said, and decided to leave it there. Although she hoped she would never be in a position where she was utterly separated from the world she knew, she thought she understood a little of the desperation that had driven Loc to go along with Nicholas Toulouse's demands. "But I still need to call them."

"Go ahead," Loc replied, although there was a sadness in his tone that worried her. "I am ready to hear whatever they have to say."

Miranda Castillo was not pleased, Loc could tell that much. Her arms were crossed and her full mouth was pressed into a flat line, and although she didn't speak as Cat did her best to recount what had happened over the past few days, it was obvious that the Castillo *prima* had plenty of thoughts on the subject of Loc and his search for someone who could assist him in returning to his own world.

Actually, it was Rafael Castillo, her consort, who spoke first. Loc could see the resemblance between him and his sister, in the glossy near-black hair, the arched brows, the high cheekbones. He sat next to his wife on one of the couches in their large living room and directed his words to Catalina. "You didn't think it was important for us to know that you had a demon lord staying with you, Cat?"

Her shoulders lifted. "Not really. I just gave him some crash space."

Human slang for a place to stay. Loc could tell she hated being put on the spot like this; although he did not know her as well as he would like, he had come to realize that she was a private person, that there were many things in her past she hadn't shared with anyone, not even the brother she fiercely loved.

"I know I was imposing on her," he said. "But I could not think of where else to go."

"You spent eight months wandering the world, and suddenly ran out of resources as soon as you got to Santa Fe?" the *prima* inquired, lip curling slightly. "I find that a little hard to believe."

Of course it was difficult to believe, because it wasn't so much that he'd run out of resources—he always had as much ready cash as he needed—but that he'd needed someplace to stop and catch his breath, so to speak. Unfortunately, Loc guessed that trying to explain how his soul had reached out for Cat's would not go over very well with either Miranda or her consort.

He found himself shrugging, just as Cat had a moment earlier. "I realized I was in need of counsel. Cat offered me a place to stay, and I was grateful to accept."

The *prima*—who was young and beautiful, but whose beauty did not seem to affect Loc at all—and her husband exchanged sideways glances, but neither of them said anything for a moment. When Miranda finally spoke, she seemed willing to leave aside the problem of Loc staying at Cat's place and instead pushed on to what she plainly considered to be the heart of the matter. "Tell me about this Nicholas Toulouse. How much of a threat is he, really?"

"I don't know for certain," Loc confessed. "I

believe he is quite powerful, but he is also just one man. And, unlike Simon Escobar, he does not have access to the spell books he desires. Also, from what I have been able to tell, he seems content to stay in his house in the Garden District. He draws what he wants to him, rather than leaving to seek it out elsewhere."

"Well, that's something," Rafael Castillo said. "I'm not sure it's enough, though. I mean, it was before my time, but I'm pretty sure Escobar's father accomplished everything he did without the help of any spell books. Maybe this Toulouse character is the same way."

"Possibly." Loc couldn't say one way or another, for of course he had not been in New Orleans when the dark warlock came on the scene, which had to have been many years earlier. "I haven't seen any true demonstrations of his power, and so, as I told Cat, I don't know for sure what powers he commands on his own."

"Really, I just thought you needed to know he was out there," Cat said. She rubbed her palms on the knees of her jeans, then clasped her hands together. Although she sat next to him on the couch, she made sure more than a foot of space remained safely between them, possibly so her brother would have no reason to comment on their proximity to one another. "And the books are safe, anyway, right?"

"Safe as we can make them," Miranda said.

"Rafe's cousin thinks it's better to have them here, since she doesn't trust the de la Paz clan to guard them the way they should be, but at this point, I'm starting to wonder whether it's better if we just send the damn things back. They should never have been our problem to begin with."

Although Loc understood the truth of this statement—the grimoires were only in Castillo territory because Simon Escobar had brought them here—he wasn't sure whether sending them back to their rightful owners was the best idea. After all, the de la Pazes hadn't done a very good job of safeguarding them in the first place.

He also hadn't missed the way Miranda carefully omitted the name of the cousin who was the books' current guardian. Clearly, the *prima* still didn't trust him, despite the aid he'd provided in their last desperate battle against the Escobar warlock. Not that Loc really blamed her; if their positions had been reversed, he wasn't sure whether he would have trusted himself, either.

Cat spoke then, echoing what he had just been thinking. "It's probably better if we sit on them for a while. I mean, from what you told Rafe and me, Simon made it sound as if it wasn't too hard for him to steal them in the first place. What if the books go back to the de la Paz clan, and this Nicholas Toulouse person just goes there to steal them? At least now we know what's going on. It's been radio silence from the de la Pazes this whole time, hasn't it? You'd think if they knew where the books were, they would have reached out to us by now."

Judging by the way neither Rafe nor Miranda replied right away, Loc thought it fairly obvious that they'd already had this discussion, probably more than once, and had probably come to the same conclusion. As he gazed at their troubled expressions, an idea came to him, one so simple that he wondered why he hadn't thought of it before.

"I can go to de la Paz territory and see if there are any signs that they have missed the books, or at least are looking for them. It is simple enough for me to slip in and out of a place without being noticed."

The *prima* sat up a little straighter on the couch, even as Cat shifted where she sat and sent him a look of consternation. "You can do that? Go in and out of our territories with no one realizing you're there?" Miranda asked.

"Yes." It was easy to hide his nature from witches and warlocks, and equally as easy to make himself completely invisible, if that was what a certain situation required. "A little judicious spying is just what the situation requires, I think."

Once again, Miranda and Rafe exchanged a glance. "If you're sure...." Rafe began, then let the words trail off, as if he didn't know whether to protest or simply say "thank you."

"I am sure," Loc said calmly. "This shouldn't take me very long."

And before any of them could reply, he took himself away, to the heat and the brightness of Phoenix—or, more specifically, to Scottsdale, the expensive suburb where the *primas* of the de la Paz clan had lived for nearly a hundred years now. Like the Castillo house, the home of Zoe Sandoval, the head witch of the family, was large and built in the hacienda style, although something about its architecture felt more friendly, more welcoming, although Loc couldn't say precisely why.

What was not at all welcoming was the searing heat that greeted him as soon as he came into being in the courtyard of said house. A fountain splashed in the center of that courtyard, and bright flowers bloomed all around, and yet the air seemed hot enough to flash-fry anything it touched.

Not that he really had to worry about such things. His mind and spirit and body were here, but hidden to the eye—and to the special gift all witches and warlocks possessed, of being able to sense when they were in the presence of one of their kind.

But Loc was not one of them, and never would be.

He passed silently through the front door and found himself in an entryway with a red tile floor and dark-beamed ceilings overhead. Almost at once he heard the metallic "clack-clack-clack" of a hammer. It seemed to be coming from the garden at the rear of the house, and so that was where he headed.

As soon as he drifted through the back wall of the house, he located the source of the hammering noise. The garden was large and quite beautiful, with beds of well-tended roses and another stately fountain off to one side, but nearly a third of it had been given up to a substantial addition to the back of the house. From what Loc could tell, most of the addition's frame was now in place, and several workmen were in the process of nailing pieces of plywood over the frame.

Well, warlock workmen, that was. He could tell at once these were not ordinary humans, and neither were the man and woman who stood off to one side, observing the work as it was being performed.

They both appeared to be of some four decades or so, the woman exotically lovely with her long black hair and tip-tilted dark eyes, the man probably a little older, although there was no gray in his dark red hair. The power that emanated from both of them was quite strong, and Loc realized he was looking at Zoe Sandoval, the *prima* of the de la Paz clan, and her consort, who was a McAllister warlock but had left his clan to come live among his soul mate's people.

Despite the obvious irritation on Zoe's face, Loc noted the way the pair held hands as they watched the construction, the fond light in Evan's eyes as he gazed down at his wife.

"You'd think in a clan the size of ours, we'd have more than three general contractors," she said.

"It's going up fast," her husband replied. "I'm sure they'll have it done by the end of the summer."

"If they don't fall over from heat exhaustion first." She lifted her heavy black hair away from her neck with her free hand, as if to allow the breeze to cool her a bit, then let it fall back down again.

"They'll be fine." Evan looked away from her, over to the addition in process, and added, "But it does help that Jose's talent is calling for a fresh breeze whenever they need it."

"True." Zoe was silent for a moment, studying the building before her. "You really think it's going to be big enough?"

"We measured and did all the calculations four separate times. All the books are going to fit just fine."

"I hope so. We need to make sure they're safe."

This exchange told Loc what he needed to

know—that the de la Paz clan was all too aware of the books that had gone missing, and so they'd obviously decided to add a library onto their *prima*'s house, so that she could watch over those prized possessions and use her powers to make sure no more thefts such as the ones Simon Escobar committed ever happened again. And it also probably explained why the de la Pazes hadn't said a word about the affair. They must have been embarrassed to have lost track of items as powerful and dangerous as the grimoires that had been taken, and so wanted to make sure they had a secure place to store the books once they asked for them back.

But even with warlock contractors working on the build, it didn't look as though it could possibly be ready for a few more months, since once the outer structure was complete, they would still need to finish off the interior, install bookcases, and so forth. Loc would be the first to admit that he did not have any in-depth knowledge of human construction techniques, but he had inhabited enough different buildings in this world to know that most of them were more complicated than they appeared on the surface. At the same time, he wondered how many books would end up being stored here. The library addition looked large enough to store hundreds, if not thousands of volumes. The de la Paz clan must have a very large collection indeed.

It seemed clear enough to him that, even if Miranda and Rafael Castillo had been willing to send the books over now, the de la Pazes were in no real position to take them back. And really, even once the grimoires were ensconced here in the library that was being built expressly for them, they might not be any safer than where they were now. Loc did not know very much of Zoe Sandoval—except that once she, too, had dabbled in forbidden magic and faced some very unexpected consequences—but he knew there was no way her magic was any match for Miranda's, Miranda who was the daughter of a *prima* and a *primus,* and who had also taken on the Castillo clan's *prima* powers when it became woefully obvious that their true *prima* was not up to the task of defeating Simon Escobar.

No, it seemed Loc would have to return to Santa Fe and let them and Cat know that, while the de la Paz clan was gearing up to ask for their property back, they would not be doing so in the immediate future. Perhaps it would give the Castillo *prima* and her consort a modicum of relief to know they would not be the stewards of the grimoires indefinitely, but none of that solved the more immediate problem of Nicholas Toulouse.

If he even did anything at all. From what the witch in the jewelry shop had said, he seemed to delight in causing mental torment for others, and so it was entirely possible that the mere chance he might come to Santa Fe to wreak havoc was enough for him, knowing that it would cause the Castillos a good deal of worry and trouble.

Or he could be planning such a foray this very moment.

Since Loc knew he had seen enough here at the de la Paz *prima*'s home, he whisked himself away to New Orleans, back to the cloistered brick house in the Garden District, where the tall trees hid the darkness of what lay within those walls. This time, though, he did not walk up the front steps and knock at the door, but slid through the very bricks of the house, entering through one of the kitchen walls.

On the surface, the room looked ordinary enough, if rather stark with its whitewashed cabinets and white marble countertops and stainless appliances. Something bubbled in a large stainless-steel pot on the stove, and Loc moved closer, curiosity driving him to discover what the warlock was cooking for his next meal.

An acrid odor rose from within the pot, and when he looked inside, he saw a dark, viscous substance that filled it nearly halfway. Not soup, though.

Blood.

His nose wrinkled. Loc was certainly not what one could call squeamish—on many occasions he'd calmly dispatched demons who had somehow failed in their duty to him or otherwise showed that they were not worthy—but at least he had never made a soup of their blood, or worn the bones of his fallen enemies like beads around his neck. What precisely Nicholas Toulouse was doing with this blood, Loc didn't know, but this was dark, dark magic, even if the blood in that pot had come from an animal and not a human being.

The kitchen door opened, and the dark warlock entered. His appearance was quite altered from the last time Loc had seen him—now strands of silver showed in his black hair, and his smooth brown skin was smooth no longer, but furrowed with lines around his eyes and mouth. For a second, he paused, his strange, pale eyes scanning the kitchen, but then he seemed to dismiss whatever had been bothering him and headed straight for the tall stock pot and its grue-some contents.

Had the warlock detected him somehow? Loc couldn't be sure, although it appeared that even if he had sensed something strange about his surroundings, it hadn't been enough to keep him from his original errand here. Toulouse retrieved a large silver ladle from where it had been lying on a spoon rest next to the stove, then dipped it into the pot as he murmured something under his breath. That near-whisper wasn't loud enough for Loc to hear clearly, but he guessed it was some kind of incantation.

Spell recitation complete, the warlock lifted the ladle from the pot and blew on it gently, then swallowed a large mouthful of the hot blood. Almost at once, the silver disappeared from his hair, and the lines on his face smoothed themselves away. Now he looked much as he had when Loc first encountered him, although possibly even younger. Smiling, he drank down more of the viscous liquid, then went to the sink and rinsed off the ladle. However, he made no move to clean out the pot itself, but instead placed a lid on it and turned off the gas burner underneath.

These tasks done, he exited the kitchen with much more spring in his step than had been there when he first entered it, while Loc remained where he was, a frown pulling at his invisible brow.

Obviously, the blood and the spell combined in some sort of ritual to restore Nicholas Toulouse's lost youth. Precisely how often he had to perform this ritual, Loc didn't know for sure. However, it was still helpful to know that the dark warlock relied on such a crutch to maintain his health and vigor. Such a reliance was a weakness.

And weaknesses existed to be exploited.

12

LOC REAPPEARED AS PRECIPITOUSLY AS HE HAD vanished, and Cat startled. So did Miranda and Rafe, although Miranda recovered herself quickly enough and said, "Well?"

"The de la Pazes are building a library at their *prima*'s house, a library to store all their magical books," he replied. His gaze moved to Cat for a moment, and she felt a flush touch her cheeks, even though the glance he gave her lasted only long enough for her to realize he was looking in her direction. "They obviously know what was stolen from them, but they have no wish to take the books back until they have a safe place to keep them."

"Well, good," Rafe put in. "I guess we can wait to hear from them. I suppose I should be glad they're trying to be proactive, but I'd sure as hell like to know what took them so long."

"It was probably harder than we think to figure out exactly what was missing," Miranda said. Although she was frowning slightly, her tone was milder than Cat had expected. Then again, she knew some of the de la Paz witches and warlocks, because there had been a good bit of intermarrying between the southern Arizona clan and its northern counterparts. Probably, she was doing her best not to be too judgmental. "If those books were scattered amongst the various households, and if people didn't keep very good records, I can see why it might take months and months to get everything sorted out."

Rafe didn't seem as if he was quite so inclined to be generous. A frown of his own creasing his brows, he said, "Still, it all seems pretty sloppy to me."

"But they are working on trying to fix the problem," Loc put in. Once again, he was sitting next to Cat on the sofa, although not too close. Even so, she was acutely aware of him, of the longish dark hair brushing against the collar of his black T-shirt, the way his hands rested lightly on the knees of the worn Levi's he wore. He seemed so human, and yet every once in a while she could catch some movement or gesture, a certain strangeness, as if he was speaking or reacting that way because it was something he'd studied and not because he'd done the same thing all his life. "That's something. Now all you have to do is wait, because eventually, they will reach out to you to have their clan's books returned to them. There is something else, though."

"What?" Cat asked. The information he'd given them about the de la Paz clan and their library hadn't been bad news, not really, and yet something about the way his expression shifted told her that he had something far worse to relate.

"I returned to New Orleans to see what Nicholas Toulouse was up to—if anything. I saw him perform a blood ritual, something to restore his youth and vitality. He is obviously far older than he looks."

Miranda let out a huff of a breath. "Great. Which means he could be a lot more powerful than any of us guessed."

"Possibly," Loc said. "Although having to rely on those sorts of compromising rituals also means he is vulnerable in a way we hadn't expected. His strength is not entirely his own. If he brings an attack against the Castillo clan—and I am still not sure whether that is what he has planned—then we can do what we can to cut off his supply, so to speak."

"Of blood, you mean," Cat said, feeling a bit queasy. Oh, sure, she knew there were dark witches and warlocks who used blood in their rituals, thought nothing of dispatching a pig or a cat or a dog to further their black magic, but no one in her own clan had done that sort of thing for hundreds of years. And of course, there were other kinds of blood....

"Yes," Loc replied. He looked calm enough, so clearly he hadn't been grossed out by what he'd witnessed at Nicholas Toulouse's house. Then again, demon lords probably weren't known for their weak stomachs. "I don't know what kind of blood it was, but I fear it was probably human. Animal blood would do very little to restore a human's vitality."

"Excuse me," Miranda said, looking a little pale. She pushed herself up from the couch and fled down the hall to the guest bathroom, then shut the door. Loc stared after her, clearly perplexed by her behavior.

"First trimester," Rafe explained. "She's started to get a little pukey the past few days. All perfectly normal, of course, but I'm not surprised that talking about human blood put her over the edge. She can't even stand the smell of meat right now."

A little pause as Loc appeared to process this information, and then he nodded. "Of course. I'd forgotten that she was with child. I will refrain from being too graphic. But if Nicholas Toulouse is killing people to feed his rituals, then he will have a more difficult time if he tries to bring the fight here. Predators such as he always fare better when they can remain in an environment that's familiar to them."

Cat hadn't really thought about that aspect of the situation, but after all, it wasn't every day her clan had to deal with a blood-swilling dark warlock who might or might not be a serial killer, too. "I guess we have to hope that he decides the books aren't worth leaving his cozy spot there in New Orleans. I'm kind of surprised the Dubois witches haven't tried to clear him out."

"I'm not sure they're strong enough," Rafe said. "Our mother didn't talk about the other clans very often, but I remember her making a few catty remarks about the Dubois family once or twice. Then again, their situation is really different from ours. The Castillos have always had all of New Mexico to call their own. From what I've been able to tell, the witch clans are packed in a lot more tightly in Louisiana, and the Duboises never really spread out much farther than the French Quarter."

"It's not that different from the McAllisters, I guess," Miranda put in, returning to the living room. She still looked a little pale, but she seemed composed enough as she sat down on the couch next to her husband. "We've spread out from Jerome, but in the beginning, that was it for us. The only reason we could move into Cottonwood and Prescott and even Payson is that neither of the other two Arizona witch clans had any kind of a presence in those places. But witches have been settled in Louisiana for a long time."

"There are five families in the state, I think," Rafe said. "So yeah, it's probably a little cramped in there. And that's probably why the Dubois clan is having a tough time of it. Most of the time, we don't reach out to others for help, because no one wants to appear weak. Problem is, that's just the kind of situation someone like this Nicholas Toulouse guy would exploit. It's not that different from what happened to the Santiagos in California."

"Only, as far as I can tell, Toulouse hadn't done anything to attempt to take over the Dubois clan," Loc said. "It seems that it amuses him more to remain where he is and be a thorn in the side of their *prima*. Also, he has her daughter."

Miranda sat up a little straighter at that revelation. "He what?"

"The Dubois *prima*'s daughter is living with him—she is not the *prima*-in-waiting, though." Loc shrugged. "It is an odd situation, because I was told she went to him voluntarily, but he still has her under the control of some sort of spell. However, I couldn't see any sign that she was being mistreated."

"You *saw* her?" Rafe demanded.

"Yes. She made an appearance the one and only time I spoke directly with Nicholas Toulouse. She looked well enough, although rather 'out of it,' to use your phrase. Anyway, I believe she makes a rather good hostage. No matter what he ends up doing, I doubt that we should expect any kind of assistance from the Dubois *prima*, since that would most likely cause Toulouse to retaliate against her daughter."

Just great. Cat hadn't even thought of that angle, but it made perfect sense. Not only did Toulouse get to sleep with someone far younger than himself—way, way younger, if Loc's observation that the warlock must be very old was true —but he also had the perfect human shield in the *prima*'s daughter.

"So what are we supposed to do?" Cat asked, knowing she sounded far too plaintive. Still, this whole situation had made her feel far more defeated than she should.

"Right now?" Miranda responded. "Nothing. I mean, the books are safe, and so far we don't have any reason to believe that Toulouse knows where they are, except somewhere in Santa Fe. We'll let Rafe's cousin know she needs to be on her guard, and to let us know right away if she encounters anything that feels or looks strange, but there isn't much more we can do beyond that."

"We can still use Loc as our spy," Rafe said. For a second, his gaze rested on Cat and Loc where they sat on the couch next to each other, and it took a good deal of self-control to keep her from wriggling with guilt. All right, the only thing she and Loc had done was kiss each other once, but even so, she got the feeling that Rafe had picked up something of their vibe and was less than approving. "You can keep an eye on Toulouse for us, right?"

"That's dangerous—" Cat began, but Loc cut her off.

"Not really. Or rather, I am fairly confident that Nicholas Toulouse can't detect my presence."

"'Fairly confident'?" she echoed. "That doesn't sound very reassuring."

His shoulders lifted. "I saw him react to something when he entered the kitchen where I was observing him. However, it might have been something else entirely. The only way to know for sure is to try again."

"Well, that can wait, I think." Miranda glanced over at Rafe, and he gave her the barest of nods. "For now, we'll just have to be watchful." She paused before adding, her tone a little too casual, "Are you going back to Pojoaque, or did you plan to hang out in Santa Fe for a little while?"

"I think it's probably better to head back to the house," Cat replied, immediately on her guard. Had the question been an attempt at finding out whether she and Loc were going to share some kind of date night here in Santa Fe, since they were in town? Maybe. She hoped her response had been neutral enough that neither Miranda nor Rafe would be able to find much meat in it. "I still have a lot of work to do to get ready for the art reception, and Loc hasn't given up on finding someone who can help him."

"Someone who's not a dark warlock," he said, getting to his feet. "It is difficult, but it is a little better now that I know I have a safe place to come back to."

Once again, Rafe frowned slightly, but all he said was, "Yes, it does feel safe there. Cat's made a nice sanctuary out of that place."

It did feel like a sanctuary. Whether or not her refuge in Pojoaque would actually keep her and Loc safe remained to be seen, though.

Cat appeared pensive as she went to the refrigerator and poured both of them tall glasses of water. After handing one to Loc, she said, "Rafe seemed suspicious."

Yes, he had, although Loc knew that what looked like suspicion was often an attempt to seek the truth of a situation. He also understood that the *prima*'s husband tended to be protective of his youngest sister, and so was not pleased that she'd allowed a demon lord in as her house guest, even if nothing else had been going on between them.

But something was going on. Or rather, Loc wished for there to be something, although his last conversation with Cat had reached no real resolution. Perhaps she didn't want there to be a resolution, or at least she wanted to avoid the issue when neither of them had any idea of what was going to happen next.

He drank some of the water she'd given him, glad of its coolness against his dry throat. Miranda and Rafe had not offered any refreshments, most likely an oversight. But still, it was good to have something to drink.

"He has nothing to be suspicious about," Loc said mildly once he had swallowed his last mouthful of water.

"Doesn't he?"

She was leaning against the warm-toned granite of the kitchen counter, lovely face troubled. It would have been good to be able to reach out and fold her into his arms, but he wasn't sure how such an overture would be received.

"We shared an embrace," Loc said, making sure the words were careful and precise. "We did not follow it with anything else. You made it quite clear that you did not want there to be anything else. Therefore, I don't see how there is anything about our relationship that should upset your brother."

"You don't know my brother," Cat replied. She still held her own glass of water, but she'd only taken a single sip out of it.

"Not very well, no."

She smiled, but there was something both

tired and strained about her expression. "Because he's my brother, he wants the best for me."

"I can see nothing wrong with that," Loc returned. Indeed, it would be odd if Rafe didn't want the best for his sister.

His comment earned him a shake of the head. "No, I suppose there isn't. But I can tell you right now that Rafe's concept of 'best' doesn't include demon lords. Not that it matters," she went on, speaking quickly and not meeting his gaze. "Because you know you're not going to stay."

"I didn't say that definitively," Loc replied. He was not offended by Cat's comment. Rather, he was more amused than anything else that a mere mortal such as Rafe Castillo would not consider someone who had reigned over an entire plane of existence good enough for his little sister. "And I certainly will not abandon you and your clan while Nicholas Toulouse poses any kind of threat."

"That's something," Cat said. "But it's still no solution. Not in the long run."

"What is it you want?" he asked gently. Not because he didn't know the answer, but because he realized she needed to hear it for herself.

A long, long pause while she stared down into the glass of water she held, as though it was some sort of scrying mirror that could reveal her heart's desire, rather than ordinary water from a pitcher in the refrigerator. "I thought this was what I wanted," she said, her tone quiet, musing. With one hand, she gestured upward, as if indicating the house that surrounded them. "And I love it here, I really do. But I suppose I realized that it isn't enough. I'm tired of watching everyone around me find their own happiness when it always seems just out of reach for me."

Without speaking, Loc set his glass of water down on the countertop and went to her, then took her glass from her so he might hold her hands in his. He halfway expected her to pull them away, but she didn't, only stood there and gazed up into his face, expression expectant.

"Have you ever wondered," he said, "how it was, out of all the millions of souls in this world, yours was the one I reached out to?"

She shook her head. "I just figured it was because I have this talent of talking to ghosts, and so I wasn't the sort of person who'd be startled by suddenly hearing a voice in my head."

He smiled, and spoke in that same way to her now. *No, Cat. It is because something in you resonated with something in me.*

Her fingers tightened on his. "Then why...?" The words trailed off, and she pulled in a breath, as though somehow frustrated with herself, at her inability to say what she was feeling.

Why what?

"If it's there, this connection or whatever you

want to call it, then why would you want to keep on trying to find a way to leave?"

A very good question, one he'd begun to ask himself more and more. He should have been troubled by his growing indecision, and yet somehow, he was not. Speaking aloud, he replied, "Because exile from the place where I was lord and master is not a terribly appealing prospect."

"Even though you wouldn't have to spend that exile alone?"

She was so very beautiful, her face tilted up toward his, dark eyes wide and sad, her near-black hair falling in lustrous waves past her shoulders. Merely looking at her like this was enough to arouse the desire in him, this body he wore responding to her nearness, to the faintly floral scent that drifted from her warm-toned skin.

"I don't—I don't know," Loc said. He had to force himself to think clearly, because his body threatened to overpower his mind with its sudden, shocking need. Not sure what he should do, he let go of her hands and took a few steps away so he wouldn't have to breathe in her enticing scent or look at the delicate shadows in the hollow of her throat.

"How long do you plan to keep looking?" Now her voice was taut but neutral, and she crossed her arms as she stood there with the granite counter at her back. "A year? Five years?

Ten? Does time even have any real meaning for you?"

He shook his head. "Not in the way that it does for you. I can sense it passing, but it does not touch me."

"So you'll be like this always, no matter what?" Her gaze seemed to take him in, this mortal form he'd assumed in order to blend in with the rest of humankind.

"No," he replied, and he saw surprise register in her eyes. "This body is as human as yours, and it will age, just as yours does. It is only that, once it has become no longer useful, I can take on another."

"And another, and another, for as long as you need to."

"Yes." Loc studied her carefully, but now her expression had also grown neutral, as though she wrestled with her thoughts but wanted to make sure she didn't betray anything he might use against her.

Her tone hardened. "Is it so wonderful, this place you come from?"

Now he could only smile. "No. It is a universe of innumerable barren worlds, of sudden storms, of cold winds and desert sands and oceans of ice. A human being would not last very long on any of those worlds, but I and those I rule are not like humans. We do not need food to eat, nor water to drink. We can consume these things, and enjoy them, but they are not required for our sustenance. But that place is mine, and it has been that way since before time began." Not for the first time, he wondered whether his demon legions had run amok in his absence, or whether they waited patiently for their lord and master's return. Since they did not possess much minds of their own, he guessed it was probably the latter.

Cat's lips twitched, but he didn't see much humor in her expression. "Better to reign in hell, huh?"

"I am not sure I understand."

"It's from a poem by John Milton...*Paradise Lost*. It's something Satan says—'better to reign in hell than serve in heaven.'" She chuckled, although the sound was still rather grim. "AP English rears its ugly head."

Loc didn't quite recognize the reference to AP English, but he thought he could understand what she had intended by quoting that verse to him. Now he was the one who crossed his arms. Frowning, he asked, "Are you comparing me to Lucifer? I am not the Devil."

"No, but you're a demon lord," Cat replied. "Some might say that was nearly the same thing."

"Your people use the word 'demon' to describe us, but we are not demons, not really. We are merely beings who are different from you."

She didn't look entirely convinced. "But you, Loc, you would rather be in that awful place you just described to me, just because you get to rule over everything there. What exactly are you ruling, if there are no cities, no kingdoms, no crops to raise, no art to be made, no…nothing?"

Again, she had asked a very good question. For the longest time, it had been enough to gaze upon those worlds and know that they and the entities which occupied them were all under his sway, that he had come into being precisely to rule those worlds. But Cat was right—there was existence, but no beauty, no wonder. Indeed, he had not known precisely what those things even were until he came here and was able to see the glory of a sunrise, the great wheeling expanse of the night sky with its innumerable stars.

Or a child's laughter, or the rich curve of a woman's lips as she smiled.

Still, what she asked of him was no small thing. The price to be paid for Earth's beauties was very high. Or rather, the price he would pay for sharing those beauties with Catalina Castillo would be very high. Eternity would no longer be his to play with—he would have to age, and die, and leave this all behind, in a span of time that was little more than a single eye blink. The thought crossed his mind that he could stay here and live a life with her, and then take another body and continue his search for someone to send him home. But doing so would be a betrayal of this feeling that had begun to blossom in him, and he knew he would never do such a thing, no matter the cost.

"You ask a great deal of me," he said heavily. "When we have shared very little so far."

"You're right," she replied. Her gaze met his, and she gave a rueful shake of her head. "Just a kiss, some time spent together…not much at all. I'm okay with leaving it there, if that's what you want. But you can't ask me for more when it's obvious you want to have things both ways. I…." She let the words trail off as her fingers played nervously with the hem of her shirt. "I've made enough mistakes that I know I don't want to make any more. Can you understand that?"

Loc thought of her confrontation with Channing Ellis, the ugly things that poor excuse for a man had said to her. He had no idea how many other "mistakes" lurked in Cat's past, and he truly did not care. If she wished to speak of them, he would listen, but nothing she told him would change his feelings for her.

The real problem was that he still didn't know precisely what those feelings were. He did not wish to see her hurt, but he also was not sure whether he could willingly let go of who he was. This body he wore now was a prop, nothing more, and he couldn't be sure whether he'd ever be able to view it as truly his own.

"I understand," he said slowly. "But…."

"But…?"

"I am not sure whether I am able to make that sacrifice."

Cat's lips pressed together, and a hurt, angry light showed in her dark eyes, but she did not snap at him, did not lash out with her anger. A long moment passed, and then she nodded, shoulders slumping. "Because I'm not worth it. I understand."

"That is not what I said." Loc began to reach out a hand, but he saw the way she flinched, and guessed that touching her in any way would be precisely the wrong thing to do right now.

"No," she replied, although she sounded more tired than anything else. "But it's exactly what you meant." Another pause, and she added, "I'm going to work in my studio. I suppose you can conjure yourself something to eat if you get hungry."

And with that, she went over to the door that led from the kitchen to the patio outside and let herself out. She didn't bang the door, however, but closed it carefully behind her.

Loc watched her go. In a way, he wished she had slammed the door. An angry response he might have understood. But she had looked so defeated, so weary. He hated to see that in a woman with so much spirit, so much fire.

Yet he still wasn't sure whether he'd ever be able to tell her what she wanted to hear.

13

CAT WANTED TO CRY, BUT CRYING WOULDN'T change the situation. Besides, she wouldn't be able to work if her vision was all blurry.

Oh, who was she kidding? Did she honestly think she was going to get any work done?

Luckily, she'd made sure the studio was a work space that could stand on its own, and that was why it had a little kitchen area with a sink and a hot plate and a mini-fridge, along with a bathroom and a comfy chair with a matching foot stool for those times when she needed to take a break and put her feet up for a while.

She headed to that chair now after getting herself a glass of water. A glass of wine or a beer probably would have been better, although alcohol was most likely the last thing she needed right now. After all, she'd had way too many glasses of sangria the night before. If she'd been stone cold sober, she probably wouldn't have allowed Loc to kiss her.

Well, that was something she couldn't change, no matter how much she might wish it. Right now, it seemed pretty obvious there wouldn't be a repeat of that kiss, so she needed to put it out of her mind, focus on more important things. There was the problem of those damn books Simon Escobar had left behind, although it seemed as though Miranda and Rafe had the situation handled as well as anyone could. Maybe this Nicholas Toulouse character was someone they all needed to be worried about, or maybe not. Frankly, since Miranda had been able to defeat Simon, who was a more powerful warlock, Cat didn't see why Toulouse would be that formidable an enemy. Besides, even if she and Loc were at odds right now, she knew he would step in to protect the Castillo clan, just as he had before. There was really nothing to worry about.

Of more immediate concern was the art show. One of her pieces was already done, but the other one still required a good chunk of embroidery to finish it, plus a blanket stitch with silk floss all the way around the edges once she was done embroidering all the wildflowers and wild grasses, and that meant another seven or eight hours of work.

If she was lucky.

She looked up at the clock. It was a little past five. If she worked for four hours, then she should be able to creep into the house under cover of darkness and avoid any confrontations with Loc. Not that he probably wouldn't know the second she set foot in the place, but she had to hope that he would get the message and leave her alone. What a ridiculous situation, to be creeping around in her own home as if she was the intruder. But, as upset as she was with Loc right now, she also didn't want to banish him, to tell him he needed to go stay in a hotel or book a vacation rental or something. Tomorrow he would go off on his quest to find a way back to that hellhole he called home, and she'd have her house back again.

Well, at least until he returned. Funny how he always managed to show up in time for dinner.

Scowling, Cat went to fetch the silk floss she needed, then sat down in her armchair and got to work. The embroidery was probably more important, but she knew she wouldn't be able to focus on it right now. Better to get the busywork done first, so she could space out and let her fingers move automatically. If the worst happened and she couldn't complete all the embroidery she had planned, at least she had the other tapestry finished. Better that than nothing at all.

The silence seemed to press on her ears, but she ignored it, her head lowered over the piece that was her current focus. Part of her wished desperately that Loc would come over to the studio and knock on the door, tell her that he'd made a mistake and realized this world would be enough for him. This world, and her.

Now tears did begin to sting her eyes, but she pulled in a hitching breath and blinked once, twice, doing her best to prevent them from hindering her work. Really, she was being stupid about this whole thing. So what if she'd never been quite able to banish the Lord of Chaos from her mind all these months, even though she'd known he was gone, and that even if he'd continued to hang around Santa Fe for some reason, it would have been stupid to keep thinking of him when he wasn't even human, was this strange, hideous being from another dimension. Yes, he'd helped to save them all, and he'd been able to touch her mind when no one else, living or dead, had ever managed to do such a thing, but still....

Goddamn it.

She set the tapestry down in her lap for a moment so she could take a sip of water. That was a little better. And after the water, back to work.

Eventually, the edges of the tapestry were all carefully bound. The clock ticking on the opposite wall told her it was a few minutes after nine. In all that time, she hadn't heard from Loc, and her phone had likewise been silent, no calls from Rafe or Miranda to check on her, nothing from Tony, making sure they'd gotten all cleaned up after the party and there wasn't anything else he needed to handle.

Well, why should they call? she asked herself as she carried the tapestry over to blanket rack she used for draping her work over when she was done with it for the day. *You just talked to Miranda and Rafe, and Tony has no reason to think everything isn't just hunky-dory over here. They probably figure you're a big girl and can take care of yourself.*

Which she was. Hadn't she just overseen the retrofit of this property, pretty much all by herself? They knew she would reach out for help if the situation arose, and until then, they all had their own problems to deal with.

Even so, she wished she didn't feel quite so abandoned.

As much as it pained him to do so, Loc did not follow Cat when she disappeared into her studio. Neither did he allow himself to go down there as the hours passed, even though his mind began manufacturing scenarios of her weeping as she tried to work. Or perhaps he was giving himself far too much importance. For all he knew, she had been working diligently the entire time, focused on her art and not bothering to give him a second thought.

That second scenario was even more worrisome, for reasons he was not sure he really wished to explore. Did he want to assume that much significance in Cat's life? Possibly she was hurting now, but he reflected that maybe the best thing he could do for her was slip quietly away. He had promised that he would watch over the Castillos to ensure that Nicholas Toulouse did not attempt anything nefarious, but that did not mean he had to continue staying in Cat Castillo's home. The city was full of hotels and vacation properties, and it would be easy enough for him to move into one of them. Then, once their current problem with the dark warlock from New Orleans was resolved one way or another, he could go back out into the world and resume his search.

While this seemed like a practical enough plan, he did not find it particularly appealing. Loc knew he did not want to be separated from Cat for any length of time. And yet, he also did not want to give up all chance of returning to the place where he was lord and master. The two goals were diametrically opposed, and he had no idea whether he would ever be able to reconcile the two.

At length he ate—worried the whole time that Cat was going hungry in her studio, but too proud to come up to the house and get anything for her own dinner—and some time after that, he retired to his borrowed bedroom, although he found sleep eluded him. He lay there in the dark, staring up at the ceiling, and finally heard a faint creak from the staircase, signaling that she had returned to the house. A moment later, there came the slightest of thumps from the end of the hall, probably from her door closing.

Well, she was back, but it seemed she had no desire to speak to him still. This realization was troubling, but Loc knew better than to go and knock on her door, attempt to talk to her.

Perhaps the morning would bring some enlightenment.

But unfortunately, even after he fell into a restless sleep and awoke feeling far from refreshed as new sunlight slipped its way past the curtains in his room, there was no sign of Cat. That is, it seemed she had awakened even earlier than he, because when he went downstairs, he found half a pot of fresh-brewed coffee sitting on its warmer, but no sign of the woman who had made it. Had she already fled to her studio?

It appeared she had, because when he peered out the kitchen window, which allowed a view of one corner of the low building that once been the wine-tasting room, he caught the barest glimpse of one of the windows there being opened to let in the morning breeze. While Loc was vaguely reassured that she was up and about, he still had to wonder how long this current situation would last. He did not wish to be responsible for driving Cat out of her own home.

However, since she had clearly left the coffee for him, he drank a cup, then summoned some bread and honey, which was all he felt like consuming right then. A shower and his regular morning routine—not for the first time, he shook his head at how much time humans spent on grooming their bodies—and then he decided it was time to go.

Her comment about his savior possibly living in a small town spurred him on, and he visited several—Hagerstown, Indiana, and Ottumwa, Iowa, and Astoria, Oregon—and found no one, no local witch clans at all. In Astoria, he bought a hot chocolate, since it was cool and damp there on the seacoast, even at the tail end of July, and sat on a bench in a park and pondered what he should do next. The absence of any witches and wizards in these places puzzled him, although he knew that of course they couldn't be found in every town and city that existed. It would be one thing if they mainly lived in big cities, to better hide their presence, but he knew that wasn't the case, not when the McAllister witches lived in tiny Jerome, Arizona.

Jerome. Of course he had never visited there, for he knew that none of the witches in that clan possessed the skills required to send him home. However, he had studied the town a little, since he was curious about a place that could produce a witch as strong as Miranda Castillo. But as Loc sat there on his park bench and slowly drank his hot chocolate, he suddenly realized there was someone in that former ghost town who might be the only other person in the world who could remotely understand his current situation. He'd known of the man's existence, but until he'd begun wrestling with his feelings for Cat, Loc had seen no reason to pay him a visit.

Now, though…Jerome it was.

Loc finished off the last few sips of hot chocolate, then disposed of the cup in a nearby trash can. Because the day was damp and not very hospitable, no one else was currently visiting the park, which meant it was safe to disappear, even out there in the open.

The contrast with Jerome could not have been more different. A bright sun blazed down from the Arizona sky, which was a deep, deep blue, studded with white, downy clouds that looked close enough to be touched with an outstretched hand. Loc had materialized in an alley next to a ramshackle apartment building, knowing he wouldn't be noticed there. However, his destination was farther up the hill.

In this part of the world, front yards were something of a scarcity. However, the house Loc approached now had a little postage-stamp lawn bordered with exuberant hollyhocks, which also grew in the flowerbed in front of the white-painted porch. The home had clearly been built during Jerome's copper-mining boomtown days, since the wood-frame structure with its wrap-around porch stood a proud two and a half stories tall and commanded an astonishing view of the Verde Valley and the red rocks of Sedona off in the distance.

A man with flaxen-pale hair was using an electric mower to cut the grass of that tiny lawn. He wore khaki-colored shorts and a blue T-shirt, along with a pair of grass-stained sneakers. To anyone else, he would have appeared completely ordinary, although handsome enough, with his bright blue eyes and regular features.

Loc knew better, however.

"Hello, Levi," he said, and the man straightened and turned off the mower.

His gaze met Loc's, and for a moment he said nothing, only stared at the man who stood by his front gate, before he gave a knowing nod. Then he said, "I didn't think I'd ever see you here, Lord of Chaos."

"Loc," he returned, since the title seemed a bit unwieldy for normal conversation. "I had never expected to visit this plane, either, but sometimes the universe enjoys a joke on us."

"That's true enough." Levi pushed a sweaty lock of hair back from his brow and made a silent appraisal of his visitor's appearance. "You look different."

"My actual form is rather conspicuous."

"True." Another of those appraising glances, and then Levi said, "If you've come here to ask me to send you back to your own plane, I fear that's something beyond my powers."

Even though he'd been expecting that sort of comment, Loc couldn't help replying, "Are you so sure of that? You're no more bound by the constraints of this world than I am."

"Oh, yes, I am," Levi said. "Because to reach across worlds in such a way is to ignore the natural order of things, and you know I have never walked that path."

That much was true. Still, it was frustrating to know that Levi possibly could have helped him, but wouldn't.

"Why don't you come inside?" Levi asked. If he'd noticed the way his response had evoked a frown in his guest, he didn't show it. "Hayley is up in Flagstaff for the day—she and my daughter Brianna are scouting apartments. Bree's starting at Northern Pines University in August," he added, with some pride.

"You have offspring?" Loc responded, startled despite himself. For some reason, he hadn't thought that a being such as Levi would be able to breed with a human woman.

Levi chuckled. "Yes, Brianna, and my son Jason. He's down in Cottonwood today —summer job."

"Of course." The words sounded calm

enough, but Loc was still feeling somewhat shaken. The thought of such unions producing children had opened up a whole world of possibilities, possibilities he wasn't sure he was ready to acknowledge quite yet.

Without speaking, he followed Levi into the house, which was furnished with such care and precision, Loc thought it must have been decorated by a professional. The impression it gave wasn't stuffy at all, though, but light and breezy and welcoming, from the linen-covered sofas to the watercolors of local landscapes on the walls.

"Would you like some water?" Levi asked. "It's a hot day."

Since Loc's throat did feel somewhat dry, he nodded. "Yes, thank you."

"Go ahead and sit down."

Loc took a seat on one of the sofas while Levi left the room and disappeared down a short hallway. Within the next moment, he was back, a tall glass of water in each hand. After giving one of the glasses to Loc, he sat down on the couch opposite him and cocked an inquiring eyebrow.

"What brings you to Jerome?"

"I'm in need of advice."

This response prompted a slight tilt of the head, as if Levi was inspecting him a little more closely to determine whether he could detect the reason behind requesting such advice. "About?"

Loc gestured with his glass toward the room around them. "How do you do it?"

"Well, Hayley's the decorator, but I assume that's not what you meant."

"No, it is not. How can you live here, pretend to be human, when you are so much more?"

"I'm not sure about 'more,'" Levi said slowly. "Different, yes. Or rather, at first I was acutely aware of my differences, that I was only a spirit summoned to this world and then given shape and form, rather than born of a mortal mother, but eventually I realized something."

"What was that?" Loc drank some of his water, then placed the glass on one of the wooden coasters on the table before him. He might have come from another plane of existence, but he'd learned of the importance of coasters over the past eight months.

"No one else cared. Or rather, the McAllister clan accepted me as one of their own, and so I understood that it didn't matter where I had come from. What mattered was what I did with my life here. Even though I was not born to this clan, they made me one of their elders, were glad when I married Hayley." Levi retrieved his own tumbler of water and sipped from it, his bright blue eyes keen as they gazed at Loc from over the rim of the glass. "But why do you ask, Loc? Do you fear you will never find your way back to your own world, and so ask for advice on how to survive here?"

"That is part of it," he replied, "but not all."

For a moment, Levi was silent. Surprise flickered in his expression, and he said, "You have found someone you care for?"

It seemed that Levi's years as a McAllister clan elder had made him a little too discerning. "Is it that obvious?"

"I couldn't really think of another reason why you would be here, asking for my help."

Was that what he was doing…asking for help? Loc didn't much like the idea, because he wanted to believe that he was entirely self-sufficient, had no need of anyone's counsel. But he was out of his depth with Catalina Castillo, and Levi was the only person who had experienced anything remotely like the situation Loc was in now. Levi, who had stayed in this world, and married, and had two children. That must have been them in the photographs on the mantel, a boy and a girl as bright and blond and attractive as their parents.

What would his and Cat's children look like? They would be as dark as Levi's children were fair, but surely they would inherit her beauty, as well as the beauty of this body he had taken for his own.

"Her name is Catalina Castillo," he said, the words feeling strange on his lips, as though now the entire world must know the weakness of his heart, since he had said her name out loud. "She is the daughter of the former Castillo *prima*, and Miranda's sister-in-law."

"I've heard her name," Levi responded. "I believe Angela and Connor mentioned her after they went to Santa Fe for Miranda and Rafael's wedding."

"She is…very beautiful, and alone," Loc said. He extended one hand, fingers outstretched, and for a moment, Cat's image wavered there—her image as she'd looked the night they'd gone out to dinner, with the emeralds at her neck and her dark hair falling loose around her shoulders.

"Yes, she is quite beautiful," Levi agreed. "Does she know who you are?"

Loc nodded. "I assisted their clan in defeating Simon Escobar, who had done me the grave disservice of summoning me this plane, although he never succeeded in making me his slave. There was…something…about Cat's mind that made it easy for me to reach out to her, communicate with her. I passed on what information I could, and stepped in at the end when it appeared that the battle might not be going their way."

After absorbing this information, Levi leaned forward on the couch, gaze still intent. "Has she ever seen you as you truly are?"

"Yes."

"And she doesn't care?"

How could Loc begin to answer that question? She'd certainly kissed him willingly enough, knowing who and what he was, but then, it was easy enough to ignore such truths when the reality that confronted you was so very different. "I don't know. It does seem that her problem is not what I am or where I came from, but rather my wish to return there."

"Can you blame her? I haven't met many women who would be happy bestowing their affections on someone, only to have them disappear out of their lives."

Once again, Loc shook his head. He had thought that Cat was asking a great deal from him, but then again, he was asking for a great deal from her as well. His enormously long life hadn't given him any context for the sorts of emotions that had raged through him the past few days, and even so, he thought he might begin to grasp the sort of hurt she would suffer if she allowed herself to care for him and then lost him as soon as he was able to leave this world.

Apparently noting Loc's reluctance to reply, Levi went on, "My situation is somewhat different from yours, simply because I was only spirit when I was called here. This body is something that Zoe Sandoval, the *prima* of the de la Paz clan, conjured for me. I had to make a life for myself in this world, but I had no life to speak of in the void where I had been drifting for millennia. You, on the other hand, have been lord and master of innumerable worlds. You have something you would be forced to leave behind."

"I am glad you understand that, for I fear Catalina does not."

Now Levi smiled. "I think she probably does. Women are very perceptive creatures."

"And you do not mind…being mortal?"

Levi's gaze traveled to the portraits of his children where they sat in pale wood frames on the mantel. "No, because I know some part of me will still be here when I am gone. You and I both know we have no need to fear death, because the only thing that waits for us on the other side of the veil is a continuation of our existence, albeit one different from the life we might have lived here on Earth."

No, death was not something Loc had ever particularly feared, mainly because it was not anything he'd thought he would have to experience. "Perhaps not death," he said slowly. "But growing older, having this body succumb to the various weaknesses and ailments of old age."

Rather than look troubled, Levi only smiled. "I don't think that's anything you need to fear," he replied. "I have lived in this world for more than twenty years and have never been ill once. Oh, I have aged a bit—the man who looks back at me from the mirror is certainly not a man in his twenties any longer—but I think our otherworldly origins give us some advantages when it comes to aging. Of course, your case is different from mine, but I still believe you will have very little to fear."

Those were hopeful words, but Loc was not sure whether he entirely trusted them. Then again, Levi had no reason to lie, was only telling the truth as he had so far experienced it.

"Only you can know for sure whether this world, the love of this woman, are worth giving up what you have," Levi continued. One corner of his mouth lifted in a lopsided smile. "Although, knowing something of your world, I think I can safely say that there is far more to entice you here."

Cat had brought up much the same argument, although of course she had no experience of her own upon which to base that judgment, only her own conclusions drawn from what Loc had told her of his kingdom. He had already been gone for months and months. Had his world spun out of control, or continued serenely on without him, proving that it mattered very little whether he was there or not?

And oh, Cat was so very enticing....

"You may be right in that," he said heavily. "And I want to believe that living a mortal life is what you say, and that there will be very little of darkness and pain in it. But I still have to weigh whether a few short years lived in the light are worth giving up so much."

"I can assure you that they will be worth it,"

Levi said, and once again his gaze strayed to the family portraits showcased on the mantel. "But in the end, you're the only one who can decide whether to take that particular leap of faith."

A leap of faith. Unfortunately, Loc had had very little need for faith in his life. He had known his world, and his place in it, but here, everything was different. There was no basis of experience for him to use to weigh such decisions.

But he did know what it had been like to hold Cat in his arms, to taste her sweet mouth. Nothing in his previous existence had prepared him for those wonderful sensations. And he also knew what it was like to sit across from her at the dinner table and see the emeralds he had given her gleaming around her slender neck, and nearly be struck dumb by her beauty.

And to sit in the sunlight and see it awaken warm flickers of red and umber in her near-black hair, and to bring a flush to her cheeks and a golden warmth to her skin. To hear her low-pitched laugh and look at the beautiful tapestries she'd created, and to know they had come from her talent and her hands, her mind and her fierce, stubborn creativity.

Suddenly, she seemed more precious to him than anyone or anything he'd ever encountered in his long, long life, and Loc realized he could not give up any of those things. If he returned to his world, he knew he would always be haunted by her absence.

"I think I understand," he said at last. "Thank you, Levi."

"I'm glad I could help," Levi replied. His expression was serious enough, but again there was that small lift at the corners of his mouth, as if he'd known all along that this was the conclusion Loc would eventually reach.

"You did."

He would have to go to Cat, speak with her.

But there was one test she would need to pass first....

14

ONE THING ABOUT BEING ABANDONED BY THE MAN you thought you might just have fallen in love with—it definitely gave you plenty of time to work. Cat had thought she'd be working nearly all the way up to the day her pieces were due for the art show, and yet here she was, early on Tuesday evening, and that last pesky bit of satin stitch with alternating metal threads in silver and copper was now done. Both tapestries finished, and she still had until Thursday at five to turn in her work. She wouldn't leave it that long, though; she'd go in tomorrow sometime, hand both tapestries over, and then go on a shopping binge to reward herself for all her hard work.

And maybe have a drink and do her best to put Loc out of her mind.

She paused to take one last look at the tapestries where they hung in all their glory in the studio, and gave a weary nod. Her back ached and the tips of her fingers felt rough from working with the metal thread, but there was definitely something to be said for sitting down and putting in the work.

After turning out the lights in the studio, Cat touched her finger to the deadbolt to lock the door and began to make her way up the path toward the house. She hadn't gotten more than four or five paces before a tall, menacing shape materialized on the path before her, wings outstretched, blocking the setting sun.

Her heart was nearly in her throat before she realized what—rather, *who*—it was.

"Damn it, Loc," she snapped. "You scared the crap out of me."

"I hope not literally," he rumbled. His voice was much deeper in this form, but Cat guessed that was because it emerged from a larger throat.

"No," she said. Crossing her arms, she made herself gaze up at him. Although she'd seen Loc in his true guise as the Lord of Chaos before this, she hadn't stood so close, hadn't given herself a crick in the neck from staring up at a being nearly two and a half feet taller than she was. His wings beat gently, stirring the warm air. Although she halfway wanted to pretend that his appearance in this shape was entirely normal, she couldn't help asking, "Did you get tired of hiding who you were?"

"'Tired' isn't precisely the right word." His wings slowed, then went still before folding, bat-like, flat against his enormous back. "It is more that I needed to be sure of something."

"What's that?" she asked, although her heart rate sped up slightly, as though it knew something her brain wasn't yet ready to acknowledge.

"You said that you wanted me to stay, that it was the only way we could become any closer." His eyes narrowed, nearly hiding their crimson glare...but not quite. "But I need you to be quite sure of who you're becoming close with. This is who I am, Catalina. I can hide it behind a human body, but that will never change my true self."

"I know," she said. To her own surprise, she moved closer to him, then took one of his clawed hands in hers. His night-dark skin was covered in scales so tiny, she hadn't even realized they were there at all. The flesh beneath her fingertips was warm, almost uncomfortably so, as if he burned with a fever that would never abate. A nervous laugh escaped her lips, and then she said, "The crazy thing is, Loc, that I knew you looked like this, and yet I still kept thinking of you, kept wondering what you were doing, whether you were all right. I doubt I would have been thinking those things if I really cared what you looked like."

His fingers tightened on hers, but gently, as if he knew he could break her bones with one careless touch. "Then look at me, Cat. Be sure, before we go any further."

She pulled in a breath and gazed up into his face, at the red, lash-less eyes, the bony ridges above those eyes, the lips so thin they were barely there at all. Pointed ears under the mane of heavy black hair, and harshly carved cheekbones and a sharp beak of a nose. All those things, and yet in them she saw a certain wild beauty, the kind that made her want to get out her charcoals and note-book and sketch him, even though she mainly worked in fabric these days and very rarely did any traditional drawing.

"I'm sure," she said at last. "Oh, Loc, I'm so very sure. I know who you are, and this doesn't matter."

In the next second, his arms had gone around her, and he held her in his embrace, lifting her from the ground as if she weighed nothing at all. And then he was kissing her, yes, kissing her in his true form, and she really didn't care, only wanted to experience the clean taste of his mouth, the strength of the arms that held her, the way his coarse, thick hair brushed against her cheek, how the faintest scent of wood smoke seemed to cling to that heavy hair. She was aware of how much he aroused her, how much she wanted him, and how crazy was that, when any rational observer would have taken one look at his grotesque appearance and run away.

When he pulled away from her, his eyes glowed with red fire, brilliant as the forge her cousin the metal-worker used in the workshop behind his house. "Catalina, you amaze me," he said in his deep rumble of a voice. "And I want to love you—*make* love to you. But I cannot do it in this form, for I would only hurt you."

Cat felt a little pang then, although she really couldn't be sure whether it was from relief or disappointment. Still, what did it matter one way or another, as long as they could be together? "Does this mean you want to stay?" she asked, wishing her voice didn't sound so tremulous.

"For as long as you will have me, my brave, brilliant Cat."

Forever, she thought, but didn't say the word out loud. She didn't know where he'd been or where he'd gone, but it seemed as though he'd made peace with the idea of staying here... staying with her. Even so, she thought it might be better to leave aside the talk of forever for just a while longer.

"We'd better go inside," she said, then gave a shaky laugh. "Roberto and Miguel went home a couple of hours ago, but I'd hate for them to come back and—"

"And see me like this," Loc finished for her. "I understand."

Before she could say anything else, he'd transformed, and although he still held her, they now both stood on the flagstone path, rather than having her dangle her feet a good eighteen inches above the ground. The change happened so quickly that she couldn't help letting out a little gasp of a breath.

"That's some trick," she said shakily.

"Only one of many. Shall we go inside?"

She nodded, and he took her hand. Now his touch was entirely human, but it was enough to send a delicious little shiver through her. Because that was still Loc, no matter what he looked like, and he wanted her, wanted to stay here with her rather than reign in hell. She vowed never to take his sacrifice for granted, to always show him how much she appreciated the choice he'd made, which couldn't have been easy.

The house had been dark and quiet when she left it this morning, all the drapes still pulled shut. Now they were open, letting in the last burnt-umber shades of sunset. The warm light was echoed in the flicker of dozens of votive candles burning along the mantel in the living room, the side tables, the dining room table, the sideboard… everywhere Cat looked, she saw more candles.

"Your doing?" she asked.

"Yes," Loc replied.

Of course it was. She might be part of a family of witches and warlocks, but she knew none of her relatives had the power to pull off something like this. Maybe someday she'd ask Loc if even he knew the extent of his own peculiar talents. For now, though, she was content to have him hold her hand as he led her into the living room. Sitting on the coffee table, amongst the candles, was a bottle of wine and a pair of glasses. They hadn't been there when she'd left to go to the studio earlier in the day, but she figured she'd better roll with it.

He's here, she thought in some wonderment, watching as Loc poured wine for the both of them and then handed her one of the glasses. *He's here next to me, and he wants to stay.*

Her head was spinning, and she hadn't even drunk any wine yet. Maybe that was simply the after-effects of the kiss they'd shared. She'd kissed a demon, right there in the middle of her yard, and it had been damn good.

The words of an old, old song floated through her mind, altered for the occasion. *I kissed a demon and I liked it....*

Cat wanted to laugh but kept herself from doing so, mostly because she didn't want Loc to think she was laughing at him. She held up her glass as he raised his.

"To being together," he said softly.

"'To being together,'" she repeated.

The wine was good—a Syrah from this very vineyard, albeit a vintage from some five years back. As far as she knew, Cat didn't have anything that old in the stores she'd been given as part of the purchase of the property, but she realized that didn't matter so much. Loc could have gotten them a hundred-year-old Bordeaux if he'd so pleased.

Loc took another sip of his wine, then stared toward the hearth, his gaze thoughtful. It was far too warm to have a fire burning there, but the iron candleholder with its nine pillar candles provided its own light and warmth, a good substitute for a true wood-burning fire.

He didn't seem inclined to speak, so Cat found the courage to ask, "Where did you go today?" Because some part of her was still worried that he'd come here and told her he would stay simply because he'd gone on his search yet again, and again was unsuccessful.

His answer surprised her. "I went to seek counsel from someone I thought could give me the insight I needed. His situation is not entirely unlike mine."

"He's a demon?" Cat asked. For a moment, she imagined the world being populated with hundreds or even thousands of demons in disguise, with their spouses and partners completely oblivious to their significant others' alternate identities.

"No," Loc said. His mouth quirked, and he added, "To be completely honest, I am not sure exactly what he is. Perhaps he doesn't know, either. But he has been living a mortal life here on

Earth, a life with a wife and children, a place in his community. His example made me reexamine my desire to return to my own world."

Cat wondered who this person could possibly be. She'd never heard a whisper of anyone like that, but then again, it wasn't as if her experience was all that large. There were huge swaths of the world she hadn't visited, vast numbers of people she would never meet.

That thought didn't sting quite as much as it used to. How could it matter, when she had Loc sitting here next to her?

"Because if he could be happy in this world, then you could be happy here, too?"

"Precisely," Loc said. "How could I be happy there, if I didn't have you with me?"

She wasn't sure which one of them moved first. All she knew was that they were kissing again, lips locked as though they both feared the other person might somehow be whisked away from them at any moment. He tasted of wine, and his hands were tangled in her hair, holding her close, while the blood thundered in her veins and she thought she might drown from the sudden, overwhelming desire that flooded through her entire body.

Maybe he felt her need, or maybe he was just experiencing his own. Whatever the case, his arms went around her, and before she could blink, they were in her bedroom, where more candles shimmered on every available surface, and the room was washed with sunset's orange light.

Now that they were alone here, though, Loc seemed suddenly shy. He let go of her and took a few steps backward. His dark eyes still glittered with desire, but his hands hung at his sides, and he glanced away from her, mouth tight.

"What is it, Loc?" she asked.

"I want...." He stopped there and pulled in a deep breath. "I want *you*, Cat. This body is telling me how much it wants you. But I have never—in my world, there is no such thing—"

Even with the hot ache of need throbbing between her legs, she couldn't help but experience a wave of pity. Loc seemed so lordly, so masterful...and yet, this was his first time. Cat supposed she shouldn't have been surprised. After all, how could he have ever experienced physical love before this?

Well, to be fair, she guessed he probably had ample opportunity while he was traveling the world, but she sensed that such earthly concerns hadn't even crossed his mind. Until her, he'd never met anyone who had ever sent his thoughts along those paths.

"It's all right, Loc," she said gently. "Your body is telling you what it wants. Just listen to it. And I can show you. Come here."

She took him by the hand and led him over to the bed, then turned back the quilt and the sheet and the blanket. Slowly, she took hold of the hem of his T-shirt and pulled it up over his head, trying not to gasp at the body that was revealed. She'd seen his arms, of course, but this was the first time she'd caught a glimpse of the defined muscles of his chest, the beautifully cut shapes of his abs, such a display of shadow and light that once again she found herself wishing she could sketch him.

And another cut, V-ing down into the waist-band of his jeans….

Before now, she'd let her lovers take the lead, figuring they had more experience than she did. Now she knew she would have to be the bold one, because even if Loc had seen depictions of human sexuality in movies or books or TV shows, he certainly had never experienced the act for himself. She undid the button of his jeans, and the zipper, and worked the pants down, revealing the gray boxer-briefs he wore underneath.

Well, at least now I know he doesn't go commando….

Cat didn't allow herself to dwell on that thought for very long, though, because the bulge she glimpsed in those briefs made her realize they had more important matters to attend to. Her hand brushed against that bulge, and he moaned, eyes widening as unexpected sensations began to move through him.

"That felt…good."

"It's supposed to," she said with a smile.

He didn't respond, but, echoing her own actions, took hold of her tank top and pulled it up and over her head. For a second, he frowned as he caught sight of the plain black bra she was wearing.

"Here," she said, grasping his hands and bringing them to the front hook of her bra. "This is where you unfasten it."

"And that is all right with you?"

Cat grinned. "Loc, I wouldn't have shown you where the clasp was if I didn't want you to undo it."

Those words elicited a fierce grin of his own, and he unhooked the clasp and slid the straps of her bra over her shoulders, letting it fall to the floor. At once his hands were on her breasts, stroking her, and a moan of pleasure escaped her throat. It had been a long, long time since anyone had touched her like this, and yet Cat somehow knew Loc would be evoking this same response from her even if she'd gotten laid a few days earlier.

"You are so very beautiful," he murmured. "Is it all right if I kiss you like this?"

And he lowered his head and took her nipple in his mouth, tongue working over the sensitive flesh. Once again she moaned, the heat between her legs increasing. How he'd known to do that, she had no idea, but damn, he was good at it.

Gasping, she said, "Oh, yes…it's more than all right."

Somehow, they were falling onto the bed, his mouth still closed on her nipple even as his fingers caught hold of the button of her jeans. He got it free, then pulled the zipper down. At once, Cat wriggled her way out of the pants, kicking them to the floor. Loc's hand slipped inside her bikini underwear, moving down….

"Oh, God!" she cried.

At once his hand stilled. "Did I do something wrong?"

"No, Loc, you did something exactly right." Despite the anxious need building in her, she smiled. "Human women can sometimes be a little noisy…during. You know."

He nodded, although Cat wasn't entirely sure whether he did in fact know what she was talking about. But that didn't matter, because those long, strong fingers were now slipping over her, feeling her, exploring, one of them going inside her, sliding in and out.

Oh, dear lord. Maybe he'd watched human pornography so he'd know what to do if he ever found himself in this sort of situation. Cat had no idea, and it wasn't long before she found herself not really caring where he'd learned how to do this, because she could feel the orgasm building in her, warm, swimmy heat increasing in her body as he touched her and continued to suckle her breast.

And then it was happening, and her body was spasming around his fingers, her own fingers buried in his long, silky hair. She held on to him and rode the wave, and then, when it had finally dissipated somewhat, she fell back against the pillows, gasping.

Loc shifted so he was propped up on one elbow, starting down at her. "Is this what an orgasm is?"

Cat nodded because she wasn't sure if she trusted herself to speak. Finally she managed to say, "Yes. That was amazing."

A relieved smile spread over his features. "Good. I didn't want to disappoint you."

Not much chance of that, especially since she realized that the climax she'd just experienced was only an appetizer. The main course was yet to come...no pun intended.

She pushed herself up and said, "I am pretty much the opposite of disappointed." Leaning in, she initiated a long, slow, deep kiss, tasting him again, breathing in the warmth of his skin. One hand moved down to caress the bulge in his briefs, and he gasped, a gasp that turned into a moan once she'd pulled down the underwear that had concealed him all this time.

His cock was just as magnificent as the rest of

him. Good thing she wasn't the virgin that most people probably thought she still was….

Before he could react, she bent and took him in her mouth, tongue working slowly up and down his shaft. He moaned, falling flat against the pillows while she continued to lick him, not fast enough to bring him to orgasm, but just enough that his need would continue to grow.

The daylight had begun to fail, the room lit now only by all the candles Loc had placed there. Still she made love to him with her tongue, until he groaned and sat up, taking hold of her hands so he could push her back down onto the bed.

She'd expected him to enter her then, but, to her surprise, he pushed her legs apart and kissed her up the inside of her right thigh, and then let his tongue slip into her, just as slowly and lascivi-ously as she'd sucked his cock. Cat was glad that she lived in such an isolated spot, because the cry that escaped her throat then was probably loud enough to carry outside the house.

Then she didn't have time to worry about neigh-bors or anything else, because the throbbing heat in her body was concentrating in her core, making her focus on Loc and only Loc, his dark hair brushing against her thighs, his tongue circling her clit.

This time the climax hit her with the force of a thunderbolt, her body shuddering as she buried her fingers in his hair and held on, nearly weeping from the intensity of the pleasure that swept through every limb. And as she caught her breath, tried to recover herself somewhat, he was moving, cock pressed against her entrance.

She gasped. "Yes, Loc. Yes."

He pushed in, deeper, and then deeper still, and she began to rock her hips, showing him the rhythm. At once, he picked up on it, moving with her, going deep and then nearly pulling out before plunging into her again.

Was it possible to die from pleasure? Cat didn't know, and right then she wasn't sure whether it mattered or not. All that mattered was the weight of his body on her, the intense sensation of him filling her in a way she never had been before.

At last, though, he groaned, dark eyes wide and wondering as they focused on her face. In the next instant, she could feel him come, could feel the heat of his seed going into her. Apparently, that was all she needed, because she climaxed yet again in the next second, her body clamping down on his shaft as she cried out his name and held on to him.

The storm subsided, and he fell over onto his side, breathing heavily. Cat moved toward him, snuggling against his chest.

"That was...." he began, then stopped, as if he had suddenly realized he didn't have the words to express what he'd just experienced.

"It was wonderful," she said softly. Right then, she thought she'd never felt so satisfied...so *satiated*...in all her life. Even in the afterglow, however, she was also glad that she'd gotten her contraceptive shot a few months ago, although at the time she'd wondered why she even bothered, considering the wasteland that was her sex life. But as happy as she was with how things were progressing, she doubted either she or Loc needed that kind of complication in their lives.

"Now I begin to see why human beings are so obsessed with sex," he said in musing tones. "I could never quite understand before this, even when I found myself thinking of you, wondering how you were doing."

"You did?" she asked, surprised. She would have thought he was far too busy with his search for someone to send him back to his world to have spared any mental energy on her.

His hand moved over her hair, slow, caressing. More warmth spread through her body, and Cat knew that, even as content as she felt right now, she would happily go for a second round any time in the near future. "Of course. Yours was the only mind I had been able to touch. As the months wore on, I realized I wanted to experience that again, wanted to be near someone who could communicate with me in a way I was used to."

"You haven't done it very much, though."

"No," he said. "Once I was here with you, I

realized it wasn't the mode of communication that mattered so much, but rather simply being able to speak with you at all. And, after so many months of being here in your world, being around your people, I began to understand what a rare jewel you are, Catalina Castillo."

As much as his words pleased her, Cat felt as though she should offer up some form of protest. "I'm not that rare."

"I disagree." He moved then, shifting so he was mostly on top of her, his hands holding her arms down against the mattress.

A thrill of need went through her. Normally, she would have said she didn't much care for being put in a position where the man was so dominant, but Cat liked him holding her down like this, his straight dark hair falling around his face, black eyes boring into hers. It was probably just a reflection from one of the candles, but for a second, she could have sworn she saw red flames gleaming in the depths of those eyes.

That thought didn't bother her at all. She loved what he was, didn't care at all that a bat-winged, red-eyed demon lurked under his outer perfection.

If she were going to be entirely truthful with herself, she loved him. Everything about him, no matter what it was.

Possibly something of what she was feeling revealed itself in her face, because he bent and kissed her, kissed her hard, tongue in her mouth strong and needy, just as his cock had been a few minutes ago. And was now, too, because once again he was at her entrance, ready to go all over again. She wrapped her legs around him and pushed him inside, glad of this chance to join with him again, to feel their bodies locked together in the sort of harmony she'd never experienced before.

This time went on even longer than the first. Cat clung to Loc, kissed him, reveled in the strength of his arms, the heat of his body. And when they came, the orgasm hit them both at the same time, the sound of their cries mixing in the still air.

Neither of them seemed inclined to part. She lay there, feeling him still inside her, smaller now but still enough to allow delicate little ripples of pleasure to pass over her body. Finally, though, she murmured, "I need to get up," and Loc rolled away so she could push herself off the bed and go to the bathroom, where she got herself as cleaned up as she could without actually jumping in the shower. It seemed silly to get dressed again—she had a feeling they wouldn't be leaving the house anytime soon—and so she grabbed her silky, knee-length bathrobe from the hook on the bathroom door and pulled it on, pausing at the lingerie chest in the walk-in closet so she could get a clean pair of panties.

Thus attired, she returned to the bedroom. Loc was now sitting on the edge of the bed, and he smiled when he saw her, apparently not disappointed that she'd chosen to cover herself up. "It's getting late," he said. "We should eat something."

Cat hadn't really been thinking about food, but as soon as he mentioned it, her stomach woke up and reminded her that it had been at least eight hours since she'd had her meager lunch. "Probably," she replied. "I'm not much in the mood to cook, though."

"You don't have to cook a thing," he said, and stood up. Cat could have sworn he hadn't been wearing those black knit shorts a moment ago, but she supposed that someone with his particular powers could have made them appear on a whim.

Likewise with their evening meal. Of course she didn't have to cook—Loc could conjure anything they wanted. "Perfect," she said with a smile.

"What would you like?"

Still smiling, she responded, "Surprise me."

That reddish gleam was back in his eyes. "I hope I always shall."

15

Had there ever been a woman so beautiful?

Loc didn't think so, and he'd seen a random sampling during his travels.

Cat sat next to him on the sofa, smiling as she pulled bits of chicken satay off a skewer and ate them with her fingers. He'd thought she would enjoy having something different from her usual New Mexico fare to eat, and so they had satay and fried rice and wontons and egg rolls, most of which didn't have to be eaten with a knife and fork. And wine, too, of course, the Syrah that had been grown here in this very vineyard.

It was hard not to merely sit there and stare at her, at this wondrous being who had shown him heights of pleasure he could never have even imagined before this day. As he'd told her, he'd understood that human beings placed a great deal of emphasis on physical relations—and he'd even attempted to watch a few videos of the act in order to clarify this particular obsession—but those sweaty, awkward couplings seemed light-years from the intimacy he and Cat had shared.

Perhaps it was simply because he loved her. That realization had come to him as she'd emerged from the bathroom wearing that silky blue robe, her rich dark hair loose on her shoulders. He'd gazed into her face, and a sudden, piercing ache went through him. Not need for her physically, although there was something of that as well. No, it was more that he was struck by the wonder of her, that this incandescent being somehow wanted him in her life, wanted to share her days with him. Loc was not sure if he could call himself worthy of her, but he knew he would do his utter best to prove that she had not made a mistake in choosing him.

Candlelight flickered all around them. He thought that the usual practice was to have the candlelit dinner first and the lovemaking afterward, but he was very glad they hadn't delayed. Glad, too, that this body hadn't failed him, had made the experience as pleasurable for Cat as it had been for him.

"Both of my pieces for the art show are done," she said, voice deliberately casual, as if she knew they needed to speak of commonplaces right now. As much as Loc wanted to cry out his undying love for her, he thought it best to be at least somewhat restrained for the moment. He nodded, and she went on, "I thought I'd drop them off tomorrow, since waiting until the last minute usually isn't a good idea."

"That sounds reasonable," he responded. "Do you want me to come with you?"

She shook her head. "No, I don't think that's necessary. It'll just be a quick trip to the gallery that's hosting the show. But I thought that after I was done, maybe we could head up to Abiquiu for the day. It's some really beautiful country around there—Abiquiu Lake, for one thing, and then we could go on the Ghost Ranch tour, maybe horseback riding. Ghost Ranch is where Georgia O'Keeffe once lived," she added, as though he should know who Georgia O'Keeffe was.

"That sounds like it would be enjoyable. However, I have never ridden a horse."

"Oh, it's easy," Cat assured him. "These are horses ridden by hundreds of tourists every year, so they're really mellow. Basically, all you have to do is sit in the saddle and let the horse follow the guide. But it's a fun way to get into the back country."

Loc wondered whether a horse would truly bear him. He'd noticed on his travels that dogs seemed to get edgy whenever he was near, either growing nervous and visibly shaking, or being overly friendly, as if they thought they could get on his good side by being ingratiating. Perhaps they somehow were able to sense his other-worldly nature, no matter what he looked like on the outside. He hadn't been near enough any horses to tell whether they would react in the same way. If they did, attempting to go on this tour at Ghost Ranch would prove difficult. The only reassurance was that Cat most likely would guess why the horses were restive, and wouldn't ask any awkward questions.

"I like that idea," he said, and left it at that. No point in worrying about something that might never happen.

"Then it's a date." She picked up her wine glass and took a sip, then set it down so she could retrieve an egg roll from the plate where they rested. "My errand won't take very long—the gallery opens at ten, so I'll head out around nine-thirty and should be back by eleven at the very latest."

Loc nodded. He wondered what he would do with himself during that time, but he supposed he might enjoy merely sitting in the sun and breathing in the air and listening to the birds until Cat came home. Certainly there was now no reason to continue looking for someone to send him back to his world. The very thought made him go tense, for now he knew this was where he wished to be, in this little corner of the world, secluded and lovely and serene.

Likewise, he knew that Nicholas Toulouse still

lurked out there somewhere, but he did not appear to pose any sort of imminent threat. If Loc never returned, the dark warlock would probably realize that he had given up on his quest, and so Toulouse would also have to abandon his notion of acquiring the de la Paz clan's lost grimoires. Certainly he had gotten along very well all these years without them, and so he had no real reason to bring down the wrath of the Castillos by attempting to steal the books.

"Are you going to say anything to your brother?"

Cat paused just as she was reaching for a wonton. "Say anything about what?" she asked, but her tone was just a bit too off-hand for him to believe she didn't know what he was talking about.

"About what has happened between us."

She straightened, although Loc noticed how she remained facing forward, rather than turning so she could look him in the eyes. "Um, I've never discussed my sex life with Rafe, and I'm sure as hell not going to start now."

"This is not merely about sex," Loc replied calmly. "That is, he is sure to notice something if I continue to live here with you."

This comment was met with a long silence, one so long that he began to fear his feelings for her were not reciprocated, that all she'd wanted was a few moments of intimacy with him, rather than the lifelong commitment he'd imagined. He held himself still, for the last thing he wanted to do was let her know how much her reticence alarmed him, but he couldn't quite prevent himself from letting out a relieved breath when she spoke next.

"Yes, he'll notice," she said. "And I know I'll have to tell him—and the rest of my family—something soon enough. But for now, I just want to get through this week. Rafe and Miranda and my father are supposed to come to the reception on Friday evening, and while I'm not going to go into the gory details at a public event, they're definitely going to notice that I have you there with me as my date."

"Your date?" Loc asked, feeling absurdly pleased. Cat must be proud of her connection with him, or surely she wouldn't invite him along to a party where he would meet a great many of her friends and colleagues and family members.

"Yes, my date," she said firmly, then leaned over so she could plant a kiss on his cheek. Afterward, she drew back a little and sent him a questioning look. "You didn't really think I was going to leave you sitting here alone on a Friday night while I went to the reception, did you?"

"To be honest, I hadn't thought that far ahead."

She put her hand on his knee and gave it a reassuring squeeze. "Well, I had. And I totally want to show you off. It's just that there's no reason for you to come along tomorrow."

"I understand." He rested his hand on top of hers, felt the smooth skin and the warmth of the flesh beneath. Cat was so very real, perhaps the realest thing he had ever experienced. After the intimacies they'd shared, he felt as though he didn't want to lose a single precious second together. But he'd seen enough of human interactions to know that such behavior was not precisely the norm, and so he told himself that it was only an hour or two at the most, and afterward they would spend a wonderful day together.

Assuming, of course, that the horses at this Ghost Ranch didn't bolt as soon as they caught wind of him and realized they had a demon in their midst.

It felt a little strange to pull her Mercedes SUV out of the garage and realize that Loc was staying behind at the house, but Cat told herself it was good for him...good for both of them, really. They couldn't spend the rest of their lives continuously joined at the hip. She hoped that as he stayed here and became a part of her life, he would make friends both within her clan and without, would find a way to stitch himself into the fabric of existence here in northern New Mexico. They would have to decide how much of his background could be known among the clan, but of course to her civilian friends he would have to remain Loc de la Cruz, the artist from Spain who had found a way into her heart.

She'd awoken in the middle of the night to hear his deep, even breathing next to her—and what a relief it had been to see that he really did sleep—and she'd murmured the phrase in her mind, even though neither of them had yet said it to the other.

I love you.

Because she knew she did love him, his strangely generous heart, his enthusiasm for the world around him...the way he looked at her, as though she was the most perfect work of art ever created by god or man. It didn't matter that he had come from a world she could barely begin to imagine, that underneath his model-handsome looks he hid the face of a devil. He was simply, uniquely Loc, and she wondered how she had ever lived without him.

The morning was a sunny one, but thunderheads were already beginning to build up behind the Sangre de Christo mountains, promising afternoon thunderstorms. Would they reach as far north and west as Abiquiu? Maybe, but Cat figured they'd chance it. Worst case, they could still go to the visitor's center at Ghost Ranch, maybe have a late lunch at the Abiquiu Inn, which had great food. They would have at least gotten out and about for the day, explored a different corner of New Mexico than what Loc had seen previously.

And she knew she'd be lying if she didn't admit to herself that she wanted to be seen in public with him, wanted to show him off a bit... except someplace safe where she was pretty sure there wouldn't be any other Castillos around. Yes, they'd have to hash all that out eventually, but she really didn't want to be forced into it when she was still enjoying the afterglow from their love-making of the night before.

The gallery was located on Paseo de Peralta as it began to curve toward the north and east. Luckily, it had plenty of parking, so Cat pulled into an open spot, then went around to the back of her SUV to retrieve the two tapestries.

She'd called as she was leaving the house to let the gallery manager know she'd be stopping by with her entries in a half hour or so. He was a tall black man with a faint Jamaican accent, about as rare in Santa Fe as a unicorn, but over the years he'd managed to become a part of the somewhat insular community there, and Cat knew he did an outstanding job of running the gallery.

He came out into the parking lot just as she was raising the tailgate of her SUV. "I thought you might need some help with those," he said.

"Thank you, Jacques." Truth be told, the tapestries were kind of unwieldy, and she was glad of the help. Loc had given her a hand back at the house, but of course he wasn't here now.

And whose fault is that? she asked herself as Jacques took the larger of the two tapestries from the cargo area of her vehicle. *Loc could have been here helping you, but you told him to stay home.*

The excuse she'd given him was that this was going to be a quick trip, just to the gallery and back, and so there was no real need for him to tag along, but there was another reason besides that. The gallery was in nearly the heart of Santa Fe, and she hadn't wanted to risk running into someone from her clan and having to explain Loc's presence. It wasn't as big a deal with Tony, because Tony knew who Loc was—and, more importantly, he could be trusted to keep quiet on the topic. But with almost anyone else, well, she just didn't feel like going into it right now. She wanted to hold the amazing night she'd shared with Loc close, and introducing him to anyone else in the clan would somehow feel as if it was impinging on their newfound intimacy.

Cat pulled out the second tapestry, then shut the tailgate. It locked automatically as she walked away, following Jacques to the rear entrance of the gallery where his office was located.

"You can go ahead and hang those in the exhibition space in the north wing," he told her. "I already have your information pulled up on the computer, so I'll log your entries as being received. I'll be along in a few minutes to bring you the information cards for both of them."

"Sounds great." Cat picked up the second tapestry from where Jacques had laid it down on top of a worktable, then headed off in the direction he'd indicated. Carrying both of the pieces was a little cumbersome, but not too bad now that she didn't have to wrangle the lift gate of her SUV at the same time.

The exhibition space was a large wing of the gallery, windowless but exquisitely lit. Cat located the spot toward one end where she knew her tapestries were supposed to hang. Jacques had already left behind magnetic hangers that would carefully hold the heavy fabric in place without allowing it to crease and wrinkle. She got one up and was just about to start on the second when he appeared with the foam core–backed information cards for her entries in the competition.

"I'll just leave these for you here," he said, setting them down on the long polished juniper bench placed at the very center of the exhibition space. Pausing, he gave both tapestries an appraising look with a practiced eye. "You might have outdone yourself this year, Cat."

"Thanks," she replied as her cheeks heated slightly from the praise. "I wanted to try a few new techniques, see how they blended together."

"They look very good. The eye keeps moving from texture to texture, color to color." The phone clipped to his belt buzzed, and he sent her an apologetic smile. "A client. I need to take this."

"No problem," Cat said.

He nodded and left the room, his voice trailing back to her as he left. "Yes, Mrs. Goldsmith. It will be delivered on the fourth as promised. You are back in town, then?"

That was all she heard, but Cat could guess at the rest. Jacques was the type of person who never seemed to get ruffled, even though a lot of his clients were extremely demanding types with more money than they knew what to do with. Then again, she supposed she would get a little anxious, too, if she was awaiting the delivery of a piece that probably cost more than most people's cars.

With a slight lift of her shoulders, she went back to finish hanging the second tapestry, then carefully affixed the information card that accompanied it to the wall a few inches away. Once she had the other card mounted as well, she'd be done here, and she could go home and collect Loc.

"Hey," said an unfamiliar voice, and Cat turned, information card still in her hand, to see a woman maybe a few years younger than she was standing near the entrance to the exhibit space. The stranger had warm blonde hair that fell in careful waves down her back, and she was very pretty in a sort of scrubbed, all-American cheer-leader sort of way.

"Hi," Cat said, smiling at the unknown young woman. "Can I help you with something?"

"Are those yours?"

"Yes," she replied, still feeling a bit flushed with pride, thanks to the compliments Jacques had just paid her work. "But this part of the gallery isn't really open yet. We're still getting all the pieces hung, as you can see. The actual exhibit and juried show starts on Friday afternoon—there'll be a reception, if you're going to be in town that long." She figured the strange young woman must be a tourist, because she had a faint trace of a Southern accent, although it didn't sound as though she was from Texas, which was where Santa Fe got a lot of its tourists.

"Oh, no, we won't be here," the woman said. "This is sort of a lightning trip, you see."

"That's too bad," Cat replied. "The reception should be pretty good—Jacques always makes sure there's lots of great food."

"We have plenty of that in New Orleans," came another voice, a male voice, and Cat whirled to see a man behind her, someone who hadn't been there a second earlier. He was tall and had black hair slicked straight back, and icy blue eyes that contrasted with the warm brown of his skin.

Her shocked brain registered his words almost as soon as it logged the man's presence.

New Orleans. Nicholas Toulouse lived in New Orleans.

Oh, no—

She turned to bolt, to run back toward the spurious safety of Jacques' office, but before she could take a step, the warlock's hand had grasped her by the bicep, holding her with fingers so cold, they felt like bands of ice around her bare arm.

"I'm afraid not, my dear," he said, amusement flickering in his pale eyes. "Your lover and I have some unfinished business."

And even though she opened her mouth to scream, no sound came out. It was as though her vocal chords had been as frozen as her arms.

Nicholas Toulouse laughed, and laughed, and the walls of the gallery disappeared as the world went black.

16

LOC GLANCED AT THE DIGITAL CLOCK ON THE STOVE and felt a frown crease his brows. Cat had now been gone almost two hours, and he knew that was far longer than she'd said her errand would take. Perhaps she had gotten delayed while talking to the gallery manager, but he doubted she would have allowed herself to be delayed for such a significant amount of time.

He'd come into the kitchen to fetch himself a glass of water, but now that he'd realized how much time had passed, he realized he was not as thirsty as he thought. Worry coursed through him, although he tried to tell himself that there was probably a perfectly logical reason for why Cat was taking so long to get home.

It wasn't as though he could call her to find out what was going on, because even though he could summon a phone for himself easily enough, he didn't know what her number was. He supposed he could call the gallery, but he had a feeling she might not much like the idea of him keeping tabs on her in such a way.

But something might have gone wrong, he thought as he went to the kitchen window and peered out through it. Far off to one side, he spied Roberto and Miguel as they made their rounds through the vineyards, checking on the progress of the several varieties of grapes planted there, and yet there was no sign of Cat's SUV.

Well, she might not be happy about him checking up on her, but he knew he would never forgive himself if she'd had an accident of some sort and he'd sat here meekly waiting for her to return. He shed his human form and took to the air, making sure he was carefully shielded from human eyes, although he could feel his heart beat a little faster at the risk he was taking. As best he could, he followed the route she would have taken into town, moving along the little two-lane highway to something that more closely resembled an actual freeway, tracing its path until it ended on the north side of Santa Fe. In all those miles, he saw no sign of a dark gray sport-utility vehicle pulled off to one side of the road, nor were there any indications that there had been an accident of some kind.

Frown deepening, he passed over the heart of the town, peering down at the Plaza with its scores of milling tourists, at the streets which encircled that open area, but again, he didn't see a vehicle that looked like Cat's. Luckily, she'd described the gallery to him, its position on the northward curve of Paseo de Peralta, the large enclosed garden to one side with its multitude of bronze statues. However, as he descended, then assumed his human form again and threw off his concealing veil of invisibility, he did not see her vehicle parked in the large gravel lot that faced on the street.

So had she come here and left? It was possible she hadn't taken the highway out of town, had driven some other, less direct route, but he saw no reason why she would have done such a thing, not when she knew he was waiting for her.

He did his best to assume a calm demeanor, then went to the front door of the gallery and let himself in. The building was cool and shadowy, its interior lighting all focused on the art which hung on its walls. He sensed the presence of a human toward the back of the structure, but there didn't seem to be anyone else inside at the moment.

As he moved farther into the gallery, he noticed a large, airy space off to his left, one that had some art hanging on the walls, although large gaps still existed, as though they were waiting for other pieces to be displayed there. Two of the pieces caught his eye at once, because he knew they were Catalina's work. At the same time, a miasma of evil seemed to drift toward him, thick and choking as the fetid air from a swamp.

Nicholas Toulouse. Loc had sensed that same evil surrounding the house in the Garden District, and he knew without a doubt that the warlock must have come here, had to have taken Cat away. It was the most rational explanation for why she hadn't come home on time, why he hadn't been able to detect any trace of her on the roads between her house and this place.

The sound of someone approaching made him turn, reflexes buzzing. He wished it might be Toulouse, so they could have this out here and now, but Loc knew it wouldn't be that easy.

This man was much darker-skinned than Nicholas Toulouse, and older in appearance, with a frosting of gray on his close-cropped curly hair. "Did you need something? This exhibit is still being installed, as you can see."

"Cat Castillo," Loc said, all too aware of the urgent rasp in his voice. "I...was supposed to meet her here, but I can't find her."

The man frowned. "She was here earlier, putting up her pieces." His attention was caught by something lying on the ground, and he moved into the room, bent, and picked it up. Now Loc could see that it was a small piece of card stock mounted to some kind of backing. "That is strange. She has one of these mounted here, but it appears that she dropped the second one."

Most likely it had been in her hand when Nicholas Toulouse kidnapped her, but of course Loc couldn't offer that explanation. "Possibly she had to take a phone call," he said, knowing how weak the explanation sounded.

"Is her car still here?"

"No." And how Toulouse had managed that, Loc wasn't sure. The warlock was strong, but was he truly strong enough to make a large SUV vanish? Realizing the other man was watching him with some concern in his eyes, Loc added, "She probably got a call and had to go take care of something. I'll check with her brother."

"That's probably a good idea. I'm sorry you couldn't find her here."

"It's fine." There wasn't much else Loc could say, so he mumbled a thank-you and hurried out of the gallery, walking swiftly along Paseo de Peralta so he could turn up Canyon Road and head toward the house that Cat's brother shared with the Castillo *prima*. It seemed simpler to do that than to find a sheltered place where he could assume his true form, especially since the distance he had to cover was less than half a mile.

The day was warm, though, and he found himself perspiring by the time he turned down the side street where the *prima*'s house was actually located. Loc paused on the corner and brushed a hand across his brow, annoyed with this body's reaction to the heat even while he understood the physiological reasons behind it.

Now that he wasn't dripping with sweat, he let himself in through the gate of the Castillo property and made his way up the front walk to the deep, shadowy porch. This was certainly not the way he had planned to meet with Cat's brother and sister-in-law, now that his and Cat's relationship had changed so drastically, but there was little he could do about that. Her safety was paramount. The mere thought of her caught in Nicholas Toulouse's dark web made his blood boil with anger.

He knocked on the door, then waited. A few minutes later, it opened, and Miranda Castillo looked out at him in surprise, her big green eyes widening slightly as she realized who her visitor was.

"Loc!" she exclaimed, then peered past him, as if she expected to see Cat hiding somewhere behind his shoulder. "We weren't expecting you."

"This isn't a courtesy call," he said, and something about the tone of his voice must have told her he was serious, because she immediately opened the door wider and stepped out of the way so he could enter.

"Come in," she said quickly, then shut the door. "What's going on? Where's Cat?"

He saw no reason to attempt to varnish the

truth. "I fear that Cat has been kidnapped by Nicholas Toulouse."

Miranda's cheeks went pale. "*What?*"

"Where is Rafe?"

"Right here," he said, coming into the entryway from the living room. Dark eyes narrowed, he went on, "What did you just say?"

"Cat went to the gallery to get her works for the art show placed. I waited at her house." Loc realized he'd almost slipped and said that he'd waited at home, because her gracious vineyard house had already begun to feel like home to him. However, he knew that even hinting at that sort of arrangement would probably start a cascade of questions he had no desire to answer, not when time was so precious. "She was very late coming back, much later than she'd told me she would be, and so I went in search of her. Almost as soon as I entered the gallery, I could sense Toulouse's evil in the place where she was hanging her tapestries. She was gone, and her vehicle as well."

"He took her car to New Orleans?" Miranda asked, brow wrinkling a bit.

"I doubt it," Rafe said grimly. "He probably just moved it away from the gallery to make things more confusing. I'll start having people look for it—I bet it's not parked too far away."

Which would answer one question, but wouldn't solve the overall problem that Nicholas Toulouse posed. "I am sure he has taken her because he means to use her to barter for the grimoires in your keeping," Loc said.

Miranda shot a worried look at her husband. "I'd be happy to give him the damn things, but they're not even really ours. I have no idea what kind of trouble we'd be stirring up with the de la Paz clan if we gave away their property."

"I doubt Toulouse cares about our relationship with the de la Pazes," Rafe remarked, his voice taut with worry. "Or at least, he's probably laughing at the bind he's put us in."

"Very likely," Loc said. In some ways, he thought the title of "Lord of Chaos" fit the dark warlock better than it fit himself. "Considering the circumstances, I believe the most important thing for you to do is to do nothing at all."

"*Nothing?*" Miranda and Rafe said at the same time, in varying tones of consternation.

"I do not mean that *we* will do nothing," Loc told them. "Only that this is a battle I must undertake on my own. Nicholas Toulouse is a very old, very dangerous warlock. Perhaps you, Miranda, could best him, but I doubt any of us want you to put your unborn child at risk in such a confrontation."

Almost unconsciously, her hand moved to rest on her belly, which still looked flat enough to Loc, with no sign of the child growing within. "Damn it," she said, but she offered no other protest, for she obviously understood the dangers involved in fighting those sorts of magical battles.

Rafe's hands were knotted into impotent fists where they hung at his side. "I should be able to do something," he growled, sounding very like the wolf whose shape he sometimes wore.

"Your powers are no match for his," Loc pointed out. "I don't think there is anyone in your clan who is strong enough to take him on. But I am not a human, not an ordinary warlock. He will find his match in me."

For a few seconds, Rafe didn't reply, but only stood where he was, watching Loc closely. "Why would you do that for her? I thought you were trying to find the fastest way out of here."

Now it comes. Loc knew he could refuse to answer, or offer an easy lie. But he understood that Catalina's brother needed to know why their otherworldly guest was so invested in her fate.

"I no longer desire to leave this place," he said quietly. "I love your sister, and so, as the one who loves her, I must be the one to be her champion."

"You...*what?*"

"He loves her," Miranda said. Unlike her husband, she didn't appear displeased by this revelation at all. Instead, she smiled slightly, despite the desperation of their current situation. "I'd wondered...but we can talk about that later, once Cat is home. So what's your plan?"

Gone was the concerned sister-in-law; it was

the cool green gaze of a *prima* that Loc met now, and he was grateful for her command of the situation, for realizing that there was no need to waste valuable time on questions about his relationship with Cat.

"I'm not entirely certain," he confessed. "For now, it is enough to know that I have your blessing to go and rescue her. Before I force any kind of confrontation with Nicholas Toulouse, I must go to New Orleans and scout the area, assess his property for weaknesses. At least we're fairly certain there is something he wants from us, rather than him causing mayhem for its own sake."

"He wants something we can't give him," Miranda said, even as her husband's mouth thinned. Clearly, he thought it was worth destroying relations with the de la Paz clan—and handing over some very dangerous books to the last person in the world who should have them—if it meant getting his sister back unharmed.

"It won't come to that." Loc glanced from her to Rafe, who now had his arms crossed, his body practically vibrating with impotent fury. While he understood that fury, this was no time to worry about Rafe's feelings. "Kidnapping is truly a sign of weakness, because it shows that you have no other means of bargaining. Nicholas Toulouse daren't hurt Cat—if he does, then he loses his one stake in this game, and knows that the Castillo clan will rain fury down upon his head."

"That's for damn sure," Rafe muttered.

"Also," Loc went on, ignoring the interruption, "Toulouse is a lone wolf, so to speak. He certainly does not have the support of the Dubois clan, and therefore he walks a very dangerous line. There is no one to have his back, so to speak."

"Good," Miranda said. Although she appeared calmer than her husband, her eyes were glittering with anger, like chips of furious emerald. "And when you have Cat back, you'll make sure he's taken care of, right? If there's anything we've learned, it's that these dark warlocks are cockroaches. You can't leave them free to breed."

Considering what she and the rest of the Castillos had suffered at the hands of Joaquin Escobar's son, Loc could see her point. To tell the truth, he didn't know whether Nicholas Toulouse was even capable of fathering a child. His age was still unknown, but the spells he cast and the potions he drank to prolong his youth had to take a toll somewhere.

"He took Cat. His life is already forfeit," Loc said casually, and Miranda and Rafe shared a single satisfied glance.

"Good," Rafe said, but that was all.

Since there seemed to be little else to discuss,

Loc thought it time to go. "The next time you see me, I will have Cat at my side."

He disappeared then, leaving the Castillo *prima* and her husband behind.

Now all he had to do was make sure those final words to them weren't a lie.

She lay somewhere in semidarkness, although Cat realized as soon as she opened her eyes that the dimness of the space around her was due to the heavy curtains that covered the windows, and not because night had fallen. With a little groan, she pushed herself up to a sitting position, then waited for a few moments before the spinning sensation in her head dissipated somewhat. Whatever spell Nicholas Toulouse had used on her, it was a doozy…and she feared he had plenty more like that one in his arsenal.

To her relief, she was alone. The bed where she'd been placed was narrow, not much more than twin size, but with an enormously tall carved headboard. The rest of the furniture in the room was just as ornate, and faded silk wallpaper in a damask pattern covered the walls. Air whistled faintly in the air conditioning vents, sending the crystal chandelier that hung in the center of the ceiling to sway slightly, its prisms tinkling into the silence.

Even if Cat hadn't already known that Toulouse lived in New Orleans, that would have been her first guess, based on her surroundings. This sure didn't look like anyplace she knew in Santa Fe, or New Mexico itself, for that matter.

Her limbs felt heavy, as though someone had hung invisible weights on her body. An after-effect of the spell, or some kind of other charm that he'd placed on her to make sure she couldn't get away? She didn't know, but she also knew she wasn't going to sit here calmly and wait for her captor to come check on her. No matter how impaired she seemed right now, she was going to do what she could to get the hell out of here.

Gritting her teeth, she swung her legs over the edge of the bed, then made herself stand up. Everything felt wobbly, but she took one step, and then another, and as she progressed across the room toward the three tall windows that took up most of one wall, it seemed as though the stiffness slowly began to leave her body. That was a little encouraging. Right now, she figured she could use all the encouragement she could get.

Cat stopped at the middle window and pushed aside the heavy moss green velvet curtain. The room was obviously on the second floor of the house where she was being held, since she now looked down on a front yard dominated by several tall trees she thought might be elms, trees so thick she could barely see the green grass below them.

A wall surrounded the property, and just past the wall was a narrow street with cars taking up almost all the available curb space. That surprised her; even though she knew Loc had said Toulouse lived in New Orleans, for some reason she hadn't thought his home would be in such a busy and obviously populated neighborhood.

Across the street was a walled-off square with a bewildering variety of low stone structures, structures that were so foreign to her eyes, it took her a minute to realize they were all sarcophagi of some sort. Right—she remembered reading somewhere that the water table in New Orleans was very high, and so their cemeteries were full of these above-ground houses for the dead.

Somehow, it seemed fitting that Toulouse would live right across the street from a graveyard. At least the situation of the property ensured that he wouldn't have any neighbors facing his house, so maybe it was more private here than she'd thought.

Had anyone seen him carrying her inside the house? Because she'd blacked out—or been forced to faint by means of some sort of spell—Cat had no idea how she'd gotten here. Maybe Toulouse had the power of teleportation, the way Miranda and her parents did, but it seemed more likely that he'd done something to make her invisible to the naked eye as he and his accomplice carried her out of the gallery. No one else had been around, after all, except Jacques, who'd disappeared into his office at the back of the building to take that phone call. He probably wouldn't have been close enough to see anything suspicious.

It did seem later in the day. Cat couldn't see the sun, but the light outside was sort of hazy and diffuse, the way it got late in the afternoon right before sundown. How far was it from Santa Fe to New Orleans? She'd never really checked, but she knew it had to be more than a thousand miles, not the sort of distance that could be covered by a car in a single day.

Not that it mattered. Toulouse could've knocked her out, taken her to Santa Fe's small airport, and then flown her across state lines. Not all private planes had the kind of range to cover that sort of distance in a single hop, but there were enough that she figured it would have been fairly easy to find a charter jet for that sort of trip. Hauling a comatose woman aboard might have presented its own problems, but she had no doubt that the dark warlock and his blonde accomplice could have concocted a plausible story…or a not so plausible one, if enough money changed hands.

All right. She was in the hands of a ruthless warlock who'd obviously realized that Loc had changed his mind about delivering the de la Paz grimoires in exchange for a return trip to the world he'd once ruled. Stealing her must have appeared to be the logical next step, because while her own ability to talk to ghosts could be amusing sometimes, there wasn't anything all that special about her.

Except that she was the sister-in-law of the clan's *prima*...and the woman Loc loved.

Loc. He must have been frantic with worry by that point, the time she'd promised to return home long since passed by now. Cat tried to reassure herself that Nicholas Toulouse would be the logical suspect in such a disappearance, and so she knew her lover must already be working to find her.

Lover. The word sounded odd when she thought it, but that was precisely what the two of them were. Lovers. Loc wasn't exactly the sort of person you could refer to as your "boyfriend."

Even if he was already on the case, that didn't mean she couldn't do everything in her power to get the hell out of here. Her fingers found the window latch, and she fumbled with it, trying to get it open. Unfortunately, it wouldn't budge. Cat shifted her position slightly, thinking that maybe her angle of approach was all wrong, but no matter what she did, that latch wasn't opening.

She stepped back a pace, fingers throbbing. Obviously, Toulouse must have put some sort of spell on the window to prevent her from exiting that way. No doubt if she tried the other two, she'd meet with the same resistance.

Her gaze moved upward. Didn't big old houses like these have attics? Maybe this one did, but she couldn't see any sign of an access panel in the water-stained plaster. This house had clearly once been beautiful, but it appeared that Nicholas Toulouse wasn't overly concerned with making sure everything was just so.

A woman's voice came to her in the silence. "Looks like you're in a bit of a pickle."

Cat whirled. Standing on the other side of the room, underneath a portrait of a slightly consti-pated-looking man in a dark Victorian suit, was a girl who didn't appear to be much more than seventeen or eighteen. Her shining brown hair fell in fat sausage curls past her shoulders, and she wore a blue silk dress with a lace collar and an enormous hooped skirt. As Cat's gaze focused on this new arrival, she realized the newcomer was floating several inches above the floor.

A ghost. Not so strange, considering how old this house must be.

"Hello," she said, glad that she was used to talking to those who'd long since departed this mortal coil. "I'm Cat—that's short for Catalina. What's your name?"

"I thought you looked Spanish," the girl said in slightly disapproving tones. "Your clothes are dreadful."

Cat cast a quick glance downward at her faded jeans and tank top. It had been a warm day in Santa Fe, and she'd figured that she would change into something nicer before she headed out on her date with Loc. Then again, she had a feeling even her best wouldn't have passed muster with this haughty little Southern belle.

"They are, aren't they?" she agreed cheerfully. "I'll do something about that just as soon as I get out of here. You wouldn't have any idea how I might go about that, would you?"

The condescending expression on the girl's face disappeared abruptly, replaced by something that looked almost like fear. "Not with *him* around," she replied, her voice lowering to almost a whisper. "He told me once if I ever interfered with him, he'd banish me straight to hell. And I've never done anything to deserve being sent to hell," she added almost tearfully, big blue eyes suspiciously bright.

Interesting. Apparently, Toulouse could speak to spirits, just as Cat herself did. "Does he talk to you a lot?"

"Oh, no." A shake of her head that sent her glossy curls bouncing. "It wasn't so much that he told me *directly*, you know. It was just when he moved into this house, he informed all the spirits here that we would be banished if we tried to get in his way. Dreadfully rude man."

"Are there many other spirits here?" Cat

asked. She couldn't help but be a bit relieved by this latest piece of information. It appeared that Toulouse wasn't a ghost-talker after all. While it was certainly not the sort of gift that would help with a full frontal assault, she was still glad to know she had a weapon in her arsenal the dark warlock lacked.

"Not here in the house," the girl said. "Leastways, my mama and my brother died of typhoid fever the same time I did, but they moved on. I've been here alone since."

Cat wanted to ask the girl why she'd remained when the rest of her family had "gone into the light," so to speak, but she knew that would be rude. Ghosts were often happy to volunteer information, but they tended to evaporate as soon as you started asking too many personal questions.

"But there are other ghosts around, even if they're not here in the house?"

The girl nodded, and extended a pale hand toward the wall with all the windows that looked down on the cemetery. "Oh, yes. Across the street are as many as you could possibly want." A pause, and she gave Cat an inquiring look, head tilted to one side. Cat had a feeling that that particular posture had worked its magic on quite a few young men back in the day. "It's very curious that you're not afraid of me. Why, the family that lived here twenty-five years ago had a little boy who screamed and screamed as soon as he caught sight of me."

"Why would he do that?" Cat asked. "You're a very pretty girl."

Ghosts couldn't exactly blush, but the girl gave Cat a pleased simper. "Well, it might have been because he startled me, and so I showed him my other face...you know, the one from the day I died."

At once her blooming prettiness shifted into a terrible gauntness, cheekbones standing out, eyes circled in dark shadows, lips as pale as the skin surrounding them. Even though Cat had witnessed this phenomenon once or twice in the past, she couldn't help startling a bit. Finding her voice, she said, "I can see why that might have upset him."

"I know," the girl said sadly, shifting back to the face she'd first shown Cat, all big blue eyes and rosy lips. "I tried to tell him it was an accident, but he wouldn't listen to me. Had so many nightmares that they moved out only a few months later. The house was empty for a while, but then *he* moved in."

No need to ask who *he* was. "He's been here for twenty-five years?" That was also a surprise, since she didn't see how the Dubois clan could have possibly put up with having such an interloper camped on their front step, so to speak, for so many years.

"No, not that long." Another wave of her hand. Cat could almost imagine a gossamer-thin handkerchief being brandished in that hand, although right now the ghost girl held nothing. "I said the house was empty. It could have been years. I don't always keep track of such things. Time passes strangely when there's no one around to keep you occupied."

Cat hadn't thought of it that way, but she could see what the girl meant. Maybe she'd gone into a kind of ghostly hibernation, waiting for someone to buy the house and move in and once again give her something to pay attention to. If it had stood empty for a long time...years or even decades...that would explain the faded wallpaper, the stains on the ceiling.

"But then Nicholas Toulouse moved in," she prompted.

"Yes, he did." The girl's lips pressed together in distaste. "Always doing terrible things in the kitchen, and worse things in the bedroom that was once my mama and papa's, he and that little witch slut he brought here a while back."

Now was certainly not the time to discuss why slut-shaming was wrong, so Cat held her tongue. Besides, she'd be the first to admit that the blonde woman had terrible taste in men, if she truly was shacked up here with Nicholas Toulouse. But the blonde was a witch? Cat hadn't sensed that about her, but again, she knew it was possible to block other witches and warlocks from detecting one's true nature, since Simon Escobar had taught Miranda to do that very thing.

"He is a very bad man," Cat said. "He kidnapped me because he wants to use me to force my family to do something terrible, to give him something that will make him even more powerful. I can't let that happen. That's why you really need to help me get out of here."

The girl's eyes went wide and frightened. "I told you, I can't do that," she said in a terrified whisper. "He'll banish me, he said he would."

Cat didn't know whether that was even possible, despite Toulouse's threats, but she had a feeling her reassurances wouldn't go very far with the ghost girl. "But if you help me, I know people who are also very powerful, who would drive him from your house. Wouldn't you like to have him gone?"

For a moment, a terrible hope glimmered in the girl's eyes. Then she shook her head. "I can't take that risk. I am sorry."

And, in the annoying way that most ghosts had, she disappeared, leaving Cat staring at the empty space where she'd just been floating.

Well, crap. Cat knew she shouldn't be surprised by such a defection, but she still wasn't happy. Now she had nothing to do except wait.

Even so, she went over to a different window and began fiddling with the latch. Deep down, she knew this wasn't going to do any good, either, but right then it felt better to attempt and fail than sit and wait for the inevitable.

Come on Loc, she thought. *Get me the hell out of here.*

17

WRAPPED IN AN INVISIBILITY THAT NOT ONLY obscured his body, but his very nature, Loc returned to New Orleans. He took up a position on the roof of one of the sarcophagi in the cemetery across the street from Nicholas Toulouse's house, then crouched there, eyes narrowed as he reached out with his senses.

It was as though he hit a wall of brick as solid as that which encircled the property opposite him. He let out a low growl of annoyance, then once more sent his otherworldly senses questing toward the dark warlock's house. This second attempt was just as fruitless as the first, however, and he frowned, wondering what fresh deviltry this was.

A new spell, a very powerful one. It seemed obvious enough that Toulouse wanted to make sure no one would be able to detect who or what was inside the house, which told Loc that almost certainly Cat was there. There would be no reason to expend so much energy if the warlock was not hiding a valuable prisoner somewhere within those walls.

Rubbing his chin with invisible fingers, Loc contemplated the problem at hand. If the dark warlock had cast a spell that strong, it probably meant he did not have much energy left over for other uses. Loc supposed there was a chance that he could make an all-out assault, with no finesse but a great deal of force, and surprise Nicholas Toulouse before he could do anything to harm Cat.

Unfortunately, there was a great deal that could go wrong in such a scenario, the most obvious being that Toulouse would strike out at his captive the second he realized such an attack was under way. Loc knew he didn't dare take such a chance. No, he would have to come up with something else, something that took advantage of the warlock's weaknesses…whatever those might be.

But he thought he might know exactly who would be in possession of that knowledge.

Mouth grim, he blinked himself away from Lafayette Cemetery, and over to a certain jewelry shop in the French Quarter. This time, the witch working there didn't even seem surprised to have him materialize in front of where she stood, dusting one of the shelves covered with expensive trinkets—gilt jewelry boxes, carved stone spheres on stands, porcelain eggs that looked like jewels themselves, with their golden scallops and embedded crystals. She only set down her duster, put her hands on her hips, and gave him an arch look.

"I should have known you'd come pokin' around here again," she said, but there was no malice in her voice. "What is it now?"

"Nicholas Toulouse has kidnapped a Castillo witch," Loc replied. Although he hated to speak of her in such casual terms, he did not feel it necessary to go into detail about how important that one particular Castillo witch happened to be to him. "I fear he has brought the war to your city."

The witch didn't seem particularly impressed by this revelation. She gazed at him for a moment, then lifted her shoulders almost imperceptibly. "I'm sorry to hear that, but have you forgotten that he also has our *prima*'s daughter under his roof? We can't risk her life just to help you and your Castillo witch." She paused, then added, voice softening a bit, "What'd he kidnap her for?"

"Leverage," Loc replied, doing his best to keep the mounting anger out of his tone. "He is trying to force the Castillo *prima* to do something that would be very dangerous for everyone involved. Something that could have ramifications for the

Dubois clan as well." Since this revelation didn't seem to overly impress the shopkeeper witch, he went on, "Perhaps I should speak to your *prima*."

"Oh, I don't know about that. She's not been feeling so well of late. Something like this might upset her."

His teeth ground together. "I care little whether I upset her. Tell me where her house is. Or not—I can find that out for myself, although it would be easier for all of us if you would just give me the information I need."

A moment passed, then another. The witch didn't much like his ultimatum, that he could tell, but he could also see that she was quickly realizing there was no true way out of this situation. At last she let out an exaggerated sigh before saying, "It's 1520 Marais Street. I doubt she'll be happy to see you."

"I care nothing for that." Almost as soon as those words left his lips, he took himself away, going to the address the witch had provided. It was a large mansion in the classical revival style, with stately columns and colored walkways that wound around the almost impossibly green lawns.

Most humans would have found such a residence to be overly imposing, but, as Loc had just told the shopkeeper witch, he cared little as to whether the building was impressive or not. The only thing he cared about was the *prima* who dwelled inside.

Because he knew he might have to rely on the goodwill of Estelle Dubois to get some of the assistance he needed, he didn't materialize somewhere inside her mansion, but rather on the lofty covered porch, which provided some relief from the sun but did nothing to hold back the moist heat of the afternoon. He found himself longing for the dry air of Santa Fe, which felt much closer to what he was used to. If the universe were just at all, he would be back at Cat's house in Pojoaque, with her next to him on the patio as they sipped wine and spoke of the outing at Ghost Ranch they should have taken.

Instead, he was here in New Orleans, doing whatever he could to free the woman he loved from the grip of a very dark warlock.

Jaw clenched, he touched the button to one side of the door and listened to the resulting chimes echo somewhere deep within the oversized house. Only a few seconds passed, and then a woman who appeared to be around Cat's age opened the door and looked out, her gaze both surprised and somewhat appreciative. Her coloring was so similar to Celeste Dubois' that he guessed they were probably sisters, although this woman's blue eyes were clear enough, not fogged by a terrible spell to cloud her mind and make her susceptible to Nicholas Toulouse's every whim. The aura of magic around her was quite strong.

"I need to speak to Estelle Dubois," Loc said. "It is very urgent."

Now the woman's face went shuttered, as if the mention of her mother had upset her in some way. Voice crisp in spite of her soft Southern accent, she said, "I'm afraid she's indisposed at the moment. Maybe you could tell me why you're here, and I'll decide if it's worth waking her from her nap."

"Are you the *prima*-in-waiting?" he demanded, and she started.

"How could you know that?"

"Because I've come from the Castillo clan with urgent business, and I don't need to be left waiting on Estelle Dubois' doorstep."

"But you're not—" The woman paused, her light brown brows pulling together. "I mean, you don't feel like a warlock."

"Because I'm not," he said crisply, and at once the woman's puzzled expression shifted to one of sudden comprehension.

"Oh, you're *him*," she said. "Come inside. Roxanne told me about you."

"Roxanne?"

"The woman who works at the jewelry store on Dauphine Street."

Of course. Loc realized she'd never given him her name. Then again, he'd never asked for it. Somehow, it hadn't seemed all that important.

He stepped inside the foyer, which was decorated with dark, fussy antiques. From somewhere in the house came a sweet, almost cloying scent, as if someone had been burning incense.

"I'm Martine," the Dubois *prima*-in-waiting told him. "My mother is in here."

She led him from the foyer and down a short corridor, then into a sitting room furnished with the same overwrought Victorian antiques Loc had seen in the entry hall. On a chaise longue upholstered in striped satin lay a woman wearing a silk dressing gown, her head back against the pillows, eyes shut. Her graceful features were similar to those of her daughters, but she looked drained and tired, even in repose like this.

Her bluish eyelids barely lifted as Martine approached with Loc at her side. "*Maman*, this is the man Roxanne told us about."

Now her eyes opened a bit wider. They were deep blue, the same as her daughters, but they had an almost yellowish tinge to them, as if she suffered from some sort of disease that had affected her internal organs. "The demon lord." Her voice was cracked and tired, but there was still a trace of authority to it, as if she was the sort of woman used to getting her own way.

Which naturally she would, as *prima* of this clan, small as it might be. "Some have called me that," he said, then added formally, "I am sorry to see you are not well."

She waved a languid hand. "A temporary indisposition. What did you wish to see me about?"

Loc hesitated. He was not sure how much help this tired, obviously ill woman could be.

Obviously noting the way he'd paused, Martine leaned close to his ear and murmured, "She's been like this for several weeks. Neither our healer nor the civilian doctors we took her to could find anything wrong, but…."

Although Loc could not claim to know all that much about human physiology, he'd learned a few things during his travels, one being that this world's healers and doctors were skilled at treating an astonishingly wide range of ailments, and so it was odd that they hadn't been able to detect what ailed the Dubois *prima*. Eyes narrowing, he gazed down at her, then reached out with his senses, trying to see if he would have any more luck.

Almost at once, he detected the web of dark magic that had wrapped itself around her heart and lungs, weakening her, making every movement, every breath, an ordeal. And as soon as he'd found it, he knew exactly who had cast that spell.

It would not be a difficult thing to undo, but for a moment Loc hesitated, wondering if he should tell the Dubois *prima* what was wrong with her, and then inform her that he would only lift the spell if she promised to put her clan's resources behind freeing Cat from the dark warlock's clutches. But no—he suddenly realized that Cat would not wish him to resort to that sort of petty blackmail, not even for her own sake. He would help Estelle Dubois because it was the correct thing to do, not because of what he might get out of it.

He reached out with his own magic, the power that lived within him because it was as much a part of his essence as the blood that flowed within his veins. Using that magic, he took hold of Nicholas Toulouse's dark spell and unwound it carefully, making sure it was entirely free of the *prima's* slender body before he banished it forever, breaking the pattern that had given it strength.

Almost at once, she sat up, pushing herself so she was almost upright. Blood flowed into her pale cheeks, and her blue eyes took on a sparkle he guessed was far more usual for her. "What...?"

"It was no ordinary illness that struck you," Loc said, "but rather a spell sent by Nicholas Toulouse to keep you from offering any sort of threat to him. I have no doubt that it would eventually have killed you."

Estelle's hand went to her throat. "That bastard." Then she shook her head. "I suppose one of us should have thought of that, but when the doctors kept finding nothing, I think I began to believe it was all in my head."

"It was not." Loc glanced from the mother to her daughter, whose previously troubled expression was now one of utter relief. Her mother's illness must have weighed especially hard on her, since she would have become *prima* far too soon if Toulouse's spell had been allowed to run its course. "You should be back to your normal strength very soon. But you asked earlier what I wanted. It has to do with Nicholas Toulouse. He has kidnapped a witch from the Castillo clan and is using her as a hostage to gain control over some very dangerous books. For obvious reasons, the Castillos cannot comply with his demands. I hoped you might be able to do something."

"I?" Estelle gave a short, bitter laugh, then slowly got up from the chaise where she'd been lying. "I haven't been able to do a thing to that devil since he came to my beautiful city. And since he also has my own daughter under his spell, you can see why I don't dare lift a hand against him. While I know Celeste went to him willingly"—the *prima's* lips tightened with long-buried anger—"I also know she did it to spite me. As upsetting as that is, I know her actions were more childish rebellion than anything else. But I also know Nicholas Toulouse does not love my daughter and wouldn't hesitate for a second to hurt her if doing so served his purposes. He is a monster, but I am not. I can't do anything that might endanger her."

"If not you yourself, then someone else in your clan?" Loc asked.

"That would still come back on us," Martine said. "Celeste is a spoiled brat who's put all of us in a very difficult position. Besides," she continued, giving him a speculative look, "why would you need our help? If you're really what Roxanne thinks you are, then you should be able to handle that carpetbagger on your own."

Loc was not sure he understood what "carpetbagger" meant, but, judging by the compressed set of Martine's lips, he guessed it couldn't be anything good. "Power against power, yes, I can easily best him," he replied. "But a direct assault poses too much risk to Cat, and—"

"Cat?" Estelle inquired.

"Catalina Castillo, the daughter of the late *prima* and sister-in-law to the current one," he said. "She is being held captive in that house…or at least I believe she is. Toulouse has wrapped it with spell upon spell, dark enchantments that block even my sight. I could break them down, just as I destroyed the spell that was making you ill, but it would take time, and I would lose any advantage of surprise."

"So you were hoping we might be able to provide some sort of distraction?" Martine didn't look too pleased with that assumption, as though her clan wasn't fit to engage in an outright magical battle.

"Something like that," Loc admitted.

The two witches exchanged a glance. For the first time, he realized he hadn't seen any men in this household, no consort for either the *prima* or her daughter. Possibly they were out, although Loc knew if Cat were ever as ill as Estelle had seemed to be, he would not leave her side until she had improved.

"Perhaps your consort...?" he began delicately, not sure of the best way to ask.

Estelle's mouth tightened. "Edgar was a strong warlock," she said, her tone quiet but hard. "And brave. He went to confront Nicholas Toulouse, told him to hand over our daughter." She stopped there, as if she couldn't quite bring herself to go on.

"He didn't come home," Martine said then. "The police found his body in an alley off Bourbon Street. Not a mark on him. The coroner said it was a heart attack, but we knew better. Nicholas Toulouse killed my father."

The grief in her face was plain to see. Even now, tears glittered in her big blue eyes, but through some sort of rigid self-control, she didn't allow them to fall. Loc knew he should offer some words of sympathy, but he found himself unable to speak, sure that anything he said would never be enough to assuage their loss.

"And my stupid sister still stayed with that bastard," Martine added. "Even then."

"We don't know that she knew anything about it," Estelle said. Some of the pallor had returned to her face, but her voice was steady enough. "I am sure Nicholas Toulouse has plenty of secrets he keeps from Celeste." A quick flicker of a glance at Martine, and she went on, "Martine's consort is from the Calhoun clan in the southwest, along the Texas border. We sent him back to stay with them after we lost Edgar, because we feared Toulouse might strike out at him as well. It would be a good way to end our bloodline, after all, because Martine and Clay don't have any children yet."

So much loss, almost as terrible as what the Castillo clan had suffered at the hands of Simon Escobar. "This has been going on for how long?"

"Almost a year," Estelle replied. "My illness… less than a month. I suppose Toulouse began to grow tired of the status quo and wanted to see what other mischief he could cause."

Very likely. Or perhaps he had thought to rid the clan of their *prima*, then capture Martine before she'd come into the full strength of her inherited powers. It sounded like something the dark warlock might try…and after all, Joaquin Escobar had done much the same thing to Marisol Gutierrez of the Santiago clan in California, proving that it was possible to suborn a newly minted *prima* if you got to her quickly enough.

"So you see, we don't dare do anything more," Martine said. "Nicholas Toulouse has no scruples, doesn't care who he hurts or kills. We're a small clan. We just can't afford to get involved in that kind of fight."

"I see," Loc said, and indeed he did. These women had suffered enough; he couldn't ask them to take on any more risks, not when the very survival of their clan was at stake. Whatever he did to Nicholas Toulouse, he would have to do it on his own. "Then I won't trouble you any further. I will find a way to defeat this man and return your daughter to you."

Estelle offered him a sad smile, while Martine still looked angry. He had a feeling she wouldn't be particularly happy to see her sister again.

Well, that was a family conundrum they would have to manage on their own.

In the meantime, he had a dark warlock to defeat.

Sometime after dusk, the blonde girl appeared at Cat's door, a plate with a sandwich on it in one hand and a glass of water in the other. "I'm Celeste," she said as she set the food down on the nightstand next to the bed. "Don't try anything."

"Or what?" Cat returned, eyeing the other woman. Celeste was several inches shorter, and very slender. Cat figured she could take her in a fight, if it came down to that.

"Or this," Celeste said. She raised a hand and made a pushing motion, and the next thing Cat knew, she was flying backward a good three or four feet before landing on her ass—luckily on the big faded Aubusson rug, and not the hardwood floor.

Damn it. That had hurt, but not enough to cause any permanent damage. Holding back a wince, Cat pushed herself upright. "Handy talent."

The girl shrugged. "It's okay. Anyway, enjoy your dinner. Nicky says if your clan cooperates, you could be home by this time tomorrow."

"Cooperates with what?" Cat asked, trying to play innocent.

However, it seemed Celeste was on to her game, because she just sort of rolled her eyes and walked back out again without replying.

"Bitch." Cat went over to the door and tested the handle, but of course it was just as locked as the windows.

Scowling, she crossed back over to the nightstand and inspected the sandwich on its plate. Muffuletta, she realized, only recognizing it because one of the local breweries served the cold-cut sandwiches there. She supposed it could have been poisoned, but she didn't think so. Nicholas Toulouse probably had about fifty different ways of killing her, none of them as clumsy as poison.

The sandwich was good. Since it had been partially wrapped in wax paper, Cat guessed it had been ordered from a local restaurant.

And thank God for that, she thought as she munched away, glad of the food after a nearly eight-hour fast. *Because after hearing Loc talk about what "Nicky" Toulouse cooks up in his kitchen, I sure as hell wouldn't want to eat anything prepared there.*

She finished the sandwich and drank about half the water. Already she was beginning to feel as though she needed to pee, but this room didn't have an *en suite* bathroom. Maybe Celeste would come back at some point and provide an armed escort so Cat could go take care of business.

In the meantime, she would just have to hold it. In terms of problems she had to deal with, going to the bathroom wasn't even at the top of the list.

After throwing away the sandwich wrapper in the trash can next to the nightstand, she got up from where she'd been sitting on the bed and went back to the window. Now that night had truly fallen, there wasn't a lot to see except the warm glow of the street lamps and the occasional headlights of a passing car. It was strange to think that there were people driving down this street, maybe even taking their dogs out for walks or whatever, with absolutely no idea that a woman was being held captive in this house.

What if she broke the window and started screaming for help? Glaringly obvious, true, and something that would have Nicholas Toulouse on her ass in a heartbeat, but....

No, that wouldn't work. Cat had a feeling that if he'd enchanted the window latches so they wouldn't open, he would have also done something to the glass to ensure it was unbreakable. Even if she did manage to break the glass, and even if someone actually heard her and called the cops, she guessed that Toulouse would come up with some story to explain everything away. Maybe offer a little bribe; she seemed to recall reading somewhere that New Orleans cops were pretty corrupt, but that story could have been just internet rumor-mongering. Either way, things weren't looking so great on the escape front.

And beyond her worry and her fear was her longing for Loc, her need to have his arms around her again. They'd barely had a chance to spend any time together, and then Nicholas Toulouse had to come along and screw everything. If only she'd taken Loc along when she went to the gallery...there was no way that bastard Toulouse could've gotten the drop on her if she'd had her demon lord lover along. What would the dark warlock have done then?

Retreated and waited for another opportunity to

catch you alone, she thought, going back to sit down on the bed. Sooner or later, something would have come up. A trip to the salon, or another shopping expedition to the home design center where she'd already dropped an alarming amount of money. It didn't really matter.

How he'd managed to track her at all was another mystery, but once you were dealing with someone whose magical gifts went far beyond those of other witches and warlocks, then all the cards were on the table, weren't they? In the end, the how of the situation didn't matter all that much, only that she needed to find a way to get herself out of this.

After what felt like hours and hours but was probably about forty-five minutes or so, Celeste returned, a smirk on her glossy lips. "Need to pee?" she asked.

"Yes," Cat said shortly, and got up from the bed. Without saying another word, she followed the other witch down the hall to the bathroom.

"Don't try anything funny," Celeste said. "You have two minutes."

Good thing all she had to do was pee. The bathroom didn't have any windows, and, unlike the bedroom where she was being held captive, it appeared to have been updated fairly recently, with yellow paint on the walls and a newish-looking vanity with brushed-nickel fixtures, not a very good match for the overall character of the house.

Like it mattered one way or another.

Business taken care of, Cat came out into the hallway. Celeste was leaning against the wall, looking bored. "All right," she said, "time to go back to your room."

"How long are you planning to keep me here?"

Another smirk. "Well, I guess that depends on your clan, doesn't it? You'd better hope they think you're more valuable than those moldy old books."

Cat knew she was, but the math of this particular situation wasn't quite as simple as that. Instead of replying directly to Celeste's comment, she said, "What is it with you and this Toulouse guy? He's a little old for you, don't you think?"

The contemptuous look disappeared, and Celeste's mouth thinned. "Nicky is a very great warlock."

Yeah, a great big asshole, Cat thought.

"Besides," the other witch went on, "you're not exactly one to talk. Aren't you shacked up with a demon?"

"Demon lord," Cat corrected her.

"Whatever. If he was that great, he would've rescued you already." By that point, they'd reached the door to the bedroom that had become Cat's prison. Celeste opened the door, one corner of her lip curling. "Have a nice night." And as soon as Cat was inside, the door shut behind her and the lock clicked.

She didn't bother to try it, because she already knew she wasn't getting out that way. Frowning, she went over to the bed and paused to take off her boots, since she figured she should try to get some sleep. However, just as she bent over to tug off the second one, a pale figure appeared before her.

The boot dropped to the rug.

"Shh," said the apparition. "It's only me."

Standing there—this time with both her feet firmly planted on the rug—was the Southern belle ghost Cat had met earlier that day. "Oh, hi," she said. "I was just getting ready for bed, since there doesn't seem to be much else I can do."

"About that," the girl said, then paused. "I realized that I hadn't told you my name before. It's Elizabeth—Elizabeth Beaufort, but my father always called me Lizzie."

"Well, hello, Lizzie," Cat responded. Sure, it was great that she now knew the girl's name, but that wasn't going to help her get the hell out of here.

"I didn't come here to tell you only that," Lizzie informed her. "I was thinking about what Mr. Toulouse had done to you. I thought I should do something, but I still worry that he might banish me from the house. Then I realized that even if I couldn't help you directly, I could find someone who would. That's why I brought *him* along."

Out of the shadows came the shape of a tall man. As he approached, he seemed to solidify slightly, but his feet hung about an inch off the carpet, indicating that he was no more mortal than Lizzie herself. He wore modern clothes, a white shirt and charcoal slacks, and was handsome in a distinguished way, with his hawkish nose and the streaks of gray in his dark hair.

"Hello," he said. "My name is Edgar Dubois."

18

Cat blinked at this new apparition. "'Dubois'?" she repeated. "You're part of the witch clan here in New Orleans?"

The man offered her a sad smile. "I was the *prima's* consort. I came to take my daughter away from Nicholas Toulouse—"

"—and he stopped you."

"Killed me, actually." Edgar's gaze shifted downward, as if he was looking at the ground floor of the house. "Down in the foyer. He is... very strong."

Well, Cat knew that already. "Does Celeste know?"

"As far as I can tell, no. While she might have gone with him to spite her mother and me, I know she wouldn't remain loyal to him if she knew the truth." He paused for a moment, mouth tight, as though he wrestled with inner doubts that he didn't want to share with her. "I can only imagine what you must think of her, but remember, she is very young."

Not that young, Cat thought. Although she had to guess at Celeste's age, she thought the Dubois witch must be at least twenty-one. Old enough to vote, to drink, to get married and do a whole host of other things that constituted acting like a proper grown-up. No, sorry…she didn't have a lot of sympathy for Celeste or her shitty choices.

But since arguing with a ghost about what a crummy human being his daughter had turned out to be felt like a very low blow, Cat thought it was probably better to move on to something a little less fraught. "Lizzie said you could help me?"

He glanced over at the girl ghost, who suddenly appeared nervous, hands in their crocheted mitts smoothing down the silken folds of her oversized skirt. "I said I *thought* you might be able to help her. You want your revenge against Mr. Toulouse, don't you?"

"Very much," Edgar Dubois replied, his face set and grim. "But I don't see what I can do. Unfortunately, a ghost doesn't have too many options when it comes to harming the living."

"That's where you're wrong," Cat said. For the first time, she experienced a flicker of hope, a way they might be able to retaliate against Nicholas Toulouse. "Ghosts can act against physical objects if they're motivated enough. My cousin Tony's house is haunted by a ghost named Victoria. Before Tony took over the house, his uncle Max lived there. He tried to turn the dining room into a game room, and that seriously pissed her off. She took all his new furniture—including the foosball table he'd just bought—and dumped it in a big heap in the backyard. Needless to say, Max put all the original furniture back."

"What's a foosball?" Lizzie asked, but Edgar Dubois now appeared thoughtful, one hand rubbing his clean-shaven chin.

"A ghost really picked up all that furniture and moved it?"

"Oh, yes," Cat replied. "She came right out and told Max she'd done it, and that she'd do it again if he messed with anything in 'her' house. He didn't try any redecorating after that, but I guess he got tired of the situation after a while and sold the house cheap to Tony. Anyway," she went on, realizing that certain bits of family history really weren't germane to the current discussion, "Victoria is a ghost, and she moved big pieces of furniture around."

"Inanimate objects," Edgar pointed out.

"I don't think it matters. Victoria wouldn't assault a person because she's way too ladylike for that, but I'm pretty sure the same principle applies."

"So Edgar could do something to Mr. Toulouse?" Lizzie asked, appearing somewhat disappointed that no one had yet explained what foosball was to her.

"I think so." Cat studied Edgar Dubois' expression for a moment. He looked thoughtful more than anything else, but he didn't seem as enthused by the idea of a full frontal assault on Nicholas Toulouse as she'd hoped he would be. "What's wrong?"

His shoulders lifted slightly. "Nothing. That is, I'm a ghost. The worst has already happened to me. At least, I hope it has. But Lizzie has talked about his threats of banishing her. What if he really does have some way of sending souls to a place outside the world? I stayed here because I didn't want to leave my wife and daughters behind, but this sort of half-life is still better than utter nothingness."

A little chill went through Cat, even though the room was slightly stuffy despite the central air conditioning churning away in the background. Still, she tried to sound as confident as she could as she replied, "I honestly don't think he's capable of that. It's just another threat, something to make him seem even more powerful and in control. I've spent more than half my life talking to ghosts, and none of them have ever said anything about getting banished from this plane. Either they're here, trying to work out their issues, or they've moved on to the next place."

"'The next place'?" Lizzie asked, her face now bright with curiosity. "Do you mean heaven?"

"I suppose you could think of it as heaven," Cat said. "But it's not some kind of a reward for a select few. Everyone can move on if they're ready."

"Even bad people?"

"Even bad people." In a way, it was too bad that there wasn't really a heaven and hell, because if anyone deserved to go to hell, it was Nicholas Toulouse. "The next place is where you can become a better version of yourself."

Now Lizzie's tone was plaintive. "Then why didn't I go?"

"Because you wouldn't let yourself," Cat said gently. "Something held you here. Once you figure out what it was...what it still is...then you can move on."

"Hmm." The girl walked away from Cat and Edgar, going to stand by one of the windows so she could look down at the cemetery across the street. Her expression was very thoughtful.

"All right," Edgar said, his voice firm. "I'm willing to try. What did you have in mind?"

"I—I'm not totally sure." Now that she actually had an ally, Cat realized she hadn't done much planning. It wasn't as though she had an attack skill like Celeste's, something she could use directly against Nicholas Toulouse. "I'm hoping that Loc will come and try to break me out of here, but—"

"Who is Loc?"

"A-a friend," Cat faltered, not sure she could adequately explain Loc—or her relationship with him—to this stern-faced man, someone a movie casting director probably would have put in the role of the President, or at least a senator or something. "He's very powerful."

"A warlock from your clan?"

"Not—not exactly."

Edgar Dubois' steel-blue eyes narrowed slightly, but it appeared he wasn't going to press the issue, because he said, "Well, I don't think we can wait around for this Loc. We'll just have to see what we can do on our own."

"Um...." Cat hesitated for a moment, not sure whether this plan was the best idea or not. Hedging, she said, "You really think the two of us can do much against him?"

Now Edgar smiled, although there was something thin and cold about that smile, like the calculating grin of a shark. "Oh, it won't be just the two of us."

"It won't?" Cat cast a dubious glance in the direction of Lizzie Beaufort, who still stood by the window. "But Lizzie said she wasn't able to help us."

"I'm not talking about Lizzie." In a few quick strides, Edgar was across the room, where he pulled aside the curtains at the window next to the one where Lizzie lingered, gazing out into the night. Clearly, he could affect the physical world if he wished to. With his free hand, he pointed toward the cemetery across the street.

"I'm talking about *them*."

Loc had once again assumed his position on top of one of the mausoleums, keeping the shroud of invisibility around him but taking on his natural form, as it felt more comfortable. In his mind, he kept seeing the haunted faces of the two Dubois witches.

He had to defeat Nicholas Toulouse. Not just to rescue Cat, but to relieve those women of the burden they'd been suffering under for far too long.

As he crouched there, he reached out with the power that lay coiled within him, but delicately, with no more than a feather touch of his magic. It brushed up against the spells that cloaked the house Toulouse had taken for his own, then, ever so gently, began to unwind them, pulling on them as one might tug on a single thread to begin unraveling a sweater.

It was a risk, but one he knew he must take.

With a great many spells, they tended to be set by the user and then left alone until such time when they must either be strengthened or undone altogether. Loc could only hope the enchantments that shrouded the house were of this sort, and that Toulouse would notice nothing wrong until it was too late. He did have a great deal to manage, after all, between casting the other spells that maintained the façade of his youth, holding Cat captive, and doing what he must to keep Celeste Dubois occupied.

Really, with all that on his plate, would he notice his spells of protection and concealment slowly falling apart around him?

They had already thinned enough that Loc could now sense the occupants of the house. A dark and malignant pulsing on the ground floor seemed to indicate Nicholas Toulouse's position, and nearby him was another presence, one lighter and brighter but also somehow muted, as though its power was being damped down somehow. A brilliant glow on the second floor could only be Cat, and Loc experienced a wave of relief then unlike anything else he'd ever encountered. She was alive, and unharmed.

And also…not alone? There were two other presences with her, beings so insubstantial, he couldn't at first identify what they might be. Then it came to him.

Ghosts.

Her talent was speaking to the spirits of those departed, so Loc supposed he shouldn't be entirely surprised by her current company. In fact, he hoped she had derived some comfort from their presence, wasn't as alone in her captivity as he'd feared she would be.

The next thing he realized was that those two ghosts weren't the only spirits stirring this night. As he watched, dark shapes began to emerge from the sarcophagi and crypts that surrounded him, becoming more substantial after they passed through the walls of the cemetery and began to march with purposeful strides toward the house Nicholas Toulouse occupied.

Loc didn't know quite how she'd done it, because he hadn't yet had the privilege of observing Cat as she used her talent. Somehow, though, she'd called out to these ghosts, had reached out to use them as the only weapon she had. Now they were walking through the wall that surrounded Toulouse's property as though it was made of mist, men and women, some in the uniforms of the war that had been fought on this land so many years ago, others in civilian clothing of every era from the past two hundred years. They had come to answer Catalina's call, this army of the dead.

Emboldened, Loc spread his wings and took to the air, flying above them, reaching out once again with his magic so he could tear away the last of

Nicholas Toulouse's concealment and protection spells just as the cavalcade of spirits reached the front porch of the house. Instead of following them through the front door, however, he maintained his current course, then swerved off to the side, heading toward the room where he'd sensed Cat's presence. A heavy enchantment had been placed on the windows there, but it, too, was melting away like mist under the morning sun.

A wave of one clawed hand, and the glass in the middle window disappeared, allowing him to enter the room and come to rest on the floor there, wings folding behind him. Standing a few feet away was Cat herself, her beautiful face alive with a mixture of astonishment and joy at his unexpected arrival. To either side of her were the ghosts he had sensed, one a young girl in the extravagant costume of long ago, the other a tall man who stared at him in utter shock.

Before either of the ghosts could say anything, Cat had run forward and thrown herself into Loc's arms. He held on to her tightly, breathing in the sweet scent of her hair, feeling the lush shape of her body pressed up against him. "Are you all right?" he asked in a quick, urgent murmur, all too aware of the two ghosts watching them.

"Yes, I'm fine. Or at least, I'm fine now that you're here." She pulled away slightly and sent a quick smile at the two onlookers. "Lizzie, Edgar, this is Loc."

"Edgar?" Loc repeated, looking closely at the male ghost. "Edgar Dubois?"

"Yes." The man straightened and did his best to appear composed, although it was fairly obvious he was still a bit shaken by the sudden appearance of a demon in their midst.

Well, that could be remedied easily enough. Loc transformed into his human shape, eliciting a gasp from Lizzie and a raised eyebrow from Edgar.

"Your wife will be glad to know that you are here and ready to fight," Loc said.

A sudden light went over Edgar's features. "You've seen her?"

"Yes, her and your daughter Martine. They are both well."

At that point, the conversation was interrupted by a piercing scream coming from somewhere below. Lizzie started, and Edgar exclaimed, looking like he was ready to rush to her rescue, "That sounded like Celeste!"

"Oh, it probably was," Loc said. While he doubted the ghosts converging on the house would do anything to harm the younger Dubois daughter, they were probably giving her quite a fright. He glanced down at Cat. "Are you ready?"

She nodded. "Almost. I need to put my boots back on, because it's time to stomp out this cockroach."

Although she knew it was a total cliché to say that she'd never been so happy to see anyone in her life, in this case, it was the simple truth. As soon as Cat watched Loc burst through that window, bat wings flapping at the humid air he brought with him, she somehow knew it was going to be okay, and her heart sang with relief.

Well, all right, they still had to figure out a way to face Nicholas Toulouse and bring him down, but that outcome now seemed much easier to achieve, thanks to the presence of her demon lord.

They all went down the stairs, Cat and Loc in the front, Edgar and Lizzie behind them, although Lizzie seemed to lag a bit, as though she wasn't quite as eager for this confrontation as the rest of them. The bottom floor of the house was filled with a bewildering variety of ghosts, but they all moved out of the way as Cat's little group approached, possibly understanding that she and Edgar were the ones who had called them.

When they had pushed past the crowd of specters and finally entered the kitchen, Cat saw why Celeste had screamed. A contingent of ghosts in the uniforms of the Confederate army had her and Nicholas Toulouse cornered, their pale faces grim and implacable. She had her hands up and kept pushing at the air, as if she was trying over and over again to use her magical talent to shove the spirits away. However, Cat knew that wouldn't work, because they were incorporeal, had no physical bodies for her to push against. When ghosts acted upon inanimate objects or the living, it was because they were using the sheer strength of their will, not the physical bodies they once possessed.

Nicholas Toulouse's warm brown skin didn't look so warm now, was more a chalky brownish gray. Was that fear, or his youth spell wearing off?

Edgar pushed past her and Loc, his expression pleading. Somehow, the squad of Confederate ghosts knew to part enough so his daughter would be able to see him. "Celeste," he said, "please get away from Toulouse. He's not what you think he is."

Celeste had already been pale with fright, but now she seemed to go even whiter, if that were possible. "D-Daddy?"

"Yes, sweetheart. It's okay. It's time for you to go home."

"But you're—"

"Yes, he's a ghost," Nicholas Toulouse cut in. "What a protective father you are, Edgar, to remain in the place where you were killed and make sure your dear estranged daughter didn't come to any harm."

"You—he—" Celeste looked wildly from

Toulouse to Edgar, the import of her lover's words beginning to sink in. "You *killed* him?"

"Of course I did," Nicholas Toulouse said, his tone so off-hand, he might as well have been talking about a fly he had swatted. "He was making a nuisance of himself."

"You—" She raised her hands, but Toulouse caught her by both wrists, holding her in place.

Voice silky, he said, "I thought you told me you'd renounced your family, that you didn't care what happened to them."

Edgar moved forward, face white with rage. "Let go of her!"

"Or you'll do what, ghost?"

"This."

It wasn't the most elegant tackle in the world, but it did catch Toulouse off-guard, causing him to stumble and let go of Celeste's arms. She backed away, shaking, and Loc took advantage of the dark warlock's moment of distraction to grab her by the wrist and yank her away from his grasp.

"Watch her for me," he commanded, stepping forward so he could join the fray.

Startled, Cat took Celeste by the hand, since she didn't quite know what else to do. It appeared that the other witch wasn't in any hurry to get back to her lover's side, because she remained where she was, body still trembling.

Good thing that Loc had decided to take action, because Nicholas Toulouse now had his hands locked around Edgar's throat, was somehow holding him with his feet dangling several inches off the ground, even though technically he shouldn't have been able to hold Edgar at all. Grabbing a ghost was like grabbing a handful of air.

But somehow the dark warlock had managed that feat. Not for long, though, as Loc made a waving motion with one hand that slammed Toulouse up against the wall, holding him there like a bug stuck to a piece of cardboard with a pin. Edgar reeled away, gasping, and staggered over to where Celeste stood next to Cat.

There wasn't any time to ask him whether he was all right, though, because a strange red glow began to work its way down Loc's arm, the one that held Nicholas Toulouse in place. Loc gave a grunt of pain, but he didn't let go.

"Clever," he said, and, to Cat's surprise, he even smiled. "But although human flesh clothes me, I am not human, warlock, and your petty spells will not stop me."

A brilliant white light flared out of nowhere, and the red glow was gone. Toulouse's strange, pale eyes narrowed in fury.

"This fight is not yours, demon," he said. "Besides, we had a deal."

"Did we?" Loc asked, his face a study in innocence. "I don't recall ever committing to a formal agreement."

"It was implied," the warlock gritted.

"Ah, well, it seems we have suffered a misunderstanding here. Those books are far too valuable to give to a petty charlatan like you, so they will stay where they are."

Toulouse's hands clenched into fists, although he was so thin, they looked more like claws. "Very well, demon. Stay here and rot. Stay and watch that body you wear crumble as old age tears at it, stay and watch as that young woman you probably think you care for becomes old and wrinkled and not so lovely anymore. You would give up your kingdom for *that?*" He sent a venomous glance in Cat's direction, as though he thought she was to blame for Loc's change of heart.

Maybe she was. And thank God for that.

Loc smiled, eyes crinkling at the corners with sudden amusement. "You think I fear old age? I know what awaits me, Toulouse, but unlike you, I am willing to accept all the changes that come with a mortal life." He looked over at Celeste and his smile faded, replaced by a reddish glint in his dark eyes. "Perhaps you do not know what your lover was hiding from you. He offered you excitement and rebellion, an attractive way to thumb your nose at your family. Unfortunately, he is not quite as handsome as he would like you to believe."

"No—" Toulouse put up a hand.

But while he might have been a powerful warlock, he was no match for Loc's unearthly powers. Loc placed his hand on the man's forehead, and it was as though he was drawing out of him all the unnatural youth he'd stolen for himself by means of forbidden magic and unholy potions. Lines and cracks appeared in his face, and his thin form grew even more gaunt. In less than a moment, his head was little more than a skull, and as Cat—and probably Celeste—looked on in horror, he at last crumbled into a pile of dust at Loc's feet.

And in that same instant, the watching ranks of ghosts also disappeared, as if they now knew there was no reason for them to stay any longer.

Well, almost all the ghosts. Lizzie stood where she'd been this whole time, a few feet behind Cat, and Edgar remained standing next to his daughter, who now had a hand held up to her mouth. Maybe she'd meant to scream and then realized there was no point.

Loc turned back toward all of them, then wiped his hands on his jeans, clearly doing his best to get rid of Nicholas Toulouse's dusty remains. "He was a very old and very powerful warlock," he said, his tone strangely gentle. "He hid what he was by means of terrible potions, blood spells he used to create a façade of youth and vigor."

Celeste swallowed, face still pale. The black cat-eye liner she wore stood out in harsh contrast to her pallor. "He was always telling me to stay out of the kitchen."

That made sense. Cat somehow doubted Toulouse would have wanted his girlfriend to see what he was cooking in there.

Edgar turned toward his daughter. "You're going to go home now, aren't you?"

Her lips pressed together. "D-daddy, I'm so sorry. If I'd known Nicky was capable of any of this—"

Oh, she'd probably known. Cat had a feeling Celeste Dubois would never admit it to herself, but on some level, she must have realized how ruthless Nicholas Toulouse actually was. But that was something she'd have to work out with her family. It certainly wasn't Cat's place to comment here.

Really, she just wanted to go home.

It seemed as though some of the same thoughts had been running through Edgar's mind, because his stern expression didn't change. "Celeste, you need to go home and fix things with your mother and sister. This clan can't function with such deep cracks running through it."

Once again, her mouth compressed. Then she nodded. "Okay, Daddy. I'll do my best."

"That's what I wanted to hear." His gaze moved to Cat and Loc, who had come to stand next to Cat, his fingers twined with hers. "And now I don't think there's any reason for me to stay here. My daughter is safe, thanks to you."

"I am glad we could help," Loc said.

Edgar nodded, and he looked over at Lizzie. "I think it's time for you to go, too."

At once she put her hand to her throat. "Oh, I don't think so. I've been here so very long—"

"All the more reason for you to leave. We all have to move on at some point." His hand extended, he said gently, "Don't you want to see your family again?"

Her eyes were suddenly bright with tears. "You're sure I'll see them?"

"Yes," he replied. "Just as I'm sure I'll see my own family, when the time comes for them as well."

A tremulous smile, and she went to Edgar, her silk skirts swishing on the scratched linoleum floor. He took her by the hand, and a warm, pale gold glow enveloped them. Then they were gone, and the only sound in the room was Celeste's sudden sobbing.

"It's all right," Cat said, her tone a little rough because she realized she wanted to cry, too. Why, she couldn't even exactly say, except that she'd always hoped that one day she might be able to see one of the unquiet souls she spoke to finally move on to the next world. Now Edgar and Lizzie had just proven that wasn't a vain hope at all, but something all those restless spirits might someday achieve.

"Come along," Loc told Celeste. "It's time to go home." His eyes met Cat's, and he added in a murmur, "For all of us."

19

A PAIR OF BLUE AND GOLD RIBBONS HUNG FROM THE tapestry that she'd known was her better work. *Sangre de mi Madre: Blood of My Mother.* A paean to the mountains and the sky, to the city and the landscape that had brought Genoveva Castillo to life, done in hand-dyed linens and silk floss and rough, glittery gemstone beads.

"That is quite an accomplishment, isn't it?" Loc asked in a low murmur.

Cat nodded and forced herself to turn away from the tapestry. After taking what she hoped was an appropriately casual sip of champagne from the plastic flute she held, she said, "Yes. I've won best in my category a few times, but this is the first time I've gotten that and best in show, too. Usually that award goes to painting or sculpture."

His hand slipped into hers, squeezed it gently.

"I am very proud of you."

Color rose to her cheeks, but she made a deprecating gesture with the hand that held her champagne flute. "Oh, I guess if you enter enough times, the odds of winning start to get better."

Loc raised an eyebrow, as if he'd guessed she was uncomfortable with the praise and so was doing her best to deflect it. His gaze shifting to the tapestry, he said, "Where shall we hang it?"

"Oh, I don't usually keep my pieces," she replied with a chuckle. "It'll stay here in the gallery until it's sold—which probably won't take very long. I've seen several people eyeing it."

"Well, then, if you don't wish to keep it for yourself, I want to buy it from you." He let go of her hand and reached into his pocket so he could pull out his wallet, the one with the ever-renewing supply of hundred-dollar bills. "How much is it?"

"Loc!" After glancing around to make sure no one had heard her outburst, Cat added in slightly calmer tones, "You don't have to buy it. I'll ask Jacques to put an NFS sign on it until we can take it home."

"'NFS'?"

"'Not for sale.' Come on."

She dragged him away from the tapestry to hunt down Jacques. After she briefly explained the situation to him, he smiled and said he would take care of it.

"All right, that's handled," Cat said, going in search of a waiter so she could get her champagne flute refilled.

"Not completely," Loc returned, a glint of amusement in his dark eyes. "You haven't said where you want to hang it."

"Well...." There was still a blank wall in the living room, mostly because she'd been holding out for a very special piece to hang there. She'd told herself she would scour the galleries for the right art once the house was really, truly finished, but she'd never gotten around to it. Then again, what could be more special than the tapestry she'd dedicated to her mother, the one that had obviously captured the judges' imaginations as well?

Besides, she'd been working on that piece when Loc came into her life, and she knew she'd think of him as well every time she looked at it.

"The living room?" she suggested, and he nodded, clearly pleased with her solution.

"That would be perfect. Everyone will see it as soon as they come in the house."

He was so proud of her, so eager to face their life together. After they'd gotten back from New Orleans, they'd fallen into bed and made fierce, desperate love, as if trying to reconfirm their bond, to prove that everything they'd gone through to get to this point was worth it.

And of course after that, Cat had phoned

Miranda to let her know Nicholas Toulouse wasn't going to be a danger to anyone ever again, and that the de la Paz books were safe. What she hadn't said was anything about her relationship with Loc, although she wondered if Miranda had been able to read between the lines.

At any rate, since Cat had Loc with her now, as her date at a very public reception, she figured the cat—no pun intended—was out of the bag anyway. She hadn't yet seen Rafe and Miranda, but several of her cousins were here, including Tony, who was never one to say no to free food and booze.

"I was rooting for you kids," he told Cat with a grin, before wandering off, champagne flute in hand, to chat up a very pretty blonde who was standing in front of an impressive oil of a summer monsoon storm.

Cat could only hope that her brother would handle the situation with the same insouciance, but she had her doubts. Rafe had never really been the easygoing type.

There they were now, coming through the crowds, Rafe dressed up in a real shirt and some dress slacks, Miranda in a knee-length dress in a summery floral pattern. Almost at once, Miranda's gaze went to the emerald necklace Cat wore around her throat, and her eyes were suddenly full of questions.

Not as many questions as Rafe, though. He

glanced at Loc and then back at Cat, and his brows drew together. However, his voice was casual enough as he said, "It looks like you two make quite a team."

"I think we do," Loc responded, his hand stealing into Cat's once again.

Rafe didn't miss the gesture. "So, is this a formal arrangement?"

"Well, we didn't sign any paperwork, but yeah, Loc's living with me now." *And our mother is probably turning over in her grave, although I honestly don't know what would upset her more—me being romantically involved with a demon, or the fact that I'm "living in sin."*

"Is this going to be a problem?" Loc asked in low tones.

Miranda broke in, saying firmly, "No, it's not a problem at all. I'm happy for you—*we're* happy for you. And also very grateful for that business in New Orleans."

"I was glad to help," Loc said.

Rafe still didn't appeared overly thrilled with the situation, but at least he was gracious enough to say, "And congratulations on that best-in-show win, Cat. Jacques told me as we came in. That's quite the accomplishment."

"Well, I guess I was inspired," Cat said, hoping they would all leave it at that. "But let me snag a waiter for you. The hors d'oeuvres are really good tonight—I think Jacques is stepping up his game."

"But no champagne for me," Miranda replied, looking regretful. "I hope they have sparkling apple cider."

"I'm sure they do," Loc put in. "Let me go find the waiter, Cat, so you can speak with your family."

He went off before she could protest, weaving skillfully through the crowd. It was hard for Cat to look away from him, he was so damn handsome—and she noticed how quite a few heads turned as he went.

She supposed she would have to get used to that.

Miranda watched him go, too, but apparently not for the same reason. Smiling a little, she said, "I think you've found a keeper."

Cat halfway expected Rafe to make a sarcastic comment, but instead, his expression was thoughtful. "I kept expecting him to cause all sorts of chaos—I mean, it's kind of built into his name—but it seems like he's the one who keeps chaos in check. Maybe that's what his name really means."

She hadn't thought of it that way, but Cat found herself agreeing with Rafe. Loc might have turned her life upside down, or at least made her reexamine what she really wanted out of her life, but otherwise, he'd brought stability to the

Dubois family, had made sure that old wrongs were righted and the unjust found their just reward. She couldn't think of anything less chaotic than that.

"I think you might be right," she said. "And I know he's given up a lot to be with me, which is why I have to make sure this world—this life—are everything he hoped for and more."

Miranda offered her a reassuring smile. "I know you will. He looks at you the same way Rafe looks at me. You can't really ask for much more than that."

And there Loc was, maneuvering skillfully through the crowd, two flutes of golden liquid clutched in one hand, a plate full of hors d'oeuvres balanced carefully on the other. Cat imagined that was pretty much how he would navigate the rest of his life in this world, walking a thin line with natural grace…and the confidence that he would always, no matter what, be the Lord of Chaos.

The Witches of Canyon Road will continue with Tony's story in *An Ill Wind*.

Don't miss out on any of Christine's new releases —sign up for her newsletter today!

ALSO BY CHRISTINE POPE

THE WITCHES OF CANYON ROAD

(Paranormal Romance)

Hidden Gifts

Darker Paths

Mysterious Ways

A Canyon Road Christmas

Demon Born

An Ill Wind (May 2019)

THE WITCHES OF CLEOPATRA HILL*

(Paranormal Romance)

Darkangel

Darknight

Darkmoon

Sympathetic Magic

Protector

Spellbound

A Cleopatra Hill Christmas

Impractical Magic

Strange Magic

The Arrangement

Defender

Bad Blood

Deep Magic

Darktide

THE DJINN WARS

(Paranormal Romance)

Chosen

Taken

Fallen

Broken

Forsaken

Forbidden

Awoken

Illuminated

Stolen

Forgotten

Driven

Unspoken (June 2019)

THE WATCHERS TRILOGY*

(Paranormal Romance)

Falling Dark

Dead of Night

Rising Dawn

THE SEDONA FILES*

(Paranormal Romance)

Bad Vibrations

Desert Hearts

Angel Fire

Star Crossed

Falling Angels

Enemy Mine

TALES OF THE LATTER KINGDOMS

(Fantasy Romance)

All Fall Down

Dragon Rose

Binding Spell

Ashes of Roses

One Thousand Nights

Threads of Gold

The Wolf of Harrow Hall

Moon Dance

The Song of the Thrush

Snow Fall (Second half of 2019)

THE GAIAN CONSORTIUM SERIES*

(Science Fiction Romance)

Beast (free prequel novella)

Blood Will Tell

Breath of Life

The Gaia Gambit

The Mandala Maneuver

The Titan Trap

The Zhore Deception

The Refugee Ruse

STANDALONE TITLES

Hearts on Fire

Sympathy for the Devil

Taking Dictation

Night Music

Golden Heart

* Indicates a completed series

ABOUT THE AUTHOR

USA Today bestselling author Christine Pope has been writing stories ever since she commandeered her family's Smith-Corona typewriter back in grade school. Her work includes paranormal romance, fantasy romance, and science fiction/space opera romance. She makes her home in Sedona, Arizona.

Christine Pope on the Web:
www.christinepope.com

facebook.com/ChristinePopeAuthor

twitter.com/ChristineJPope

pinterest.com/ChristineJPope